DANCE IN NIGHT

AN UNSEEN MIDLIFE
BOOK 2

LAINIE ANDERSON &

USA TODAY BESTSELLING AUTHOR L.A. BORUFF

DANCE IN NIGHT

AN UNSEEN MIDLIFE
BOOK TWO

LAINIE ANDERSON
&
USA TODAY BESTSELLING AUTHOR L.A.
BORUFF

RILEY

My little garden grew beautifully. Squash and zucchini, corn, and tomatoes, all in neat, orderly rows. I hummed as I weeded, soaking up the summer sunshine that was a source of energy to me, like the plants. *Maybe I'm turning into a pumpkin. I certainly feel like one.* I rubbed my growing stomach fondly.

Once again, I cursed the laws that forbade an Unseen creature from studying our genetic heritages. I should've known why the sun gave me energy. All of the Sárkány knew it, but nobody knew why—it wasn't the same in Galdiart, the homeland of my people. I held out hope that one of the Sárkány we brought through the portal to live on Earth might end up being one of their famed scientists.

The dragons I'd begun to help save the year before had once been a thriving and proud people, even more advanced than we were on Earth. But their civil war had destroyed all of that, leaving them a shell of who they once were, without enough people to keep their civilization going. Much knowledge was lost or burned, and there weren't enough people to carry the tomes of information to the small village they'd gathered in.

We'd promised to destroy the last remaining portal once all the dragons were through, but I found myself second-guessing that decision. We could send expeditions into Galdiart. There was so much information to be had. I groaned and sat up, rubbing my lower back.

"Are you okay?" Anthony sat in a lawn chair beside the garden, the sunlight bringing out caramel highlights in his dark hair, reading a book on programming. He was searching for a way to combine human technology with magic. "Are you sure you won't let me help you weed?"

"No, but thank you. I enjoy the sunshine and having my hands in the dirt. It's weird, I never had any desire to do such a thing before we went through the portals and my dormant Sárkány side was awoken, but now I love it. I feel connected to the Earth."

"In all the years I watched you and learned about you, I never noticed you spending any amount of time outside," he replied, face pensive.

I gave him a sharp look. "Don't say it like that. I know you *now*, I love you, and I'm so happy to be your wife. But that was creepy."

The months after we returned from Bolivia were, in some ways, a nightmare. I'd grown to care for Elias and Anthony, to love them. But the shock of losing Michael was raw after watching his persona burn. And once I'd had time to really think and contemplate how everything had happened, the pain of Elias's betrayal cut me deep.

Anthony's role in the whole ordeal didn't bother me quite as much, since he didn't integrate himself into my life with lies, but him watching me for so long before I knew him was still an intrusion into my privacy.

Even months later, the betrayal and lying was still a major wedge in our relationship. I sighed and attacked the sparse weeds with renewed vigor. Elias, though I'd married him and loved him, wasn't my favorite person at the moment. He'd taken to traveling with the Sárkány, throwing his energy into helping them come through the portal and integrate.

After so many years apart, we told my sons the truth as soon as we could find a private room to sit down and talk to them. We made it a family conversation, knowing they'd need all of us in the coming years. We didn't know how they would progress as they aged, whether their Sárkány or Supay lineage would dominate or somehow meld into some new species. As adults, we had decided to resolve our issues so we would all be available to support the children.

In the early days, I couldn't let my guard down enough to let Elias or Anthony close. Axoular, who was also in an overwhelming situation, became my companion. The kids had continued their studies with their Aunt Tammy and weren't around as much as I would've liked.

Axoular filled a need, giving me a purpose. I'd taught him the basic history of Earth. We'd driven to the home I'd shared with Michael, about a half an hour away, and I'd taught him to use technology that he'd encounter in his everyday life in our society. He'd mastered the television, and I'd gotten him his own cell phone. We had plans to go get my laptop as well.

I'd put Danyelus on the scent of solar power over the winter, and he'd been obsessed until he completed the setup for the manor. It had previously been run on generators and gasoline, but they'd had to be sparing. Most of the lighting came from the sun, and they'd live without television or internet access. I wasn't about to live that way—I needed my TV fix.

"When will Elias be home?" I asked tentatively, without looking up. He'd run off on another trip to Bolivia a few days before, after we'd had a pretty nasty fight.

"I talked to him this morning. He'll be back tomorrow."

Guilt, my constant companion. I sighed and allowed the emotion to overwhelm me again. Guilt that my children were only just beginning to know me. It didn't matter to me that I couldn't have done anything sooner to reconnect with them.

Guilt that Axoular was miserable. Minda, his long-time girlfriend, took off soon after reaching Earth. I taught her a little about technology and she took to it. She'd loved figuring out how electronics worked and stayed holed up in my old home for days at a time tinkering. Eventually, she turned up at the manor, took the starter kit we offered every Sárkány, consisting of a new ID, ten thousand dollars, and a cell phone, and took off. We'd texted a few times, but she seemed to want nothing to do with any of us.

Guilt that I couldn't get past Elias's betrayal. I'd managed to forgive Anthony, though it was still a touchy subject. I just couldn't quite forgive Elias for ingratiating himself into my life without telling me my children were safe.

And worst of all, guilt about what sort of world I'd be bringing my little one into. I rubbed my belly. If he—I was convinced he was a boy—was a Shapeshifter, what would the other Unseen think of him? How would they treat him? What if he needed some sort of special treatment only Shapeshifter children required? If Peter really was his father, we might have problems.

"I think your weeds are gone. You're pulling up vegetable roots now." Anthony's voice broke through my thoughts again and I jerked my hand back. He was right; I held tiny carrots in my hand.

After shoving them back into the dirt in hopes of having them grow again, I stretched and got to my feet. Anthony jumped up to grab me, pulling me up so it wasn't so difficult to rise. At eight months pregnant, my stomach was enormous and cumbersome. When I found out I was pregnant, I'd hoped my newfound powers would help me thrive through the nine months, but no such luck. I'd been miserable since about week four, unlike with my other boys.

Anthony hugged me, putting one hand on the back of my head in comfort. The baby kicked hard enough for him to feel it as he pressed himself to my front. He laughed and drew back, bending to talk directly to my stomach. "Don't worry, little one. There are plenty of hugs waiting for you when you come out."

He kissed my stomach before taking my hand and tugging me toward the house. "It's lunchtime, and Axoular made your favorite."

Mmmm. Mini pizza bagels. I'd been craving them. "Great."

Axoular had fit right in at the manor. He got along well with everyone but spent most of his time by my side. He'd been teaching me about our heritage, and I'd continued to teach him about Earth.

Anthony and Elias became fast friends with Axoular. They shared many interests, namely the continuation of our combined races and my well-being. If I allowed myself to think about it, I knew I was attracted to Axoular, but I wasn't sure about the can of worms that would open.

I waddled my way in the back door, which

opened into a washroom. Stepping into the utility sink built into the floor, I strained to clean my hands and bare feet.

Anthony followed me into the room and laughed at my attempts to lean against the wall and reach my feet. He bent over and took the water sprayer from my hands. "Clean your hands, Coya. I'll take care of the rest."

He held the sprayer out for me to soap my hands, then rinsed them for me, rubbing with one hand and spraying the water with the other. When they were clean, he took a knee and set down the sprayer. With sure, firm hands, he massaged soap into first one foot, then the other, careful not to tickle me. His touch sent tingles up my legs, straight to my sorely neglected happy place.

"How many more days?" I asked, naughty bits aching from lack of use.

"The doctor said once you reach thirty-two weeks, we could have sex again. So, four more days." I'd gone into premature labor and one of the Unseen healers had been called in. She had primitive medical equipment, but it was sufficient to hear a heartbeat and determine the baby was healthy. My body had a hard time holding the little guy inside, so I was put on strict bed rest until thirty weeks, and on pelvic rest until thirty-two weeks.

"That's an eternity," I said with a groan.

"For us, as well. Elias has expressed more than once how he longs for you, Riley." He finished my feet and dried them with a towel kept nearby for that purpose. I'd been spending a lot of time in the garden. He gripped my arms and pulled me close. "When will you forgive him?"

I stiffened and turned, making my way toward the smell of cheap pizza sauce. *I'll forgive him when I'm good and ready.* My shoulders slumped. I was tired of being mad at my best friend and love. I needed to find a way to move on, but the anger wouldn't cool.

"Thanks for lunch, Axo." I smiled at my friend as I entered the kitchen.

He chuckled and patted my belly in response before walking around the kitchen island to the sink. He loved doing the dishes, thrilled with the ability to use a dishwasher. "I'd heard of dishwashers in Galdiart, but never had one. By the time I was old enough to help with the dishes, we had no electricity."

I sighed, troubled by the fate of the Sárkány. They believed me to be their savior, and in a sense I was. I ensured their survival, but on Earth, they faced the danger of the Shapeshifters hunting them down, and they would probably suffer the same fate as the Supay. Their intermarriage with other species was a likely outcome. But I was only part Sárkány and I was just fine, so maybe their genes would dominate similarly to the Supay.

"Any news from the Junta?" Axoular asked. We were waiting on a formal invitation for him onto their council. I both looked forward to and dreaded the invitation. It would mean he'd move to New Zealand.

"Nothing. I expected word from them weeks ago," Anthony replied, shaking his head. "It's pretty typical of them to keep us waiting though."

"Well, that's in poor taste," I said around a mouthful of bagel. "I don't know, Axo, do you really want to do it? Let Drest or Maedoc do it." I hated the idea of him being gone. *You'll have to let him live his life. He's not yours.*

"They refuse to cross until every other Sárkány has come through, and I'm glad. With Boudicca and Morcan searching for Boudicca's progeny, someone needs to be there to lead those left behind. We can only bring through one or two every week or so, and that leaves the rest of them to be protected in Galdiart."

"How many are left?" I asked. We'd brought them through in small groups every week since the previous October. Basically, the length of my pregnancy.

Axoular did a quick mental calculation. "A hundred and three."

I moaned. "So, another eight months." Those poor people. "We need to organize another supply run. The last I checked they'll need them within the next few weeks."

"I already started the list, Coya." Anthony patted my hand.

"Thanks." I finished my lunch in silence while Anthony sipped a cup of blood. Once we'd returned home, they drank blood supplied by a regular delivery from a Supay controlled blood bank. It still rankled a bit that they used blood donated by unsuspecting humans, but at least they weren't taking their meals directly from the source.

Elias's face drifted through my mind. His expression had been hurt before he'd turned and walked away from me to go through the portal on the latest Galdiart run. I could tell he'd wanted me to ask him to stay, but I couldn't say the words. He took my heart with him, goodness knew I loved him, but his betrayal had festered until it was something ugly inside me.

I was ready for him to come home. "I think, when Eli comes home tomorrow, I'd like to have a couple of days just me and him. Maybe we can go stay at my place in town?"

Anthony shared a look with Axoular and nodded his head. "I think that's a wonderful idea, Coya."

"What's with the look?" I asked. "You've been talking about my relationship with Elias?" I wasn't sure how I felt about that. Axoular had become a dear friend to us all, but still, he wasn't my husband, and they were. I felt a bit betrayed, though I knew they'd have my best interests at heart. I grumbled to myself. It was difficult differentiating hormones from true feelings.

"It was my fault," Axoular said. He moved around the island to put a hand on my shoulder. "I overheard part of your last fight and asked Anthony to explain."

"Why didn't you just ask me?" I furrowed my brow at him. We talked about nearly everything, why not that?

"You haven't exactly been easy to talk to late-ly." He grimaced and took a step back as if expecting me to blow up. "I didn't want to upset you."

I blew my hair out of my face in exasperation. "I'm under a fair amount of strain, but that's nothing new for me. Being stressed while carrying an unknown species in my womb is a bright, shiny new level of worry." I put my hand on his. "I'll try to be more reasonable and recognize when I'm just being hormonal."

"Actually, Coya, we've talked about that too."

I raised an eyebrow.

"We don't want you to worry about that, the hormones. Don't try to curb your emotions or wonder if you're being irrational. You're pregnant with an Unseen child. Those pregnancies are always more difficult than a human pregnancy. The hormones seem to be wilder. Just feel how you feel and don't apologize for it."

"We can handle it, Riley." Axoular squeezed my shoulder and Anthony took my hand.

He had his eyes on Axo's hand but didn't seem upset by the gesture.

"Well, I'm not going to argue with that. I *have* been worrying over absolutely everything, and it'll be nice to have at least that one thing off my fret list." My relief at not having to curb my emotions was overwhelming and tears leaked from my eyes. "I'm sorry, it's still the hormones."

Anthony laughed and pulled me close. "Not much longer now, Coya. Do you feel like a nap?"

I smiled and nodded my head gratefully. A nap sounded wonderful. He took my hand and we walked slowly up the grand staircase to the bedrooms. My bare feet sunk in the plush carpet.

Tammy and Danyelus had the master suite, but given there were three of us, they'd renovated and combined three of the bedrooms on the right side of the hallway. We had our own bathroom and den, as well as a spacious sleeping area. Anthony joined me, pulling down the comforter and top sheet so I could slide into the crisp, fragrant bed.

"There's nothing like clean sheets," I said with a sigh, my eyes already closing.

He wrapped his arms around me from behind and I felt his head nod. "You are absolutely right."

———

I woke gently, my mind peaceful and calm. Before I opened my eyes I stretched and languished in the warm bed.

"I love you." Elias's voice sent shock waves through me.

I was surprised and pleased at how thrilled I was to find him lying on the covers beside me. "I love you, too," I whispered. "You're back early?"

"I couldn't stay away." He smoothed my hair, no doubt a rat's nest from the nap. "I hated the way we left things."

"So did I." I turned my cheek, so it rubbed against his hand. "Let's go away this weekend, just you and me."

"That sounds amazing."

I stretched forward with my lips puckered.

He chuckled low in his throat, but ignored my outstretched lips, instead scooting close and nuzzling my neck. "How much longer?"

I moaned. "Four days."

"That's too long." He nipped my neck playfully. "But I'll survive. I don't want little Elias Junior coming too early."

"This weekend will be perfect, but Anthony

might be jealous. Maybe he can follow us down to the house the second day."

After giving me a long, toe-curling kiss, Elias sat up. "Sounds great. Do you need me to plan anything?"

"No, we'll just go spend a few days at my house."

Elias shook his head. "I don't think so, Riley. First of all, the house has too many bad memories. When are you going to let me clean it out for you?"

"When I'm ready, I'll tell you." I grimaced. I had no idea when I'd actually be ready to go through Michael's belongings.

"Right, then. We can talk about that again after we go away. We're going somewhere relaxing, and private. Leave it to me. Just be ready when I tell you."

I chuckled at his excitement and hated to bring him back to Earth. "Don't forget I can't fly, and we really need to stay within a thirty-minute drive of the hospital in case I go into early labor."

He stiffened. "Riley, you can't have the baby in a hospital."

His words knocked the air out of me.

Of course, I couldn't. What if the baby's dragon genes dominated and he burst into flame as soon as he was born? Or if he was a Shapeshifter, who knew what he'd look like at birth. We had no idea what a Shapeshifter's true form was.

"How had I not thought of that?" I whispered. We'd seen the healer, and I'd just assumed everything would be like with Michael. We'd gone to the local hospital to deliver.

Elias's eyes widened. He looked terrified of my reaction. "I just assumed you knew. It'll have to be a home birth. We have midwives, and the healer will come back. If you'd like, we can have a witch present as well. We won't take any chances." He reached around and rubbed my back soothingly.

"My deliveries with the boys were uncomplicated, it should be fine. I just hadn't considered it." How had I not thought ahead?

"You had them in a hospital? What about ultrasounds and stuff?"

"I had no reason not to. Michael never pressured me to have a homebirth or anything."

He was silent for a few moments, contemplating my words. "That could've gone very badly if they'd thought there was reason to do genetic testing."

"They did. At least, they wanted to. We refused it. Michael said he didn't want to know the future, and what would be would be. It seemed important to him, so I allowed it."

"I wish I knew what he was thinking. By our laws, he should've made sure you didn't see a conventional doctor."

I shrugged and searched my memories, but Michael had just acted like any father to be. Another thought popped in my mind, and I let out a cross between a moan and a cry. "That means no epidural, doesn't it?"

Elias chuckled. "You'll do great. You're the strongest woman I know."

"Thanks for the vote of confidence, but I still want to stay close to home."

He winked. "Leave it to me."

I left it to him. I had no desire to do anything but spend time with my kids and rest. Everyone else could handle things for a while.

———

The classroom was chilly on the top floor of the manor. Seven children, well, six children and a teenager, sat in comfy chairs behind school desks. They worked on various lessons, from colors for Talem, Danyelus and Tammy's adopted three-year-old Sárkány son, to the —now revised—history of the Supay for Stephen,

Anthony's thirty-four-year-old pubescent son. By Supay standards, he still had another twenty-six years before he reached his maturity and could be considered an adult.

My eyes drifted repeatedly to the blonde highlights in both David and Daniel's hair. David's hair had darkened a little over the winter since he wasn't spending much time outside and was more of a light brown than a dark blonde. Daniel's strawberry blonde mop was unchanged, much like my own. I might grab a few extra highlights if I spent an excessive amount of time outdoors, but nothing like Michael's did, and now David's.

My boys worked on Supay history as well. Daniel, only seven, had vocabulary words relating to the old god Supay, the Inca, and Bolivia. David seemed to be writing an essay but straightened when Axoular walked into the room.

Tammy sat in the front corner, scribbling away in a notebook while her adopted Sárkány daughter, Rose, snoozed away on her back. I couldn't help but imagine her with Daniel on her back when he'd been brought to the manor, while I was back at home mourning the loss of my children and husband.

I shook off my torpor. It wasn't her fault, and

she'd done everything in her power to give my boys a happy childhood.

Axoular winked at me, nestled into a rocking chair in the reading corner in the back of the class-room. It had become a favorite spot for me to rest so I could be near my boys without disrupting their studies.

"Come on, double D. It's time for your Sárkány lessons." David and Daniel jumped up excitedly, thrilled to learn about their previously unknown dragon lineage. "Kohbi, you too." Axoular would take them down to an empty field usually used to graze the horses, and teach them to control and master their Sárkány powers. Daniel was still too young for any of his powers to manifest, but Axoular said Sárkány children began their educations as soon as they could behave themselves. I'd join them after I had the baby.

Talem jumped up. "When can I come, Axo?" Frustration was plain on his face.

"When you're six, little man. You stay up here with your mama for now." Axoular nodded to Tammy, who gave him a warm smile. He'd really grabbed the hearts and friendships of everyone in the house.

Talem sat back down with a huff. Jaime, Anthony's daughter, patted him on the back. "At least you'll get to go eventually. I'll always be stuck in this classroom."

"Oh, pooh," said Tammy. "Nothing wrong with learning about your history, Jaime. We're different creatures, living under the same roof. We have to learn to embrace our heritage and celebrate each other's differences."

Jaime pursed her lips but nodded. She'd be respectful, even if she didn't like it.

I stood and patted Talem on the head on my way out the door. "I'll see you later, Tammy," I murmured to her as she began writing math problems on the chalkboard.

"Bye, Riley," she called.

Smiling, I began the trek to the main floor of the manor. Halfway down, on the second floor, I was waylaid by a grinning Anthony. "Wait 'til you see where we're going, Coya!" He laughed as he picked me up and carried me down the stairs. "You're going to love it."

I swung my feet and grinned up at him. His dark hair had gotten longer, brushing his shoulders. I twirled my finger in a strand of it. "Dollywood?"

"No!"

"I told Elias I want to stay close to home." I arched an eyebrow in warning.

"You forget, my little spitfire, we have the ability to use portals."

My eyes widened in excitement. "That's right! I hadn't even considered using a portal for leisure."

"Grease the palms of the right witch and you've got yourself a vacation." He deposited me in a recliner in the family room at the back of the manor, beside the kitchens. On the coffee table in front of me was a tray complete with a citrus soda and peanut butter crackers. "I thought you might be hungry."

I nodded enthusiastically and grabbed the crackers. "I am, but geez, I've been eating enough for four or five, not two."

"You're beautiful and perfect. If you're unhappy with your weight after the baby is born, we'll help you. You love to spar and fight, why worry? Any pounds will melt away."

"I'm more worried about how I'll look until they're gone." I eyed him, worried he might be turned off by my after-baby belly. Those things tended to take on a jiggly life of their own.

"Don't worry on my account. I love you so much, Riley. I'd love you if you turned into a troll."

I stopped munching on my cracker. "Are they real?"

"Yes, and uglier than any of the story books recount. Stinky, too." He shook his head ruefully. "They give the Junta a job, trying to keep their presence quiet."

I was about to ask more questions about trolls when the den door burst open, and Elias ran in, cheeks red. "It's all booked!" he exclaimed.

"When do we leave?" I asked, excited about a few days to reconnect and hopefully finally forgive my husband.

"Tonight. As soon as you're both packed."

I jumped up and glanced at Anthony who was grinning from ear to ear. "Anthony, too?"

"Yep. We're all going, and the healer will be here momentarily to hopefully clear your pelvic rest."

I clapped my hands, thrilled. "What do I pack for? Heat or cold or rain or what?"

"Pack for a week of heat." He grinned evilly.

"Are you going to tell me?" I asked.

"Nope. Now go." He smacked me on the butt to get me moving. "Anthony and I will pack our own clothes, just worry about yours," he called as I waddled from the room. I flashed him a thumbs up and trudged up the stairs. Unfortunately, my excitement didn't lessen the pain in my lower back or pelvis.

———

Bags packed, shower taken, light makeup applied, I laid on my bed in a robe, waiting on the healer to make her way upstairs. She looked about seven hundred years old, and I wasn't entirely sure what species she was. She rapped my bedroom door twice, then entered the room in all her wrinkled glory, her back stooped over, white hair secured in a bun, and gold-rimmed glasses.

Healer Rakesha grunted in response to my excited, "Hello!" She opened her black bag and took out a stethoscope, fetal heart monitor, and gloves.

Snapping the gloves on her age-spotted hands, she smiled. "Ready to have this baby, are you?" she asked with a raspy, overused voice. Almost like a long-time smoker.

I nodded, amused by her nature. She was simultaneously caring and not about to take any nonsense. "Yes, but it's still early."

She nodded her head and put some goo on her hand. "Ready?"

"As I'll ever be." I pulled my feet back to give her

access to check my cervix. I looked up at the ceiling, distracting myself by trying to guess where we'd be going. Maybe the Bahamas or somewhere else in the Caribbean.

She finished quickly. "All good, love." I gave her a relieved smile.

Removing the gloves, she took a tape measure out of her pocket and measured my big belly. Then she turned on the heart monitor and I got to hear the steady, fast heartbeat of my baby boy.

She smiled at the tears in my eyes as I relished the sound of his heart. "Are you sure about the pregnancy timing?" she asked.

"Positive." I couldn't be any further along than thirty-two weeks at the most.

"You're measuring a little bit bigger than thirty-two."

My stomach dropped. "Is that bad?"

"Not really. Your cervix is closed up, tight as a drum. And the heartbeat is strong and steady. You've probably just got a little bit too much amniotic fluid."

"Is there anything to do about it?"

"If you start swelling, get a headache, or any other odd symptoms beyond the normal pregnancy tiredness and achiness, call me immediately. But I think you're fine, and so will be your babe."

She began packing her instruments back into her bag while I covered up. "And the pelvic rest?"

Chuckling low in her throat, she snapped her bag shut. "Enjoy your vacation. Your pelvic rest is lifted."

"Wahoo!" Without any advanced medical equipment, it was the best news I could hope for. "Thank you, Healer Rakesha."

"My pleasure, girl. I'll see you in a few weeks."

Just a few weeks to go. Excitement bubbled up my throat until I wanted to squeal. I refrained and rolled off the bed so I could get dressed. *Vacation time, baby! Yeah!*

2

RILEY

Elias and Anthony carried our bags, of course, while I stood beside them in a sundress and big floppy hat. We waited in the back garden. Cindy, the witch who helped our family with portal travel, twirled her arm clockwise, then counterclockwise while muttering words in a language I didn't know.

Anthony bounced a little onto his tiptoes then settled. "You ready, Coya?"

I nodded. We were due a little rest and relaxation. The kids were lined up so I could kiss them goodbye, including Elias and Anthony's brood. They had warmed up to me, except for Stephen. He regarded me with cool disdain, too old for a step-mom, I supposed.

It didn't help that we were very close to the same age, but he was viewed as a child, and I was his step-mother. It would take time, but I was confident I'd win him over.

Stephen stepped up first, holding Jaime. "Well, see ya," he said.

Jaime held her arms out for me to pick her up. "I'll miss you, Riley."

Anthony grabbed her and I snuggled close. "I'm sorry I can't pick you up right now. As soon as I have this baby I will." After getting a kiss from me and her dad, and a pat on the head from Uncle Elias, Anthony put her down and she ran across the yard to a swing set to wait on Kohbi.

She stepped forward next. "Why can't I go?" Her lower lip trembled.

"I'm sorry, sweetie," I said, feeling like the worst mother in the world for leaving her. "We'll all take a vacation soon. Wouldn't that be fun?" I'd make sure it was the best vacation ever.

She shrugged, still sad, and I didn't know what else to say.

Anthony crouched down beside her, and she turned her big heterochromatic eyes on him. "We won't be gone long, then we'll do something together, princess. I promise."

"Can we go to the beach?" she asked, blinking.

"Of course," Elias said as he crouched down

beside Anthony. "Now go play with Jaime and we'll be back before you know it."

Charlie ran up and threw his arms around me. "It's okay, Riley. I know you gotta go. My dads have to go places all the time. It's part of being Supay." He took off to play with the girls.

I threw them a dirty look. I didn't care what the Junta had expected of them, or how much they'd felt like they had to be around me in the past, our children would learn they could depend on us.

David and Daniel were the only two left. "Boys," I said.

They smiled, and Daniel mimicked Charlie, running forward for a hug. "Have fun, Mama!"

He was tall, and his head bumped against my big belly. The baby kicked back in response, making him laugh and bump it again on purpose.

David stepped forward to put his hand on his unborn brother. "Don't be born until you come back, kid."

I beamed, thrilled that they were excited about the baby. "I love you two."

Daniel grinned up at me. "I love you too, Mama!" That was all he needed. He ran off to join his friends.

David scuffed his toe, glancing toward Elias and

Anthony. "Yeah, have fun." He gave me a quick sideways hug and loped off toward Stephen.

"He's not totally opened up yet," I whispered, saddened by his reluctance to show affection.

"He will," Anthony said. "We have all the time in the world now."

"Just step through," the blonde, Cindy said, interrupting my sadness and reminding me of the fun to come. "It'll take you straight to Ba—"

"Don't say it!" Elias barked. "It's a surprise."

Cindy clapped a hand over her mouth before splitting her fingers and talking through them. "It'll take you straight to your destination." She winked and nodded her head toward the portal, which showed me a beach, but it was like I was looking at it through a waterfall.

With a wave at Axoular, who gave me a sad smile I didn't want to analyze, I stepped through, and like every time I'd been through one, it left me with the feeling of being soaked. Once I was on the other side, I was bone dry.

I walked out into intense summer heat, tempered by a salty sea breeze. Clapping my hands, I waddled toward the water, the urge to get my feet wet overwhelming. Leaving my sandals on dry land, I splashed into the surf, not caring that the hem of my dress was getting soaked.

Elias and Anthony laughed behind me, and soon their arms were around me on either side. Elias wore khaki shorts, but Anthony had on jeans, which he'd rolled up to the knee to join me in the water. We looked ridiculous, so excited to be on a beach.

No matter how hard I looked up and down the coast, I couldn't see another person. "How'd you manage a private beach?"

"This stretch of coastline is owned by the Junta. It's made available to all Unseen for a cost. Sometimes we just want to get away like anyone else, but it can be difficult to arrange a vacation when you have some of our limitations and special dietary needs."

I was delighted that they had such a thing. A vacation destination away from humans. "Where are we staying?"

"Look behind you," Elias said with a laugh.

I hadn't even turned around since we arrived, I was enthralled with the water. I'd only ever been to the beach a few times. Turquoise water swelled into low, frothy waves. The colored water was also somehow clear, and the floor of the ocean lured me with colorful fish and golden sand.

Behind us was a large cottage. Every window was lit up, making it homey and welcoming. "This is ours for the next week, Coya." Anthony pulled me toward the house, which was almost entirely made of glass. The windows were so large they took the place of the walls. The roof was thatched in grass, most likely for looks. He let me go so he could help Elias grab our bags, and I walked leisurely past a pristine blue in-ground pool. *I'll be with somebody in that pool if I have my way.*

The inside of the house was magnificent. High ceilings and plush furniture, it was made for relaxation and beauty.

Peeking inside the fridge, I found it fully stocked with food and blood. I made my way to the back of the house, poking my head into rooms along the way. There weren't many rooms to see since the downstairs was an open floor plan.

A bathroom and pantry off the kitchen-living room combo, and a coat closet by the front door. The entire rest of the downstairs was split between the kitchen, dining area, and living area. Wide, pale wood stairs led to the bedrooms, and I climbed them carefully to continue exploring.

A hand touched my back as I walked up the stairs. I looked back to see both of them following me up. "I won't fall down the stairs."

"We know," said Anthony.

Elias rubbed his hand on my back. "We just wanted to see the upstairs, too. It's the first time we've stayed here."

"Why haven't you stayed before?" Surely their parents had at some point.

"It's very expensive to rent, and usually booked for years in advance." Elias took my hand at the top and pulled me to the right.

"How'd we get it?" I asked as I looked around a basic bedroom with an ensuite bathroom.

"You're a bit of a hot topic right now, sweetheart," said Elias. "They were quick to free up the week for us."

"I hope we didn't kick someone out of their vacation." I didn't want to put someone else off their fun just for me. We could've gone anywhere.

"They said the Junta leader, Alexander, had it booked and said he was thrilled to be able to do the leader of the Sárkány a favor, so he moved his vacation elsewhere." Elias shrugged. "I didn't question the gift."

"Now I'm the Sárkány leader. I told them I didn't want that title or responsibility. Give it to someone that's used to it, like Boudicca or Drest."

"It seems you've gotten it." Anthony led the way

to the master bedroom, in the front of the house. It was striking, following the light, airy colors of the rest of the house. The view from the balcony, streaming in through the floor-to-ceiling windows, was breathtaking.

I plopped down on the enormous bed to watch the ocean and sank into the blankets on the obviously expensive mattress. "This is heaven. Come feel."

Anthony launched himself from across the room and bounced twice before landing beside me. "This *is* nice!" He flopped around a few times until he was settled with his head on one of the pillows. "Why don't we have a bed like this?"

"I'll get right on it," Elias said as he sat beside me. "How are you feeling?" he asked as he put a hand on my belly. "Little man, okay?"

"You're both so sure it's a boy. I still say girl," Anthony said from behind me.

I grinned at them both. "I'm great, wonderful! Let's go swim before it gets dark."

Anthony sat up and scooted over until he was pressed against my back. "Are you sure there isn't something else you'd rather be doing?"

He moved my hair to the left side of my neck and pressed his lips against the right side. His lips shot a bolt of lightning directly down south, and my interest in the pool waned.

"I can't imagine what else we could do." I turned my head so that his lips were presented with my hair, and I was looking at Elias. "Do you have any ideas?"

The pupils of Elias's eyes widened, the iris in each narrowing to almost nothing. I pulled back, bumping into Anthony. "Elias! Your eyes!"

Anthony chuckled when Elias blinked a few times. "He's aroused, Coya."

"I've never seen him do that before!"

"Well, Riley, it's been a while, and I've been dreaming of you for weeks. I'm so excited that you seem to want me again, I feel like I could lose control."

Anthony rubbed his hand over my back soothingly. "When was the last time you ate, Elias?"

Elias rubbed his eyes. "Sorry, Riley, I'm trying to make it stop. It *has* been a while since I've eaten, I was so wrapped up with getting home then planning our trip. I just left Bolivia this morning, and now here we are."

I felt like a dunce. He was exhausted and hungry, and I'd just realized I didn't even know where we were. "So, um, where are we anyway?"

Elias chuckled, "I wondered when you'd ask."

"I was so happy to see the beach and the house!"

"It's okay, Riley, we loved how excited you were. It was nice to see some joy on your face after all the stress we've been through." Anthony started kissing my neck again.

"We're in Bali, Riles."

"Indonesia?" My heart sank. I'd thought I made myself clear that I wanted to stay close to home. "I thought maybe Florida, or possibly California. I didn't want to go so far from home!"

"Riley, relax. With portal travel we can be home in minutes. We just have to call Cindy and she'll be here in a jiffy." Elias tried to placate me, but I was already mad.

"Why couldn't you listen to my wishes?" I knew my voice sounded whiny, but I couldn't stop myself. "You just do whatever you want to, don't you Elias?"

"I thought I was doing what *you* wanted. I mentioned portal travel, and you perked up, and I thought that was my green light to go wherever."

I fought back tears as I listened to his perfectly reasonable words and placating tone. I was being irrational. I took a deep breath and counted to five. "I'm sorry. You're right, this is wonderful."

Anthony leaned back into my neck. "How do

you feel now?" he asked, breath whispering over my skin.

Shivering, I tried to gauge my emotions. I was still turned on, but also still felt like crying. It might not make the best combination for our first time together in so long. "Let's have that swim."

Elias smiled at me, and Anthony tore his lips from my neck with a groan. "All right, Coya. Whatever you want is what you get this weekend."

I grinned. "I appreciate you two coddling me." I stood and looked for the bags. "I'll just change."

Elias stood and turned toward the door. "Oh, I left them in the kitchen. We'll go get them." Anthony followed.

I walked to the huge window and stared at the water. How would I get past Elias's betrayal? I loved him. I wanted to be married to him. He was my best friend, had been for a long time. I mused over my predicament until they returned with our luggage.

I pointed to the bag I wanted, the one with my underthings and toiletries. Elias put it on the bed and opened it for me. The last thing I'd packed lay on top, spread out as I'd intentionally placed it there for him to find. It was an emerald green teddy, complete with a garter belt and thigh-highs. It had a pleat in the middle to accommodate, and slightly hide, my enormous stomach.

I snorted, trying to hold in an embarrassed laugh as I watched Elias staring at the silky negligee.

He turned his head slowly in my direction, his pupils dilated again. Shivers wracked my body as I recognized the predatory gleam in his eyes. "Riley Effler, take your clothes off." His voice was deep, almost growling. I'd never seen him so aggressive.

If I didn't trust him to never, ever hurt me, I'd be sprouting scales and flames. As it was, I had to breathe deep to stop my dominant dragon from coming out to play. She didn't like being stalked, but Riley the wife and all-around lover of sexual fun absolutely did. I squealed and ran as fast as my wobbly hips would let me run. That is to say, slow.

Looking over my shoulder, I found Anthony joining in on the fun, shoulder to shoulder with Elias as I boxed myself—accidentally-on-purpose—into a corner on the other side of the bed.

"Someone help!" I cried, laughter in my voice. "I'm being attacked by vampires!" My tears were forgotten as I scrambled up onto the bed on all fours to escape my predators.

A strong hand clamped onto my ankle, and I squealed as I was gently rolled onto my back. Elias might have been serious in his stalking of me after seeing the nightwear I'd brought with me, but he was also serious about making sure I was comfortable and safe.

Elias tugged me down so my lower legs hung off the bed, bent at the knee. Anthony moved around to put my head in his lap. He grabbed my arms and slid his hands down to my wrists, leaving a trail of goose-bumps in his wake. Once at my wrists, he grabbed them and pulled my hands up to his chest, and held them in an iron velvety grip.

Elias grabbed the front of my dress— *yes, please rip it off of me*—and jerked the material apart, ripping it down past my waist. *YES.*

My breasts, swollen by the pregnancy, spilled out of the top of my bra. I hadn't gotten around to buying any new bras, or even any maternity clothes, but at least my bra and panties, both deep purple, matched.

Granted, my lace boy shorts hung a lot lower on my hips than the way they were supposed to sit, but I didn't think Elias and Anthony noticed. All they saw was my darkened areolas peeking out of the top of the sexy demi bra I'd chosen back at the manor, hoping it would be seen by the two of them.

I'd been feeling sexier since my stomach had

grown, as odd as it was to feel that way. The pregnancy smoothed out my belly pooch and I had a reason to have a round tummy. My skin glowed and I hadn't had a single pimple since the previous autumn.

I followed Elias's gaze and watched my chest heave, the fabric of my bra strained by their size and movement. He reached his hands up and scooped a finger inside each cup, pushing the material down so I sprang free. I threw my head back in anticipation, dying to have his mouth on me.

Instead of putting his mouth on me, I felt his rough chin glide over the sensitive skin. He had a bit of stubble —he'd not taken the time to shave in all the day's busyness. While Elias teased me, Anthony shifted my hands to one of his and squeezed my left breast with his other.

I arched my back, pushing my stomach into Elias's. I'd been ignoring my own desires for so long they were piling up on me and making me as sensitive as a stick of dynamite. Every nerve ending crackled, begging me to make them touch me.

"Please," I cried.

Elias pulled his face away, running his nose along my skin before bringing his face level with mine. "Please what, Riley?"

"I need you." With his face so close to my own, he pressed himself against me, and I pulled my legs further apart, needy, and desperate to feel him. "Hurry, Elias, I need you."

Anthony captured my mouth from above, bent over into an awkward angle. I broke away, unable to breathe, and he moved my head out of his lap and lay on his stomach with his head level to my chest. Elias pulled away from me and I opened one eye to see him undressing.

"Elias!" I screamed when Anthony let his teeth enter the skin on my chest. I felt his lips vibrate when he chuckled at the response he gave me. Thanks to his venom, I was in the middle of an intense orgasm.

My moans and whimpers turned into throaty yells as Elias took me while Anthony had his teeth in me. He didn't really drink from me, just gave me intense pleasure while having a taste.

Elias was too tall to bend and capture my chest, but he was able to arch his back and take my neck.

I lost all comprehension at that point. Elias did drink, hungry as he was. I knew he wouldn't take too much, and he'd never put the baby in any danger. The combined pleasure from both bites and the feel of Elias was too much. I exploded, my orgasm ending, leaving me weak and satisfied.

"More," I gasped, looking at Anthony.

"I gotta move," I said. Once I came down a little, I realized my position at the end of the bed caused my back and hips to ache.

Anthony lifted me in his arms and pulled me back toward the center of the bed. Elias climbed up beside me.

"Did you drink enough?" I asked. I would've been more than happy for more bites. I understood how humans could become addicted to the bite.

"Enough from you. I'll get some more out of a bag. If you want another bite though, you just need to ask," Elias replied.

"I'll keep that in mind," I said throatily. I turned to Anthony. "More."

He laughed at my demand. "Yes ma'am. Do you feel like rolling over?"

"Onto my knees?"

He nodded.

"Heck, yes. Help me out here." He helped me sit up and turn so I was belly down. Elias leaned forward and rubbed my backside, stuck up in the air, then gave it a little slap. We'd been together often enough since October that I wasn't squeamish in any position around them. They loved to see me naked, loved to feel me, kiss me, bite me. I loved it right back and loved to see the same from them.

I scooted over to perch over top of Elias. Partly so I could kiss him and look into his eyes, and partly so he could help hold me up.

"I love you, Riley," he whispered as Anthony took me.

"Bite me," I said to Elias, lying under me and watching my face.

"With pleasure," Anthony said above me, misunderstanding who I was talking to.

I didn't mind. Elias grinned wickedly as Anthony bit into my shoulder. The combined pleasure took me over the edge, and I came with my eyes glued to Elias's. I wanted to close them and scream, but I forced them to stay open. I knew how much he loved to watch my face as I came apart.

Anthony wasn't far behind me, having the same trouble as Eli–no stimulation for so long.

As he finished, I whispered three words I knew they could both hear. "I love you."

We collapsed in a heap of limbs and napped for a while until hunger woke me. The sun was setting, turning the ocean a myriad of yellows, oranges, and reds. It was breathtaking, and I wanted my guys to see it too. "Wake up, lazy-bones," I called. I was on the left side of the bed, and they spooned each other on the right. It wasn't unusual for that to happen, as they both liked to cuddle in their sleep, and I didn't. They'd stopped being weirded out by it a couple of weeks into us all three sharing a bed.

I made my way to the window. "Watch the sunset with me."

They rustled some clothes on and joined me, naked as the day I was born. "This is a private beach, right?" I asked.

"Yes, but didn't you notice the windows when we walked in? They're reflective on this floor. Nobody can see in."

I hadn't noticed at all. I shrugged. "Well, that's nice. I didn't give it a moment's thought earlier. It's nice to know we didn't have an audience."

"Do you still want to swim?" Anthony asked.

"Yes, but after I eat. I'm starved, and I *did* notice the refrigerator was fully stocked." I walked to my suitcase, which had been moved to the floor. "I didn't even notice you move this. Which one of you did it?"

Anthony smiled. "I did. You were distracted."

I looked down at the suitcase and sighed. I couldn't reach it. "Thanks for moving it then, but could you move it back now? I don't feel like battling my belly to reach it and get my undies out."

Elias hugged me from behind while Anthony put it back on the bed. "Get what you need, for now, Coya, and I'll unpack the rest while you eat. I'm not hungry." They walked out and I heard them laughing as they went down the stairs.

Smiling, I found my bikini—the only bathing suit I owned that fit me. I managed to get it on without having to ask for help and made my way downstairs. Anthony was sliding a grilled cheese sandwich out of a Panini press and Elias sipped a glass of blood.

Anthony set the plate of grilled cheese and carrot sticks in front of me and headed back toward the stairs. "Thank you!" I called.

He blew me a kiss.

"Do you feel better after getting your belly full?" I asked Elias.

"Much." He eyeballed my meal. "Humans eat weird."

I arched an eyebrow. "What's wrong with grilled cheese and carrot sticks?"

"Well, I know he used the cheapest processed cheese available because that's what you like. We've always argued about that."

"And?"

"Why not chips with it? And why a big glass of milk?"

"I don't know! Why the third degree?"

He sighed and dropped his head. "I just want to talk. It feels awkward."

He wasn't wrong. "I know. I'm trying to move past it. You've apologized until it'd be cruel of me to ask you to keep apologizing, and I know beyond a shadow of a doubt that you love me, truly I do."

"But?"

"But I'm still angry. I've got a handle on the anger, but I can feel it, bubbling under the surface. Except for me, it's not just anger bubbling. It's fire. And if I let it go, I'll literally catch on fire."

"And it's all directed at me?"

"No. Not even most of it is directed at you. But you seem to be the catalyst. I can't do anything about any of the other things that have happened. But you're still in front of me, a living reminder of what I... What we all went through."

"If I could go back and change it I would, you must know that. Knowing that you're an Unseen changes everything."

"Wait. You told me before you knew what I was." I felt myself heating up, anger rising.

"Yes. Because we knew you were something

different. We strongly suspected, based on David's powers, that you had to be something more than human."

"So, if David had shown no extra powers, you wouldn't have told me?"

He stared at me, expression blank. I had no idea what he was thinking, but I waited patiently for him to answer.

"I won't sugarcoat it for you, that would do you a disservice."

"Fine." *He's about to make me really angry.*

"I probably wouldn't have told you anything."

"You would've let me go on not knowing what happened to my children?"

He sighed and rubbed his eyes. "Do you really need to know all this?"

Crossing my arms in front of my chest, I leaned back in my chair, sandwich forgotten. I stared him down.

"Fine. We had a contingency plan. If you hadn't begun to move on by your next birthday we were going to have 'found' the boys in another state, dead in a car crash, too unrecognizable for anything but a DNA match, which we would have faked, of course."

My hands began to leak steam. I felt the fire

inching up the inside of my neck, itching to be released. I stood, pushing my chair back. Turning my back on Elias, I walked out the back door to the pool that lay between the house and the beach. Untying the side ties of my suit, I shed it before jumping into the deep end of the pool.

The cool water soothed my fiery nerves. Anthony opened the doors of the bedroom as I leaned back to float in the water, breasts and belly bulging out above the water. "Do you want company?" he called.

"No!" I barked.

He saluted me and went back inside. With his advanced hearing, I knew he heard our conversation, and I knew he'd realize I wasn't just angry with Elias. It was his plan, too.

THEY GAVE ME THE SPACE I NEEDED TO CALM down as I alternately floated and swam laps in the pool. When the sun was completely down, and the night was illuminated only by the moon and the underwater lights, and I'd thought it through from every angle I could, I grabbed an oversized beach towel from the huge wicker cabinet nestled against the house. Leaving my swimsuit lying on the concrete, I went back inside in only the towel.

Elias and Anthony sat on the couch, eyes glazed over, not really watching the sitcom on the television. "Okay," I said, startling them.

I chuckled. "What's wrong with you two? Didn't you hear me come in?"

They didn't respond for a few moments. "We've been talking, and we aren't sure that you might not leave us," Elias said, a miserable look on his face. "Now that you're introduced in the Unseen world, you could go wherever you wanted. With your position as leader of the Dragons, you could petition the council to provide you with money and power. You'd have influence, and basically anything you wanted out of life. Who are we to stand in the way of that, especially after our betrayal of your trust?"

My mouth dropped. They thought I was contemplating leaving them when the thought hadn't entered my mind.

"Okay. A couple of things. First of all, I want to put a pool in at the manor."

Anthony nodded enthusiastically. "We can even have it spelled to never need chemicals or get dirty, the way that one is."

I blinked. I hadn't even noticed the absence of chlorine smell or salt water. "Right. The second thing. We're married. I won't leave you so easily. Marriages are work, constant work. And yes, we're starting off rough, but that doesn't mean I would give up on us. I love you both, and we'll work through this."

"Okay," said Elias. "We agree, we want to work through this, and we'll do whatever we need to make it work."

"I think it'll have to be time. I thought a lot about what options you had in front of you while you were ingratiating yourself into my life."

"At first—" Elias said.

I cut him off. "Let me, please. Tell me if I've got the long and short of it." I wanted to see if I'd sorted it out correctly, and I didn't want him to get an opportunity to say the wrong thing and piss me off any further. "When you first found Michael, you let him know you'd found him, right?"

"No," said Anthony. "We let him have his space and occasionally threw the Junta off the scent by telling them we'd had phone calls from random countries. They thought he was gallivanting all over the world."

"That's right, you told me that. You didn't contact him until he ran out of blood and robbed a blood bank to get more." I'd forgotten that. *Baby brain.*

"Right." Elias nodded.

"So, once you found him, and he let you know he was looking for a way to make me a Supay, you helped him get blood and kept his secret?"

More nods.

"Then, the day he died—How'd you find out?"

"Some of the Junta goons turned up at the manor

with the kids. They were frightened and tired, and David was asking for his mom and dad."

My heart cracked hearing those words. "And Michael?" I asked through clenched teeth.

"They told us he'd breached the security and had the kids with a human, which we knew. They said he put up a massive fight and they had no choice but to subdue him, and eventually kill him."

I pretended those words didn't hurt as much as they still did. "Once you knew he was dead, what does protocol say you should've done?"

"By the laws of the Junta, we should've ignored your existence and raised the children."

"But you didn't. You watched me, and in a year, Elias, you were well on your way to becoming my best friend."

"At first," Anthony said, "we just wanted to know what the allure was. What was it about you that was so special that Michael was willing to give up his life for you?"

Elias took my hand. "Then I got to know you and started seeing why Michael was so enraptured by you."

I looked at my hand in his and tears formed. "But you still waited years before doing anything or saying anything."

Anthony took my other hand. "It got really, really hard to talk about revealing ourselves. We couldn't tell you the truth, about Michael, or the Unseen, or your kids. So, what would we tell you about us?"

"Next we knew, a lot of time had passed, and you still didn't know anything. Weeks turned to months, which turned to years. I got antsy," Anthony continued. "I wanted to know you like Elias did. I wanted you to know me. I needed to be *in* your life, not watching from the sidelines.

Elias reached behind and clapped him on the back. "You already had it bad, man."

"Like you didn't?"

"Anyway," I interrupted before it turned into a pissing contest. "So, before you got that far, before you suspected I might be Unseen, what was the plan?"

They looked at each other. "We hoped you'd move on. We both secretly didn't want you to meet anyone else, but when we discussed it, we always said we'd give it until you were in your mid-forties and if you hadn't started moving on, we would stage their deaths. It's something our people have been doing for centuries, though we haven't ever needed to do it before. It always worked out with our kids' parents."

"That's another conversation I want to have. Where are their parents?"

"It's a different story for each child, but rest assured, none of them went through what you did," Elias said in a soothing tone.

"So, you had no intention of telling me anything. What about your feelings for me?"

"What about them, Coya?" Anthony stood. "You have to understand. It is expressly forbidden for us to enter a relationship with a human. It's understood that there will be lusts, and one-night stands, especially given that our bites cause spontaneous orgasms. It's a hand slap if you get a human pregnant, and there are measures to prevent the human from going through too much heartache. We aren't cruel, generally speaking." He moved back and forth, talking with his hands.

"So, it's just okay to take the kids away?"

"It's not okay, but it *is* necessary," replied Elias. "Can you imagine how you'd react if David suddenly had overwhelming cravings for blood, or you took him to buy new school shoes and everyone in the mall followed him around like he was the Messiah?"

"I know. I get it. I'd already got to that conclusion

in my own mind before asking, I just wanted to hear it straight. It's a necessary evil." The baby gave an especially sharp jab to my bladder, so I stood and paced the floor opposite Anthony, hoping he'd lay off if I walked around. "But what about me? You'd already broken a ton of rules by sticking around me."

"We were going to be forced, and very soon, to let you go. But then David began showing signs of being extra special and we thought you must have something to do with it." Elias joined us, pacing around the coffee table. "Why are we walking circles?" he asked.

"It helps me think," Anthony said.

At the same time, I said, "Because the baby is kicking my bladder."

"That's another conversation we need to have again before the baby is due. Who is the father—" Anthony said.

I kept pacing without looking at him. "Elias and I woke up in the night before we left with Mama Pacha for the portal. We did it in the room next door. Which, by the way," I wagged a finger, "was totally empty! We could've used two rooms just fine and they said they were booked."

"Well, then. It could be any of us." He eyeballed Elias, who shrugged.

I nodded my head. "Yup." I sighed. Back to the matter at hand. "You were contemplating forcing me to move on. Then you found out about David and decided you'd pretend to be an FBI agent? What sort of nonsense stupid move was that? You're both smarter than that."

Anthony grunted. "I know, it was dumb. I wish we'd handled it differently. We thought we could get you to make statements and somehow get some information out of you that might indicate if you had Unseen blood or not."

"You didn't think that in the four years of conversations and time spent with Elias, in all that time I wouldn't have dropped something? If I hadn't dropped any clues by then, what made you think you could get some out of me?"

Anthony stopped and I nearly ran into him. "I told you, Riley." He turned and grabbed my arms. "I had to know you. I needed to be in your life and have you in mine."

"So that's it then. You would've followed the law and never told me anything true if I hadn't turned out to be Unseen." On either side of me, they nodded.

"I need to process. I'm going back to the pool."

I still had the towel wrapped around me, so I just

dropped it out on the patio and walked down the steps to sink into the cool water. My heat had been rising again, even though I wasn't feeling particularly angry anymore. Just confused.

They'd been raised to not consort with humans. It was preferable not to interact with them at all. They'd broken the unwritten rule by befriending me. The moment they told me the truth, we'd assumed the Junta was after us for telling, but in reality, they were after us to capture me, since they'd also figured out, somehow, that I was Unseen.

If they hadn't intervened when they did, I would be locked up in a gilded cage, having babies for the Unseen's twisted Council.

I let out a groan of frustration and rolled over to swim some aggression out. I was beginning to understand why they did what they did, but I couldn't let go of the anger.

Swimming wasn't helping. Sex didn't help. Axoular had been telling me I needed to let my fire out occasionally, or it would build up and fester inside.

Maybe he was right. He'd been trying to teach me to let go and let it out when I chose, not when my emotions overloaded, and I had no choice.

I ambled up the steps, out of the pool, and

grabbed my towel, with a little difficulty reaching it on the ground. I settled it around my waist and grabbed another to take to the beach. Once I was as close to the water as I could get without getting wet, I sat on the spare towel and crisscrossed my legs. Placing my hands on my knees and straightening my spine, I attempted to meditate.

Supposedly, if I did it correctly, I'd be able to find the flame inside myself and draw it out to do what I wanted it to do. I focused on the sound of the waves, eyes closed, and searched deep within myself. I thought I found it once, but I just needed to burp.

I blew out a big breath and tried again. Blanking my mind to the sound of the ocean was the easy part. Searching within was harder. *How does one search within? Am I suddenly supposed to be able to see inside my body?*

Why not try that? I envisioned my body, the baby inside, head down, sucking on his thumb. I had a basic understanding of where my bones and organs were located, so I imagined them where they should be. I saw breast tissue and a generous layer of fat. I saw my stomach muscles as they separated around my babe. I was so engrossed in trying to add parts of my inner body to my imagined picture that I almost missed the fire.

It was everywhere. In my blood, lapping around my baby, keeping him warm and snug. A conflagration around my organs. I saw it and I focused on it. It burned brighter, and my skin grew hot. I lifted my left hand, eyes still closed, and focused the inferno into my palm.

Cracking one eye open, I looked at my hand and squealed when I saw the flames on it. Unfortunately, my excitement made me lose focus and the flames traveled up my arm. I shook it in panic, but it kept going. Of course, it didn't burn, but I didn't want to set the towels on fire.

I breathed deep, focused on the flames again, and pushed them back into my hand, grinning when they obeyed my will. I'd done it. And Axoular had been right. I felt a lot better. More reasonable, less angry. I stood and walked toward the water, and let the flames have their way and consume me. My entire body flickered with orange and red flames, in some places the heat turning them white. It felt like I was letting loose, like the tension and worry evacuated my body in waves.

When I began to feel a little drained, I focused the flames back to my palms and then finally back inside my body, where they easily tamped themselves back into my core. I would have to make sure to let them out more, so they didn't overtake my emotions again.

As I turned to walk back to the house, exhaustion overtook me, and I crumpled. I had sense enough to twist my body, so I didn't fall on my stomach before blackness took me.

———

I woke in bed, facing Axoular. I twisted my head to see Elias and Anthony spooning each other behind me. I grinned at them, not surprised to see them cuddling, *again*.

Axoular was a surprise, though. His eyes opened when I fidgeted, and he smiled. "Glad to see you awake, Riley."

"Did I sleep long?"

"All night, all day, and it's..." He twisted around to consult his phone on the bedside table. "Three a.m. now."

"That long? That's crazy. All I did was play with my fire for a few minutes."

"You're pregnant, Riley. You're using a ridiculous amount of energy creating a life. I don't know how long you had your fire out, but it takes a big toll on our energy stores. If you'd seen us before, you'd have seen our soldiers often looked fat when they went off to war, but skinny when they came home. They bulked up, similar to the way your bears bulk up for winter then live off of their stored energy while they hibernate. You'll probably find you lost a couple of pounds if you weigh yourself.

I looked down at my body, clad in one of Anthony's t-shirts, and ran my fingers through my hair. *Ugh. I need to bathe. How can they stand to be near me with their super noses?*

"Let me up," I whispered. Axoular hopped up and pulled me to my feet. I was a little wobblier than normal, even considering the pregnancy.

He followed me to the bathroom. "Do you want to use the one in the spare room, so you don't wake them up?" he asked, nodding toward the bed.

I gave him a thumbs-up, stepped in the bathroom long enough to grab my toiletries bag, and headed across the hall to the spare bedroom. He followed.

There was no point in closing the bathroom door, he obviously wanted to talk. "Turn," I commanded.

He turned.

"Why are you here?" I asked as I took off the tee and turned the water on. I found my toothbrush and made quick work of my teeth while I let the water get warm.

"When they couldn't get you to wake up yesterday morning, they called me, and Cindy brought me right out. This place is amazing. It kind of reminds me of the old days in Galdiart. We had a lot of open floor plan homes with lots of glass."

"What did you do? How'd you help, I mean?" I spat and rinsed in the sink and stepped into the shower, closing the curtain behind me. "I'm in, you can turn now." The shower curtain was a thick black and gold material, he wouldn't be getting any peeks. *I can't say that I'd mind letting him peek once or twice.* I mentally shook that thought off. I had no business going down that road.

I worked the citrusy shampoo into my thick, unruly hair as he talked. I loved my hair, but it was definitely a pain to take care of sometimes.

"Uh, I didn't really do anything." I could hear the shrug in his voice. "But they said I'd be in for a free trip to the beach, so who was I to argue? I looked it up on my phone while I waited on Cindy to pop in and do the portal. Have you seen this place?"

I laughed at his reasoning. "Yeah, it's fantastic. Best place to turn into a raging human fireball ever."

"That's true." He sat quietly for a few minutes.

"What's going on with you, Riley? Why the inferno?"

"I was trying to channel the fire, like you taught me," I said as I rinsed my hair. "With meditation. It worked, and I had fire in my hand. I lost it for a second and it wanted to go across my body, so once I'd mastered it again, I gave it free rein to have a little fun. I just didn't realize how much energy I'd be using."

"Did you feel better? After you mastered it and before you let it loose."

"Yes! I felt so much better emotionally that I decided to let it have its head and see if I felt even better afterward." I considered my leg hair, opting to skip shaving for one more shower.

"Yeah, that happens. You've got to let it out every couple of days. Just hold it in your palm, let it burn a little, then let it go. It's simple, you don't have to go all flaming-anger-woman to keep it from overwhelming your emotions."

"You could've mentioned that before."

"Yeah." He chuckled. "Sorry."

"Go away, I'm almost done." I rinsed the lather from my body and peeked out of the curtain. He was gone. Drying off and dressing took several minutes since I couldn't even put underwear on quickly.

Then, I was on my way downstairs, with a towel on my head, to find him.

He stood in the kitchen, slicing a tomato. The fixings for a salad sat on the counter in front of him. He tilted his head as I walked in. "We didn't have tomatoes on Galdiart. Our fruits and vegetables were very different from these, but no less delicious." He dropped the tomatoes in a bowl and grabbed a cucumber, peeling it in stripes. "I've found similar veggies to almost everything I can think of from home, but nothing comes close from my world to a tomato."

Popping a piece of tomato in his mouth, he finished peeling the cucumber and began slicing it into the bowl. "I was thinking about bringing some seeds from Galdiart and trying to plant them in your garden. We might be able to get something to grow."

"What's up with you, Axo?" He was acting weird.

His hand stilled over the cucumber, then he moved on to peeling a carrot. "Nothing. Why would you ask that?"

"Come off it, Axoular. You're rambling like you're nervous. What's going on?"

He ignored me, finished peeling the carrot, and then sliced it. I let him contemplate his words. I'd learned enough about his personality over the months we'd lived under the same roof to know he'd talk when he was ready.

"I've been having some feelings," he finally said.

"Oh?" I wondered if he was missing Minda.

"Yes. For you."

My jaw dropped. I'd been having a few feelings myself, but had mostly attributed them to sex deprivation. I hadn't given them any real thought. I said nothing and he continued his chopping. He chopped an onion, a few sweet peppers, and was ripping the lettuce before I finally spoke.

"I have as well." *Well, the cat is out of the bag now. Nothing left but to own up to Elias and Anthony.*

He jerked around and stared at me. "I want to be in your life. And I don't want to be your friend, or buddy as you say."

"I don't know what I want, Axo. I do know I want something more with you. But nothing, absolutely nothing, can be done until I discuss it with Anthony and Elias."

He twirled and held his hands up, as if in surrender. "I agree completely. I would never betray their friendship that way." He dropped his hands and hung his head before turning back to his salad prep.

"I already feel as though I've betrayed them by admitting this to you."

"As long as we go to them first thing in the morning with the information, it isn't a betrayal."

Nodding his head, he placed the bowl of salad on the table in front of me before going for condiments.

I dished myself out a generous portion. "When did you realize your feelings?"

"While you were showering." I laughed at his honesty. "No, I've had the urges for a couple of months, but I think—what's the word for doing something without realizing it?"

"Subconscious."

"Okay. I think subconscious I was burying my feelings and attractions because of the potential explosion it could cause."

"Subconsciously," I quietly corrected.

He shrugged. "You know what I mean."

I nodded and ate to give me a reason to think instead of talking. We finished eating in an awkward silence before cleaning up the mess and putting the leftover salad in the fridge.

I checked the time. Four in the morning. *Might as well just stay up.*

Wasting time with Axoular was usually easy. We'd end up playing cards, or a board game, or zoning out on TV. He liked learning new words from television shows and movies. "This is awkward," I said, after we found yet another movie on in the wee hours of the morning that was just shy of porn.

I was uncomfortable, turned on, and not allowed to have the forbidden fruit until I cleared it with my husbands, though I had a sneaking suspicion they'd be okay with it. Axoular shifted in his seat several times, and I suspected he was in the same predicament I was. Horny and no relief in sight. No way I was going to go upstairs and use my husbands to relieve myself after getting turned on by another man. I wasn't that bad of a person—though to be honest, the thought had crossed my mind.

You'll live, Riley. Keep it in your pants. I stared at his pants, curious what was under his jeans. *Screw it, you're a horrible person. Go upstairs and find something to do.*

"I'm going to go read," I said as I stood. "Feel free to sleep in the spare bedroom if you need a nap. Or go swim, or whatever you want."

He nodded, expression unreadable, as I exited the room.

I tiptoed into the master bedroom and glanced at the clock. Five. We'd sat like that, uncomfortable and awkward, for an hour.

Elias heard me come in and sat up. "Riley! You're awake!" He launched from the bed and scooped me up in a hug.

Anthony joined him. "Why didn't you wake us up?"

"I was gross. I showered and Axoular made me a salad." I threw my arms around each of their necks. "We watched TV for a while, then I came up to lay with you guys and read. I'm not sleepy."

Elias grinned. "I can think of ways to occupy your time."

His words were a shot to my core, but I shook my head. "No, we need to talk, as soon as possible."

Anthony took my hand and pulled me to the bed, sitting behind me and playing with my slightly damp hair. "What's wrong, Coya?"

"Well, for starters, Axoular explained why I passed out and why for so long, so I know how to avoid it in the future."

Elias sat beside me and grabbed my hands. "That's great."

"Also, part of my anger toward you both has been exacerbated by my fire. I've figured out how to relieve my anger using my flames without hurting anyone, so any anger from now on should just be me and my hormones."

I turned to Elias. "I forgive you. I think I would have a long time ago, but I couldn't because of the fire making me so angry." Squeezing his hand, I took Anthony's hand with the other and looked his way. "I think I'll likely be touchy about the subject. I don't know for how long, maybe forever. But I recognize that you were doing the best you could, and what you thought was best. And I appreciate that neither of you ever tried to get in my pants before I knew the truth."

"Believe me, Riley." Elias laughed and shook his head. "We wanted to."

"With that being said, something has happened over the last few months that was unintentional, but you need to know about it."

Elias straightened. "Are you okay? Is the baby okay?"

The baby gave a swift kick as if on cue and I laughed. "He's kicking away and fine. No, it's about Axoular."

Anthony stroked my hand, drawing my gaze. "He's in love with you."

I looked back and forth between the two of them, shocked. "How'd you know?"

"It's obvious with every look he gives you. And I

think you care deeply for him, but I didn't think you'd realized it yet."

"I've smelled you get turned on a couple of times when you looked at him, but it never seemed to go anywhere, so I waited for you to tell me if it was something you wanted to pursue," Elias said, rubbing slow circles on my back.

"You knew? You could've told me, cos I really didn't know until a couple of hours ago." *At least they aren't freaking out. But a teensy bit of jealousy would be nice.*

"We saw it coming but weren't positive. What would you like to do about it, Coya?"

"Well, I don't really know. Polyamorous relationships are a new beast to me. What should we do?"

Elias looked at Anthony over my head. Anthony shrugged. "Coya, if it's something you want to pursue, then pursue it. We like Axoular. He's already used to living with us. We might find we don't like sharing a bed, and we might find we do. But we can work through that with him and you. If you grow to care for him and are sexually interested in him, see where it goes."

"Date him," Elias supplied.

"Date? Like...real dates? Go to the movies and eat popcorn dates?" I couldn't believe the words that were coming out of their mouths. They loved me enough to let me pursue a serious relationship with another man. It was beyond comprehension to me, who had been raised with monogamy as the only option.

"Will you be coming home to us at the end of the night?" Elias asked. Anthony nodded his head.

"Well, yeah!"

"Will we be able to worship that body pretty much whenever we want to?" Anthony asked. Elias nodded.

"Please do."

"Then date him, Riles. If it works out, it works out. If it doesn't, we'll give him the starter pack every other Sárkány gets and send him on his way."

"Well. Well, okay then." I stuttered over my words, having expected at least some drama and upset from them. "Thanks?"

They both laughed. "There's nothing to thank," said Elias. "We like the guy. We've got a bunch of kids, work, political things with the Junta. After the baby is born, we'll have to go back to real life, and we want to get busy chasing our own career dreams. And you want to work with the dragons. Having one more set of eyes in the family, on you, on the kids, on us—it's a good thing!"

I launched myself into his arms, Anthony following behind. I found myself snuggled in between them, cocooned in my favorite non-sleeping position. For sleeping I made them move and let me spread out. We laid like that for a while, whispering about our hopes and dreams for the baby and our careers, before finally getting up and going down to make a real breakfast for me and Axoular, and to warm some blood for them. My heart was light, and my anger was gone. We'd figure it all out together.

4

AXOULAR

I COULDN'T BELIEVE SHE'D AGREED. WE WERE about to go on our first date. Elias and Anthony cornered me the next time she took a shower after they had their talk, and let me know they were okay with it, but basically, they'd kill me—slowly—if I hurt her or did anything she didn't want me to do, including sex.

The thought of hurting her in any way pained me, and I told them such. I wanted to spend my life giving her pleasure, in any way I could. I told them that, too.

They'd broken out into big smiles and did a lot of punching me on the arm, which I didn't really understand. Must've been some Earth tradition, so I punched them back. Anthony growled a little when I did. Maybe I punched too hard? I wasn't sure.

A few days passed and I asked Riley to accompany me to a big Balinese pig roasting and she'd agreed. We'd just returned from grocery shopping, where I'd heard about the roast. I made discreet inquiries and discovered how to purchase tickets. I presented them to her after we unpacked our shopping, and she'd squealed in delight and pulled me into a big hug. The baby didn't like it and kicked me away.

I was dressed in Anthony's jeans and Elias's shirt, and I looked as nice as I could. I'd shaved and tried to tame my thick black hair, but it went whatever direction it wanted to.

I tapped on her bedroom door. She insisted I collect her for our outing. She said it was a tradition on Earth. I didn't care where we met, as long as we got to spend more time together.

She opened the door wearing a flowy dress in a dark purple. Her reddish hair was swept up one side to cascade down the other. She looked amazing.

"You ready?" I asked.

"Yes." She sounded excited. "I'm starving!"

"Me, too. I've never been to a pig roast, any idea what we're in for?"

"Well, I know in Hawaii, they usually entertain

you with a show of native dancing or maybe some flame-throwing."

"We could probably make a better showing than they could of flame-throwing."

She laughed, and her voice sounded like bells. Her voice was deeper than a lot of other women I'd met on Earth, or at least the ones I'd observed when out in public. But when she laughed her whole face lit up and the room got brighter.

"I'd say you're right about that."

"Where are Elias and Anthony tonight?" I was surprised they didn't tag along or at least weren't there to see her off.

"They headed to the local movie theater. There's one on the other side of the island that shows films in English."

I led her outside to the taxi waiting to take us to the roast. I'd considered renting one of the motorcycles, which seemed to be the preferred method of transport on the island, but Anthony forbade me from putting his pregnant wife on one. It was a smart decision considering I'd never driven one in my life.

The taxi driver spoke perfect English and we were soon on our way without any communication problems. Neither one of us spoke a word of Balinese.

We were staying on the easternmost part of the island, near the Taman Soekasada Ujung Water Palace. We'd played the part of tourists the day before and taken a tour of the palace. It was breathtaking. It reminded me of Galdiart before the war destroyed it.

The roast was a little further inland. When we arrived, I paid the taxi driver and arranged to have another taxi pick us up while Riley presented our tickets to the host. He smiled, hugged us both, and showed us to our seats. We were in a sort of amphitheater, complete with grass table skirts. People milled everywhere and someone immediately came and took our drink order. They returned within minutes with neon-colored glasses with umbrellas stuck in. "Riley, why are there tiny pink umbrellas in our drinks?"

She laughed and stuck mine in her hair. It clashed with the red in her hair, but I loved it anyway. "The locals, in any beach destination all over the world, think that tourists require little umbrellas in their drinks to truly feel like they're on vacation." She looked down at her avocado drink with delight on her face. We'd tried one the day before and she'd loved it. It was blended with sugar, ice, and chocolate. It had made me gag.

She took one sip and grimaced. "It's got alcohol in it."

I knew what that meant. We had spirits on Galdiart as well, and we knew not to let a pregnant woman drink more than a few sips or it could harm the babe. "I'll go get you another and make sure they understand."

I rose and took her drink over to the bar, which was across the amphitheater. I had to slip through many, many dancing bodies to get to the other side. I'd thought the pig roast would be a family-friendly type event, but I was wrong. It was just an excuse to party and drink. We probably wouldn't stay long.

It took longer than I liked to replace her drink but at least the bartender understood me and once it was my turn, made the drink quickly. I returned to the table to find Riley gone. I sat down to wait, assuming she was in the washroom, but I didn't sit for long because I spotted a handprint, in black soot, on the tablecloth, and the cloth itself was singed. Something was wrong. Riley left, and she didn't leave willingly.

I turned in circles before running toward the parking area, hoping maybe someone saw her leave. I turned the corner just in time to see her scoot into a limousine. *Why would she leave on her own?*

I took off for the vehicle, but it pulled off with a roar, leaving me in the dust. The back of my neck tingled as I stuck my hand into my pocket to get my phone. Then I felt an excruciating pain on the back of my head, but it didn't knock me out like I'm sure they intended it to. I twirled around to face my aggressor, and he backed up and pointed a gun at me.

"We intended to leave you here or kill you, whichever was more convenient." He used the gun to wave me toward another limousine that was just pulling up. "But we think she'll be more complacent if you're with her. Do I need to tell you what would happen to her if you resist?"

"No," I replied stiffly. "I'll go willingly and quietly." *For now.*

I waited patiently for Axoular to go get me another drink. I would've gotten it myself, but he jumped up and went before I had a chance. He was an old-fashioned gentleman, and I loved it. Our first date was going very well. The conversation wasn't awkward, and even though the roast ended up looking like more of a rave than a roast, I'd had fun so far.

Someone tapped on my shoulder. "Excuse me, are you Riley?"

"Yes," I replied as I turned. "Can I help you?"

An Indonesian man in a black suit held out a note for me to read. I thanked him and unfolded it.

Riley Effler,

We have your friend. Leave the table and walk

outside. Get into the limousine waiting at the gate you entered through, and we'll allow him to live.

Do it quickly.

Rage poured through me like lava. Fire flickered on my palm, and I smacked my hand down on the table and wrestled it back inside. Rising from the table, I made my way to the entrance. Sure enough, as I turned the corner, a black stretch limousine waited.

A uniformed driver waited by the door. "Ms. Effler?"

"Mrs. Effler, *if* you please." I was married and proud of it.

He nodded and opened the door. Blinking, I tried to focus on the interior of the darkened room. I looked around, and seeing no one else in front of the building, I allowed fire to hover over one finger, holding it out in front of me as I attempted to slide into the seat. My gargantuan stomach prevented me from sliding very gracefully, but I managed. *I'm gonna incinerate every person in this car.*

The flame was just enough to let me see the car was full of men, but none of them were Axoular. I took a deep breath and found the fire hovering under the surface. As I was about to release it and burn them all, I felt a little pinch in my neck and knew no more.

———

Thud, thud, thud. I squinched my eyes to block out the light. *Thud, thud, thud.* I moaned, rolling onto my side. "Anthony? I think I've caught a stomach bug." I moaned and tried to crack one eye. As soon as the sunshine hit my retinas, I regretted it. "Oh God," I whispered. "It's a migraine, not a stomach bug."

The room was silent. "Axoular?" Where were the guys? They never left me completely alone. They knew I hated it. I'd been alone for so long I never wanted to be by myself again.

I forced myself to crack an eyelid. Where the hell was I? I grunted as the baby gave a particularly strong kick to my ribs, surprising me and snapping my eyelids all the way open. "Hello?" I sat up, one hand on my head and one on my stomach.

The room was obviously someone's bedroom. It was beautiful, a room I'd decorate for myself. The walls were heather gray with a maroon accent wall. The furniture was soft and comfortable, in reds and grays. The focal point was the enormous bookshelves lining one wall from end to end. They weren't built-in, but they were stuffed full.

It was like someone built the room just for me. "Where the hell am I?" Scooting to the side of the bed and standing, I turned in a circle, looking for any clues. My headache slowly faded, and my memory quickly rushed back to me. "Oh, my God."

The flames returned, whispering to me to let them out. They hovered just beneath my skin. I ran across the room to the door, steam rising from my skin.

Shock. It was locked. "Can anyone hear me?" Silence. I went to the only other door in the room. It opened into a windowless bathroom. Closing it, I addressed the empty room. "I'm going to set this room on fire in five minutes if someone doesn't tell me what the hell is going on."

I backed up, gaze on the locked door, and sat in one of the recliners positioned around to wait. *One Mississippi, Two Mississippi, Three Mississippi, Four Mississippi...* When I got to four and a half minutes, I held my hand up and allowed it to be engulfed in flames. A hidden intercom crackled, and Axoular's voice came over the loudspeaker.

"Don't burn it down, Riles. They *say* they'll hurt us if we mess up their place. I think we could take them down though." There was a bump, and Axoular let out an angry roar-yell. The intercom went silent for a few seconds then he came back. "I'll be there soon, just sit tight."

I pulled my flames back inside and with nothing else to do—except eyeball the books—I sat tight. When sitting tight got boring, I started talking. "Whoever you are, you have to know that you'll die for your crimes today."

I got no reply. Standing, I began to walk slowly around the room, working kinks out of my back and hips. I wondered nervously what they'd used to knock me out and if it would hurt the baby. He'd been kicking up a storm, so I doubted he'd have any lasting damage, but the potential danger made my rage all that much worse.

After what felt like hours, the intercom crackled. "Mrs. Effler, are you paying attention?"

I raised my eyebrows. "What else would I be doing?"

"There's no need to worry, Mrs. Effler. No harm will come to you if you follow the rules."

There were no words capable of expressing how angry I was, so I just held up my middle finger and turned in a slow circle, so that wherever the camera was, it would see me.

"We get the point, Mrs. Effler. We are going to allow your newest pet to come stay with you to keep you complacent. The minute we hear or see anything that makes us think you're scheming, we'll remove him. If you continue to struggle after that, we'll kill him and sedate you until we get what we need."

"And what could you possibly need from me?" I asked, smoke pouring from my mouth.

"Your child." The intercom went silent with a pop and ice filled my veins, quenching the fire as if I'd been doused with water.

I plopped down on the closest chair, a rocker near the window. My brain felt like it had flies buzzing around in it, all fuzzy and overloaded.

A small table sat beside the rocker, perfect for resting a cup of tea or something equally useless. I picked it up and hurled it, using all the supernatural strength I could muster, at the closest window. It bounced off and almost hit my stomach on the rebound. I was jerked to the side just in time.

Twirling, I went on the balls of my feet and threw my arms up in a defensive gesture. Axoular backed away, his own hands up in a submissive pose. I shrieked and ran into his arms, fury and fear replaced by relief.

"What is going on?" I yelled. "Where in creation are we?"

Axoular put his hands on my head and kissed me before yanking me back into his arms. "They wouldn't let me see you. They let me talk to you and hear you, but not see you. It was to keep me from annihilating them."

"You should've done it anyway. Axo, if we burn this place to the ground, we'd walk out without a scratch. They've left us in here together, which was a huge mistake."

"This place, Riley, is made entirely of stone. And the rooms above and below this one are empty, and stone. They've laid it all out for me."

"No, Axo, I've read up on it, we can do it. You can weaken stone with fire, enough to make it collapse. Collapse a wall and we're out. And that door is wood! We just need to burn it."

"They've thought ahead. We couldn't progress the fire fast enough. They've got a ventilation system that'll pipe some sort of witchy sleeping drug into the room faster than we can get a big enough fire going. Plus, we can't spread the fire."

"We can burn the door down!"

"Riley, I'm telling you, it won't work. They're prepared."

"They want the baby." There has to be something we could do.

"I know." He kissed my hair and rubbed my back. "They won't get it."

"I'm not that far from delivery. Anthony and Elias will be looking for us, but it could take a while."

"Nah, they'll use a witch and find us in no time. Just be patient and play along." He whispered the last sentence so that hopefully their bugs wouldn't pick his words up.

"So, we just wait?"

"We just wait. I assume someone will come soon to discuss our options and exactly why you're being held."

The intercom crackled. "He's right. If you'll agree to be nice, we'll come speak to you about your current predicament."

What other options did I have? I threw up my arms. "I'll be nice," I said through clenched teeth.

"We'll be with you shortly. What would you like for breakfast?"

"Breakfast?" I couldn't believe their gall.

"It's currently two in the morning. You slept for several hours. We're happy to feed you whatever you'd like to eat. What is your request?"

The disembodied voice was trying to be reasonable, and it infuriated me. "I'd rather starve."

"No, she wouldn't," Axoular cut in. "She's just mad. She'll have waffles and bacon. I'll have the same. Don't be skimpy with the butter and syrup."

I arched one eyebrow at him but didn't argue. I was already hungry; we'd never gotten around to eating dinner. "Fine. If you want to come talk, bring me something to eat now."

Hmph. I might as well be comfortable if they're going to pretend to be sweet, nice captors. I walked over to the bookcase and read some of the titles. My favorite books were mixed among other similar books. Everything from vampires to spaceships called Malice, to historical sappy love stories, I loved fiction and loved a wide range of it.

"Do they really think I'll just settle into captivity and read until I deliver my baby and give it to them?" I turned to Axoular, the rage rising again.

He shrugged his shoulders as the intercom crackled. "Yes."

"I'm going to find the intercom and break it," I called, my eyes back on the books.

"I wouldn't advise that, Mrs. Effler. That will cause you to lose your roommate." I tried to pinpoint the direction of the voice while he spoke, but I couldn't even get a general direction.

Huffing, I walked over to the couch and sat down. Axoular followed.

"We'll get through this, Riley." He sat close to me, and I curled into him, as much as my belly would allow. "It's just a puzzle to solve. We'll solve it." I grinned at the way he thought. He had no doubts, or at least, he didn't let me see any doubts.

We sat in silence, my mind on the worst possible scenarios. What if they did a forcible cesarean once the baby was far enough along? I'd remembered all the scary news stories I always seemed to hear when I was pregnant with the boys, where the mom was kidnapped and murdered, baby cut from her womb. They always made me paranoid and scared to go outside alone in the last few weeks of pregnancy.

Now look at me. I'm likely one of the most powerful creatures on Earth and I'm sitting in a gilded cage. The more I studied the room, the more it reminded me of the story Peter had fed us of his captivity.

"This is where he got it!" I jumped up, enraged —again.

"Got what? Who?"

"I told you what Peter told us to get us to trust

him, right?"

Axoular nodded.

"Well, he described being kept in a gilded cage. I was thinking about our predicament just now and the words gilded cage popped into my mind. He said they gave him a TV, the whole nine yards. If he destroyed it, they'd knock him out and replace it all." I spread my arms and indicated the room. "He was describing all of this!"

"You think he was a prisoner here?"

"No, I think he *had* prisoners here."

Axoular's eyes widened. "I'll kill them."

"You took the words right out of my mouth."

The intercom crackled. "If you would both be so kind as to sit on the couch and don't move. If you make any moves to stand, the room will be filled with gas that will knock you both out and Axoular will be moved to a different room."

We both agreed, nodding our heads, and sitting. The door opened, and an Indonesian man of average height and build entered the room. In a crowd in Bali, he'd be totally forgettable, the perfect disguise for the locale.

"Hello Riley, Axoular." He nodded his head to us. "I am Dumadi. I'm the leader of this world's Leyak, as we call ourselves here."

"I thought you called yourselves the Humbaba," Axoular said, looking unimpressed.

"Potato, potahto. May I sit?" Sweeping one hand out, he was asking for permission to sit across from us.

"This is your place," I said with a sneer. "Sit wherever you want to." His manners meant nothing to me. I was a country girl, born and bred in Tennessee. I was raised with the best manners my mama could muster, but they were not to be wasted on the likes of him.

"I'll take that to mean, 'yes, please join me.'"

I pursed my lips. "Why are we here?"

"Axoular is here to keep you cooperative. You're here because you carry a Leyak child in your womb."

"You can't possibly know that."

"Did you sleep with my son?"

"Peter was your son?" My skin heated rapidly.

Axoular put his arm around me and squeezed. "Keep it together, Riley."

I breathed deep to try to calm myself—not an easy thing to do.

"He was. And you killed him." He pulled in a deep breath. "I was angry at first, but in retrospect, I could see why you might be a *little* angry."

I scoffed. "A *little* angry? A lot. And how could you know if the baby is his, or Anthony's or Elias's?"

"Haven't you been the busy little dragon?" He templed his hands and rested them on his chin.

"Screw you, dude. You don't know me, or my life, or my relationships." Axoular squeezed me again, a reminder to be calm.

"No, I don't. Nor do I want to. I simply want my progeny and I'll leave you in peace."

His words struck me as hilarious. I burst out laughing so hard I nearly peed myself, which reminded me I really needed to use the restroom. I fought back the laughter. "Of all the bad timings, but I need to pee. May I stand?"

The door opened and a man stepped in with a gun. Dumadi waited for him to position himself in front of the closed door and then nodded. "You may."

"I don't believe for a second you'll shoot me."

"It's loaded with tranquilizers. It will knock you out again, but not hurt you or the babe." I opened my mouth, but he cut me off. "Nor did the medicine we gave you in the car. It was specially brewed for us to make you sleep but not your child."

Well, thank goodness for small blessings. I stood, shooting both men the worst looks I could muster, and waddled to the bathroom. The weight of the baby on my hips suddenly felt like he'd added on a good ten pounds. Somehow, I was sure the stress of the day was making every small ailment seem worse because I felt like throwing up when I'd just been hungry a few minutes before.

When I'd finished and washed my hands, I walked out to find the three men staring off into space. "Couldn't find anything to talk about without me around?"

"Your defender here would only growl when I attempted to speak to him, so I gave up."

"Well, can you blame him?" I asked as I sat back down beside Axoular.

"Now, back to business. I want my son's child, and I'll happily release you back to the little harem of men you've collected for yourself."

"That's not going to happen. I'll die first."

"Somehow I don't think you will," he said smugly. "You've got two or three other children to consider, do you not? As well as the wellbeing of your new lover here. Pity to have you both die, and your children be orphaned."

"They wouldn't be orphaned and—we're going around in circles. How do you know if the baby is Peter's?"

"Our prophet told us as much."

"You have a prophet?" I asked with wide eyes. Every story book I'd ever read that had prophets described them as being rare and precious. I'd come across a book on prophets in the library at the manor. I'd only skimmed it, but I'd learned enough to know the fiction books were based on truth. Prophets were one of the rarest creatures on Earth. They transcended species and could be born to any mother of any shape, size, or ability. They were usually given power and wealth and waited on hand and foot.

"Indeed, we do. She said, 'The dragon bears the child that will both begin and end the war. The child of The Dragon and The Hidden is The Chosen.'"

"What's The Hidden?"

"*We* are The Hidden. You supernatural creatures, calling yourselves the Unseen, with your councils and rules. You had no idea we existed until Peter defied his entire heritage and training and revealed himself." He rubbed his hands over his face wearily. "I think he must have grown to care for you, Riley. I don't know how else to explain destroying years of careful planning."

My jaw dropped. "I'm glad he's dead. And I'm glad I got to be the one that killed him."

Fury crossed Dumadi's face, but only for a

moment before his perfectly controlled façade slammed back into place. "I understand your anger, but I would appreciate a modicum of respect for a mourning father."

"You must earn my respect. Kidnapping me and threatening me is *not* the way to do it."

His jaw twitched, but he didn't reply.

"What else do you have to tell us?" Axoular said, voice perfectly even, but I could hear the tension and anger in his voice, even if Dumadi probably couldn't.

"What about the Humbaba?" I asked.

"What about them?"

I gave him an exasperated look. "You said you'd explain who they are, and while you're at it, that whole backstory Peter gave us about you hunting and killing dragons because you were afraid of portals, that's a load of bull."

"It's what he believed." Dumadi gave me a scrutinizing glare. "And it was partially true."

"That's what I figured. What's the truth?"

"The Humbaba is simply one of our various names. As the Supay have been called demons, vampires, and other names across the centuries, so have we. We have kept to the shadows, to the secrets, but the humans are a discerning lot. We gave birth to rumors, and rumors, as we all know, begat legends.

Thus, the Indonesian legend of the Leyak was born, and the Humbaba, and many more. I believe in your United States we're known as skin walkers to your Native people."

I nodded my head. "And the truth? Why did you hunt the dragons? And is it something you're planning to continue doing?"

"We have no desire for war. We only want our child."

"He isn't *your* child!" I clenched my hands into fists as I tried to breathe and control the fire. "The more you piss me off, the harder it is to control my fire, I want you to know that."

"I don't wish to anger you. I understand the heartache you'll face, especially considering I so recently lost my firstborn."

"If he hadn't raped me, he might still be alive."

The color drained from Dumadi's face. "He what?"

"Raped. Me." I emphasized the consonants. "I didn't consent to have sex with him. He raped me under the guise of being my *dead* husband."

"But he did not force you to lie with him."

It was my turn to squeeze Axoular's hand as his skin heated rapidly. The subject at hand infuriated him.

"He didn't have my willing participation. He lied and manipulated me. He raped me. It might not have been violent, but it was a gross intrusion all the same."

He waved his hands, his expression was disbelieving. He was effectively dismissing me as a hysterical woman. "You'll be fine."

"This conversation is over. You'll not have my baby, and you'll not have peace. If I get a chance, I'll burn you alive as well. Get out or I'll do it now, sleeping gas or not." I allowed the flames to dance across my hand, though I kept it away from my clothes and the couch. I wasn't ready to bring the whole place down just yet. More planning had to be done.

He rose and gave us a slight bow. "We will continue this conversation when you're able to be a bit more reasonable."

I bit back the scream that fought to come out of my mouth and ended up snarling at him.

Axoular stood. "You will regret the decisions you made today," he said with finality.

Dumadi left the room. The lock gave a loud *click* as he sealed us in.

I turned to Axoular. "We gotta get out of here."

5

ELIAS

I HUNG UP THE PHONE AND CONTINUED PACING the room. Anthony had traced Riley's scent at the party to the parking lot. She'd left in a car, but he couldn't tell more than that. Our senses were heightened, but not like a bloodhound. More like a bloodhound with a stuffy nose.

My cell phone rang, and I almost threw it in my haste to answer it. "Cindy? What have you got for me?"

"She's on the island, I know that. Anything further than that would require her blood to make the spell work properly."

"How much of her blood?" I asked.

"Even a drop would do."

"Does it have to be fresh?"

"No?" she said, running her vowel into a question. "Why do you have old Riley blood?"

"Nothing nefarious. Riley doesn't like for us to use donors, so she donates blood as often as she can so we can drink her blood whenever possible. We still have to use donor blood, of course, but it makes her happy to know she's helping us keep from taking some unsuspecting human's donated blood."

"Well, that's—sweet?"

I shrugged, even though she couldn't see me. "She's got the best-tasting blood I've ever had, so I don't argue. Anyway, we're out of hers, but I have a blood bag in the garbage that has a trace amount left in it."

"That'll do," she said. "I'll be there within an hour. Gotta take my son to the sitter."

After thanking her, I hung up and rifled through the trash for the bag of blood. Riley had scribbled her name and the date she'd filled the bag on the front. Just a few days before.

I hung my head, her scent washing over me from the bag. What would we do if she was gone forever? She was the perfect companion for us. It was like we were destined for each other, even with the bumpy takeoff we'd had.

Anthony burst into the room. "Is she coming?"

He knew I'd been working to get Cindy to track Riley. "She'll be here within an hour."

He nodded and sat on the couch only to stand back up and pace with me. "There's got to be something more we can do."

"I have an idea, but I don't know if we can get it to work. Peter was able to send her messages when she slept, remember? Maybe we could try that."

"It couldn't hurt. Should we both try at the same time?"

We could possibly drown each other out, but it was unlikely either of us would even be able to accomplish such a feat. I shrugged. "Why not?"

We moved to the living room and sat on the rug in front of the fireplace and closed our eyes. I didn't know what else to do but imagine her. I used my mind's eye to picture her silky strawberry hair, the curve of her neck, how her eyelashes were blonde unless she wore mascara.

I focused for a moment on the large freckle above her right shoulder blade. She always worried about that freckle; afraid it was skin cancer. I'd reminded her several times it was unlikely with her genes that she'd get cancer. She just liked to worry.

As I pictured her, in painstaking detail, I shouted

her name in my mind. *Riley! If you can hear me, yell my name!*

I repeated that mantra with a sufficient pause each time while I focused on how she smelled, the sound of her voice. The curve of her hips. I cracked one eye when my efforts were only rewarding me with a problem in my pants. "It's not working," I grumbled.

Anthony nodded; eyes still closed. "Me neither."

"Well, I hope I can be more help than you two meditating morons." I jerked my head to see Cindy standing in the doorway from the kitchen. "What are you two doing?"

"Trying to connect telepathically to Riley."

Cindy burst out laughing. "That's not possible, guys." She flipped her long blonde hair behind her shoulders.

Anthony stood, holding a hand out to help me up. "The Shapeshifter contacted her telepathically while we were on the run."

"That shouldn't be possible. But we can figure that out later." She turned toward the kitchen. "Let's get started."

"Anthony spoke to her in her mind when she was having a nightmare."

She stopped and turned back. "Really? That's amazing. Were you touching her?"

"Yes, but why is it such a big deal? I've heard of telepathy before," Anthony said.

"Yeah, there are telepaths out there, but they're excessively rare. Either the Shapeshifter was one rare being or he used a spell."

"Maybe," Anthony mused.

"The blood is on the table," I said as she unloaded the messenger bag she wore.

Pulling items from the bag, she chanted. "*Garbitu espazio hau.*" She lit a bundle of herbs I was pretty sure was sage, for cleansing. "*Iraganekoa kendu. Negatibitatea baztertzen dizut.*"

She waved the sage around in a ritual only she understood. I trusted her ability and knowledge to do what we needed to do, and do it properly, but I wished she'd hurry.

Anthony clapped me on the shoulder. "She'll find her. And Riley is fierce, pregnant, or not. She's okay."

"I'm glad she's got Axoular with her, even so. She's been vulnerable since she's been pregnant."

He didn't reply. We watched Cindy put down a map of the island. "Where'd you get that?" I asked. She hadn't had time to stop to buy a map.

"Shhh," she said, then continued her chant.

"She probably conjured it," Anthony whispered in my ear.

She cut the top of the mostly empty blood bag open and dipped a pendant of some sort into it, rubbing it around to get Riley's blood all over it.

Her chant changed and became more commanding as she slowly circled the pendant, hanging from her closed fist, over the map. *"Erakutsi zer bilatzen dudan."*

The pendant swung for several agonizing minutes while Cindy chanted. Finally, it landed on the map with a thud.

Cindy marked the spot with a red marker and began again, exactly the same. The pendant dropped again, many minutes later, in a different spot. "What does that mean?" I asked.

"It's not good. This spell requires the caster to ask for the location three times for a reason. I'll do it one more time and let you know what it means."

I nodded and tried to ignore the panic rising in my gut.

This time, the pendant landed in the water around the island. Cindy hung her head. "She's blocked."

"What do you mean blocked?" Anthony asked, his voice higher than normal.

"Someone is using magic to keep me from being able to find her."

"So, what now?" I asked.

"Now, I call my coven here." She swung her eyes to me. "We've been friends a long time, and I come help whenever you need me because I believe you're good people, and your family is one of the few that wants to do right. But my coven will not come willingly to help a Supay."

"I know you only give us the time of day because my mother saved your mother's life. I understand what it costs to employ a coven. We'll pay double their normal fee."

She arched an eyebrow. "That's hardly necessary."

"It is very necessary. Perhaps it'll incentivize them to work faster."

She laughed. "You old fool. It doesn't work that way. But they need the money, so I won't argue. I'll have them here as soon as I can, but it might be tomorrow."

"Tell them they get a bonus thousand dollars for every hour they arrive before..." I checked my watch. It was four in the morning. We hadn't even started looking until midnight. We began to grow worried at ten but gave them time to finish their date. We didn't want to rush them.

At midnight, we'd gone to the club where they'd had the roast. The party was in full swing, but Riley and Axoular were nowhere to be found. After talking to all the cabbies outside, we found the one that was out there waiting for them. I'd returned to the cottage to contact Cindy while Anthony had continued searching.

"Eight this morning. That gives you four hours. A thousand dollars per hour before eight."

She nodded and opened a portal right there in the kitchen to take her home. Stepping through, it closed with a pop and left us alone, with nothing to do but worry.

Three days had inched by, leaving us bored and restless. We hadn't been let out of the room, and I was feeling cut off from nature, from the sun.

"I thought dragons were supposed to hibernate in caves and hoard gold and other treasures," I grumbled to Axoular. "I need to be outside."

"That must be some weird Earth legends. We aren't really dragons, not like what I've seen in your storybooks and movies. We're more like lizards."

Eww. Lizard people? "We'll stick to dragons."

"Whatever you want to call it, your legends are mostly untrue."

I turned back to the television, flipping channels too fast to really see what was on them. "Anthony and Elias are probably out of their minds while we sit here, waiting for me to have this baby. Which, by the way, they won't get their freaky hands on!" I yelled the last part toward the ceiling, where I imagined the cameras and microphones to be. In the three days we'd been in the room, we still hadn't found a camera or anything resembling an intercom or recording device. We assumed it was all done magically but had no idea why a magical intercom would sound like a real one.

"I'm about to burn this place to the ground," I said quietly, hoping anyone listening wouldn't be able to hear me.

"Not yet," he whispered. "Give them time to find us. I know they're searching."

"Of course, they are. But there's no telling how the *Leyak*—" I always said their name as sarcastically as I could muster—have blocked us. They probably can't find us with spells. For all they know, we're in Timbuktu."

"But we're not. They have money, power, and friends all across the world. They'll find someone powerful enough to break the spell."

"I'm not waiting much longer." I went back to clicking through the channels, which seemed to never end.

We'd had the same conversation a dozen times. I wanted to blow the roof off the place, he cautioned me to wait and let my husbands handle the situation. We didn't appear to be in any immediate danger, but my restlessness and craving for sunshine were getting to me.

I grabbed the book I'd found on the bookshelves and tried to lose myself in it. I'd already read five novels, and that was just the first two days.

The first day I was content, sure Elias would come busting through the doors while Anthony tricked someone into believing it was a great idea to let us out.

The second day my smile was a little strained.

This morning, my smile was gone. It was almost night, and we still hadn't heard a word from any of the Leyak.

"I'm going to take a bath," I said.

"You took a shower this morning."

"I'm not taking a shower; I'm taking a bath."

He looked at me quizzically, setting aside a word search book. He enjoyed doing puzzles and things like word finds. He said it helped him learn the language nuances.

"Girls like to soak in a tub of warm water, just for fun."

Laughing, he nodded. "Women on Galdiart did the same thing."

I shrugged. "Girls will be girls."

Leaving him to his puzzles, I walked into the bathroom and stripped. There was a small closet in the bathroom with some basic clothes to fit me, but Axoular had been an unexpected addition, so they said. He didn't have anything to change into. He'd turned his undies inside out and was now just commando.

I pulled pajamas out—they'd sprung for maternity clothes—and put my clothes into a hamper behind the door. It was almost full.

Peering around the small room, I wondered once again if someone was watching me, and if they enjoyed the show. I'd tried to keep myself covered the first day, but it grew tiresome quickly.

Once the tub was full of piping hot water, I lowered myself into it and finished my sixth novel in three days. I stayed until the water was cool and my toes were pruned.

Axoular still sat at the table in the corner, searching for more words. "Feel better?"

"How are you so calm?" I asked as I climbed into the bed. "I feel like I've been coiled up *really* tight, and I'm about to spring out and bounce all over the place."

"You forget how long I waited in that cave for

your arrival. I'm good at waiting and keeping myself calm."

"Come teach me how to do it."

My emotions had been in chaos since I'd woken up that morning. I'd finally begun to wonder if my husbands would be able to find us after all. Of course, they'd move Heaven and Earth to get to me, but what if they couldn't?

I wanted to be prepared to save myself. I would be no damsel.

Axoular slid into the bed on the other side of me and sat with his legs crossed. "Have you ever meditated?"

"Some. I've done yoga."

"I'll pretend I know what that is and that you know how to meditate." He placed his hands on his knees. "Breathe deeply and center your mind. Find your flame."

I focused on my flame and quickly found it. We'd told the room on the first morning that we had to let our flames out daily or we'd burn out, and nobody had freaked out when we did it every morning since then. No gas entered the room, so we figured they were probably listening after all.

I'd noticed that my womb seemed to be the base for my fire, and even when it was calm and where it should be, my womb was constantly burning.

"Axo, when I focus on my fire, I've noticed it always surrounds the baby."

He gave me a confused look. "You can see your fire? I feel mine; I can't see it."

"Well, then you probably can't help me."

"All I know is that Sárkány women have had babies since the beginning of time. I'm going to assume all those babies were grown in fire."

He had a point. I nodded and mimicked his pose, wondering why he felt his fire and I saw mine.

We sat in silence for a few minutes while thoughts raced through my mind. I watched my flames grow, too busy worrying to realize I wasn't meditating and calming myself. I grew more and more agitated with each minute that passed.

Before I knew it, smoke rose from my skin in whispering tendrils. I watched it rise. *Let them see. They know what I can do. They should fear me.*

Axoular's nose twitched, and his eyes flew open. "Riley," he hissed. "Do you want to get us separated? You're supposed to be calming yourself."

"I don't know if I'm the sort of person that takes something like being kidnapped calmly. I don't know if I can do calm right now," I snapped, irritated with his peaceful demeanor.

He grabbed my arms and jerked me toward him, slamming his mouth down on mine. I was so surprised I didn't even kiss him back. I just sat there, slack-jawed, while his lips caressed mine.

Once I realized what he was doing, I grinned against his mouth. "Are you trying to distract me?" I asked, his face muffling my words.

He turned his head and kissed my jaw. "Yes," he mumbled against my cheek. "Is it working?"

I considered our predicament. They were definitely watching us. If I calmed down enough to really think it through, I needed to give my husbands more time to find us. We still had weeks before I would go into labor if my previous pregnancies were any indication. I'd gone a week overdue with both of my sons.

All I needed to do was be patient, but that seemed an impossible task, so a distraction was the smartest course. I'd been given permission to bring Axoular into the fold if I wanted, and especially after being kidnapped with him, I wanted. He complimented our relationship. I wanted to know him, more and more every day.

I worked through my hang-ups and doubts

quickly in my mind while Axoular worked on my neck. Once I'd made up my mind, I pulled back and looked into his dark brown eyes. "How far are we willing to go when we're being watched?"

"There is much we can do under the covers," he said, eyes twinkling.

I laughed and pulled the blankets back. "You're right. Come here."

He joined me and I returned his kisses since I was no longer surprised by them. His mouth was hot, hotter than any other man I'd ever kissed.

He broke our kiss to pull the blankets over our heads. "It might get warm under here."

"I haven't gotten truly hot since I went through the portal the first time. My body craves heat now. The winter was miserable, I pretty much stayed beside the fireplaces in the manor," I whispered as he gazed down on me, a white blanket tenting over his head.

"You're beautiful, Riley. I never imagined I'd be in this position with you, in a bed, about to make love."

"It took me by surprise, too. My feelings for you grew when I didn't even know they were there. I love you, Axoular, and I think I'm falling *in* love with you."

He laughed; joy splashed across his face. "I'll make sure you keep falling," he said before his eyes fell to the swell of my breasts, hidden in the pink pajama top.

I lifted my hands to the top button and slowly unbuttoned the top without letting the fabric separate, teasing him. Once the shirt was totally unbuttoned, I put my hands around him and ran my fingers over the short hair on the back of his head.

He hung his head, nostrils flaring. "You're a tease." We'd been in a room together for three days, sending each other longing glances and lingering touches across hands and arms.

Suffice it to say we were both horny.

He dropped onto his elbow, breathing deeply. "Your smell," he said, turning his head sideways.

"My smell?" I'd just had a bath, I couldn't smell *that* bad.

"Haven't you noticed your sense of smell has changed?" he asked.

"Well, yeah, but I figured that was the pregnancy. I can smell *everything*. I could with my other pregnancies, too, but this is even stronger."

"I can smell you in a room full of people. I smell you when I sleep. Sleeping beside you the last couple of nights has been heaven, basking in your scent."

I raised my eyebrows. "That's heavy. You're laying it on a little thick."

His face fell, disappointed.

"No, don't be sad!" I exclaimed. "Are you being sincere? You like the way I smell that much?"

"I'm serious. Sárkány bond through smell. Can't you smell me?"

My sense of smell *had* heightened, but I'd been trying to ignore it because smells weren't always pleasant. Closing my eyes, I breathed deep and focused on the scents around me. Laundry detergent, minty toothpaste, and... He smelled like the outdoors. I laughed, delighted.

"You smell like sunshine! Like freshly mown grass and carrots pulled from the ground. How have I never noticed this?" I pulled him close and pressed my nose against his neck, breathing deeply. "What do I smell like?"

"I had to search out the spices in the kitchen to know what it is in this world. We have similar in Galdiart. Here, it's cinnamon and nutmeg. Sometimes I smell honey, too."

"But I don't bake," I said stupidly.

He laughed and popped a kiss on my lips. "We all smell like something from nature. It's just a part of our body chemistry to have a smell relating to, as you'd say, Mother Nature."

He claimed my lips again, and I enjoyed the petting, focusing on my newfound sense of smell. Smelling the outdoors on his skin made me feel closer to it, and my fire crackled happily under my skin.

He was moving down my chest when we were interrupted by the sound of the door opening and slamming against the wall. Axoular sprang up with a roar, uncovering us. I buttoned my shirt, suddenly the calm one.

When we were alone and waiting, he was the calm one, but once we were confronted with another person, he became the agitated one.

I had no reason to be upset. If they came near me, I'd burn them to a crisp.

Dumadi stood in the doorway, face red with anger. "Get out from under the blanket. You'll not fornicate here while being watched with my grandchild in your womb."

That was when I'd had enough. I smiled. "Axoular," I murmured. "Is it possible to shoot fire at someone?"

He snapped his head toward me, eyes wide. "Yes. Simply will it to be, and it'll be."

"What's that? What are you saying?" Dumadi's face was nearly purple.

I smiled and rose from the bed. "Stay close to me," I said under my breath.

"I demand you tell me what you're saying, or I'll have them release the gasses!"

I smiled at Dumadi. "Don't be upset."

"How could I not be?" he yelled. "You're a brazen woman, but you'll not expose my grandchild to any more unnatural behavior."

"It'll be all right," I said soothingly, nearly to him. He stood in front of the open door. I could see the hallway outside the door where a guard stood peeking into the room. "We're leaving now."

"You aren't going anywhere!" Spittle flew from his mouth as he tried to assert his power.

Laughter burst from my lips as I let my fire have its head. Flames erupted all over me, burning my clothes off. Lifting my arms, I focused my energy on the air above Dumadi's head, and a bolt of fire shot toward the wall, igniting the wallpaper instantly. Dumadi ducked, squealing, then ran from the room.

The guard took one look at my outstretched hand and bolted. I walked serenely out the door into the hall, an expression of peace on my face. Inside, I was screaming, terrified they'd invoke some spell to contain me and end up separating me from my only source of comfort.

Looking both ways, I wasn't sure where to go. There was a door at each end and nothing else. *I gotta get out of here.* I looked behind me, where Axoular stood, not on fire, holding the covers from the bed. I saw my clothes smoldering on the floor behind him and flames licking the door frame as they spread from the wallpaper. The room would be ash, but the hall was all stone and would not burn. He pointed to the right with a shrug, so I went that way, walking quickly, but not running. I wouldn't let them see any fear.

"Hurry," he said. "You're going to burn out soon and collapse."

Crap. He was right. I'd start burning calories at a frightening rate and probably pass out, then it'd be on him to continue our escape with me in his arms.

I ran. Throwing open the door at the end of the hall, I found a set of stairs. Heading down, I wondered why I hadn't found any more people or resistance. And where the hell did Dumadi go?

The door at the bottom opened and three enormous men ran up the stairs toward me. The lead man yelled at us. "Stop right there!"

I stopped, all right. Stopped and put energy into

making my body overwhelmingly hot. They couldn't get near me without the skin melting off of their bodies.

Halfway between us and the door, they stopped, and goon number one took a pouch out of his pocket. "Don't let him throw that at you!" Axoular yelled from behind me. I didn't even look back, I just threw fire down on the men, ignoring the panicked feeling I got for causing death. The third man dodged it and retreated to the bottom, but the first two weren't so lucky. Their clothes caught and they writhed on the stairs, dying.

"We don't have time for this," Axoular said. He couldn't touch me, or he'd risk catching his clothes and the blanket he'd grabbed for me on fire. "Go!"

I went. Goon number three at the bottom of the stairs pulled another pouch out and pitched it toward me. I brought my hand up and shot the hottest fire I could manage at it in the air. It obliterated it.

The ashes of the bag drifted down and goon Three hightailed it.

At the bottom of the stairs, I flew through the door into what appeared to be a room of worship. Dumadi ran through the door on the other side of the room. I tore through, touching my flaming hands to everything I passed. I hated lighting a sacred place on fire, but I needed any distraction I could get.

The door Dumadi exited through stood open and I saw that it went outside. I skidded to a stop when I realized people milled everywhere outside the temple. People meant safety. If we could get lost in the crowd, we could escape. I pulled my fire back inside me and threw myself to the side of the doorway to put the blanket around my body like a toga. I'd just gotten it tied when I felt the crash coming.

"Axoular! I'm about to drop. Borrow someone's phone and call them." I fought it for another second, but the exhaustion took me. It was up to Axoular to complete our escape.

6

ANTHONY

"I'VE GOT HER!" CINDY'S VOICE RANG OUT, excited, as my phone rang.

The number was unfamiliar, but it was a local number. Combined with Cindy's excited shriek, I was sure it was Riley. "Hello? Riley?"

"It's me." Axoular's voice sent waves of relief coursing through me.

Elias pushed against me. "Is it her? Is she okay?"

I pulled the phone away from my ear and pushed the speaker button.

"She's safe for now." Axoular's voice was muffled by background noise. "She passed out, but it's just exhaustion, and I couldn't stop the locals from calling an ambulance. It's on the way. I borrowed someone's phone."

"Where are you?" Elias shouted at the cell phone in my hand.

"I don't know what temple we're at, but we've been held in a temple by the Leyak."

"Are you sure you're safe?" I asked. "I knew it was those Shapeshifters."

"Our safety is the crowd. The temple was open for business when we escaped from the inner parts of it. The crowd is human, as far as I can tell, and our safety is being surrounded by them." He paused, and it sounded like he spoke to someone there at the temple. "The ambulance is pulling up, I must go."

I got the hospital information from him and hung up the phone. Elias and I stared at each other for a few minutes before rushing into each other's arms. Tears of relief coursed down my cheeks. I clapped him on the back and turned to find Cindy watching us.

"She's safe?" she asked.

"We think so. Thank you for your assistance."

"We didn't do any good. They've got some seriously powerful mojo to block us. I don't know what magic they're using, either."

"We know next to nothing about the Shapeshifters. They say they don't have magic, just science, but I don't know what to think," Elias said.

"If you get the chance to learn about them, or the magic they used here, please include me. I don't want to go up against any magic-user that can so effectively hide a person."

I strode across the room and hugged Cindy. "I know some of your people did it for money, but the appreciation is no less for it. They've worked round the clock trying to find her, and we won't forget that."

"I'll tell them." She shook Elias's hand and left the room to collect her coven and go home.

"Let's go!" Elias called from across the room. I grabbed the keys to the motorcycles we'd rented, and we ran for the door. It hadn't been easy to secure a rental for the bikes I'd gotten. I wanted us to be able to take Riley for a ride along the coastal roads but wanted her to be comfortable. The available bikes were mostly sports bikes or scooters. I'd finally found a man that owned two cruising bikes and he'd agreed to rent them to us for the week. Our week was almost over, but we had the bikes.

I skidded to a stop and turned back, sticking my head in the door. "Cindy," I called. "Can you call the Junta and let them know to expect my call after we get Riley?"

She yelled that she would, and I took off.

The weekend traffic caused us to take an hour to get to the hospital. In our eagerness to see our wife, we weaved around cars and generally made ourselves a nuisance on the roads, but we would've been much longer getting to her if we hadn't.

The hospital looked much like the ones I'd observed in the States. Doctors and medical staff bustled around while patients and visitors walked to and fro. We rushed into the emergency room entrance and headed straight for an information desk.

I got there a split second ahead of Elias, so I got to be the husband. "My wife was brought in, unconscious. She was at a nearby temple."

The clerk smiled and thankfully spoke English. "Her name?"

"Riley Effler."

She typed her name into a computer. "She's in room E4." She motioned to the doors we should walk through. "It's through there, follow the blue line to get to the emergency rooms and E4 is on the left."

Elias clapped my shoulder and squeezed as we followed her directions. With our ability to move fast, it was agonizing to force ourselves to walk at a normal pace. We had to keep up appearances.

Riley lay in a stark white hospital bed and wore a

sickly green hospital gown. Her soft red hair fanned around her head on the pillow. I choked up when I saw how pale she was: Elias flashed beside her and touched the dark blue circles under her closed eyes with his thumbs.

Axoular sat beside her, head down on the mattress.

"How is she?" I hurried to the bed, on the side opposite Axoular. Her hands were cold, and she barely moved. "She's freezing."

"I know. It worries me. I'm scared she's in a deeper sleep than before. She burned for a long time."

Elias sat beside her on the bed, near Axoular. "Why'd you let her do that?"

"She didn't give me a choice. I would've gladly done what she did, and honestly could've done it better. Though, she did a fantastic job for someone so new."

"Tell us exactly what happened and why you couldn't keep this from happening." If he didn't give a satisfactory answer, I'd kill him myself.

"We can't talk here. They can be anywhere, but I paid attention as we left that temple. Being in that place, I can't mistake that smell. I've already smelled them here. They followed us, but they can't do anything about it here. We need to get her out of here."

"Have they said anything about moving her? That would be my first move if I was trying to get her away from us."

"No, not yet. They're shorthanded, I think. She's only been seen by a nurse."

"What did you tell them?" Elias asked.

"The paramedics had the hospital gown on the rig. The nurse didn't ask why she'd been changed into it, and I didn't volunteer any information. At this point, I don't think they realize she's totally naked under there. That'll raise some questions."

I'd have to try to exert calm over the staff when we carried her out. "First, Axoular, go out and try to get a cab waiting."

He nodded and walked out of the room, shutting the door behind him.

Elias poked through the cabinets until he found another hospital gown. He lifted her up and I put the gown on her backward. We maneuvered her until it covered her and there was no risk of flashing any of the people in the hospital and raising a further alarm.

"I'll carry her," Elias said. "You do your thing if we run into anyone."

"What if he doesn't have a cab ready?"

He blinked. "I have no idea. Maybe you can convince someone to give us a ride."

"I'm going to need to drink after all this."

"We'll get home quickly."

"Wait. Let me make a call before we go."

I grabbed my phone and dialed Cindy's number. "Are you still in Bali?" I asked as soon as she answered.

"No, I'm home."

"Can you meet us at the beach house in an hour? We need to get straight back home."

"Of course. I'll be there a little early, so I've got the portal ready."

"That's great. Thank you, Cindy."

I shut off the phone. "Let's go."

He gathered her up and I opened the door, hoping to be able to exit the room unnoticed. A nurse stood at the end of the hall typing on a tablet. She didn't look like she had any plans to move anytime soon. I retreated into the room. "How fast can you run carrying her?" I asked.

"As fast as not carrying her assuming I won't have to go through any tight spaces."

"There's a nurse at the end of the hall. I'll get her to look to the left once I know the right is clear. You run Riley to the hall on the right. Hide in the bathroom in that hall if you have to, but I'll come along behind you."

I sauntered to the desk. "Hello, ma'am." I grinned, pushing the right side of my mouth down a little so my dimples deepened. At the same time, I pushed a feeling of calm acceptance toward her. My forehead tingled, as it did whenever I tried to manipulate someone's feelings.

She looked up from her laptop and stared straight into my eyes, as I'd hoped she would. Elias streaked past and around the corner, where I could see the hallway was empty.

"Where would I find a bathroom?" I asked for the room Elias was in, so she'd point me in the direction I needed to go anyway. She smiled and indicated it was down the hall behind her. "Go back to your paperwork," I said soothingly. Her eyes drifted back to her tablet, and she tapped away at it again.

I met Elias in the bathroom. Riley had her face tucked into his neck. "Has she moved?" I asked.

"She nuzzled my neck." His eyebrows furrowed. "Man, I almost dropped her when she did that. But I think it was instinctual. She's fast asleep."

I nodded then pressed a kiss to her temple. "Okay. Let's try to get out of here."

I exited the bathroom like I didn't have a care in

the world. I nodded at a passing man in a white coat, then pulled out my phone, pretending to check it. It bought me enough time for the man to turn down another hallway. "Come on," I muttered.

We walked at a brisk pace, uninterrupted until we got to the doors out to the waiting room. A woman sat at a desk I hadn't noticed on our way in. "Can I help you?" she asked, one eyebrow raised as she observed Riley.

I focused my energy on her. "This woman needs medical care at a specialized facility. We are taking her straight to an airplane that'll take her to the right doctors. Everything is fine. We have proper credentials."

My forehead buzzed; I was pushing calm onto her so hard. She blinked a few times, then smiled. "I'm sure you do. Thank you for visiting us today." She inclined her head and sat back down at her desk.

"You're getting better at that," Elias whispered behind me.

"Let's just see how well I do getting out the doors." I walked slowly toward the double doors leading to the lobby, glancing at the lady out of the corner of my eye to make sure she still focused on her papers on her desk.

"I think for now we should just fake it."

"What do you mean?"

"Walk out of here like we're supposed to be walking out carrying an unconscious patient in a hospital gown."

"It's the best we've got, might as well," I replied.

Striding the rest of the way to the doors, I pushed them open for Elias to walk through. The receptionist stood, but I just nodded at her. "Thank you for your help."

We nodded and smiled at the people waiting and made for the exit with our heads held high. I could see Axoular standing beside a cab with the back door open.

"Sir!" a man shouted behind us.

"Go," I whispered. "I'll distract him and follow on one of the bikes."

I turned to face the man that yelled. "Yes?" I replied pleasantly.

"You can't take a patient from the hospital. Stop them!" Two men ran out of a door on our right. I turned to stop them, but Elias already had Riley in the cab.

"I think you'll find we can. Who are you?" I asked.

"My name is Dumadi, and you'll regret taking my grandchild from me."

I looked around the waiting room full of humans, my blood boiling. I turned my back to the room and faced the Shapeshifter, who I was sure was the one that kidnapped Riley. Baring my considerably sharp teeth, I did my best to send panicked feelings toward him. I'd never tried my gift in reverse. I could only hope it would work.

"I'll kill you one day soon, Shapeshifter. You stole what is mine, and for that, you'll suffer."

His eyes widened, and his neck pulsed. For the first time in my life, I wanted to use my teeth to rip his jugular from his body. I'd been told it could happen, the desire to kill a human and feast on their blood, but I'd never experienced such savagery in myself.

I turned, confident he wouldn't follow. He was sufficiently cowed, even if it would only last a few more moments.

The cab pulled away from the curb as I exited the hospital. Our bikes were close, so I jogged over and hopped on. I was soon behind the cab, head swiveling as I searched for a tail.

Elias must have told the cabbie something to make him take a crazy route back to the house because he surely took us down every side street they had. It took us nearly two hours to get back, but I was confident we weren't followed.

Axoular jumped out of the car, then turned back to get Riley. Elias made sure she was steady in his arms, then reached back in to pay the man. I hurried toward the house behind Axoular. Cindy met us at the door.

"I've got the portal open. It took you so long I packed everything I could find that I was pretty sure was yours, I already took the bags through. The portal is opened straight to your bedroom at home.

We rushed through the house. I didn't even bother looking to see if we'd left anything. We hadn't taken anything important enough to waste time searching for. Axoular and Riley were the first through, then Elias, then me, and finally, Cindy.

Only when I spotted the dark red walls of our bedroom did I take a deep breath. We were home.

Riley

My eyes hurt and my bladder spasmed so much I was afraid I'd piss myself. To add insult to injury the baby kicked it. I grunted. "What happened?"

Anthony and Elias slept together on my left and Axoular on my right. The sound of my voice jolted them from their sleep and all three hovered over me, asking how I was, faster than my fuzzy mind could handle. "Give me some room to breathe, guys." They looked as bad as I felt. Axoular had black circles under his eyes, and Anthony and Elias were extra pale. Elias's blonde hair made his pale skin look worse. Anthony's hair was a mess.

The baby danced a jig on my bladder again. "I gotta pee." I tried to sit up and found all my muscles were weak and sore. "I could use a little help."

To their credit, they treated me with a velvet touch, but all three of them helped at once. I was—carefully—helped to stand beside the bed closest to the bathroom, but three men gently pushing me forward served to propel me forward. Elias was the fastest and caught me.

"I can't wait to be my limber, only occasionally clumsy self again," I grumbled as I waddled my tired, achy body toward the bathroom.

"She's a little grumpy." I stifled a laugh. I was pretty sure it was Elias's voice whispering through the bathroom door. My hearing had been improving over the past few months, I assumed because of my Sárkány side waking up.

You're being mean. They missed you and were terrified. I finished my business on the toilet and opened the door. "I want to shower, okay?" I smiled at them waiting just outside the bathroom door.

Axoular leaned in and kissed my cheek. "What do you want to eat?"

Sighing, I couldn't think of a single thing that sounded good. "Whatever you feel like making. Thank you." I grabbed his face and placed a soft kiss on his lips. He smiled as he turned and walked from the room.

Leaving the door open, I turned the water on and let it warm while I brushed my fuzzy teeth. *Gross.*

"How do you feel?" Elias asked.

I shrugged, mouth full of toothpaste. Scrubbing my teeth thoroughly didn't leave much room for talking, so I waved my hand back and forth in a "so-so" gesture while I grimaced around my toothbrush.

At least I was alive, and the baby was turning somersaults, so he was okay. I spat and rinsed. "How are my boys?"

"Fine. Worried about you." Anthony pulled the ponytail holder out of the end of my hair and combed his fingers through the braid Tammy had probably put in to keep it from tangling.

I looked down at my pajamas. One of my guys had definitely dressed me. A silky, lace-edged nighty would not have been my choice of sleepwear considering the situation. I would've put on one of Elias's worn-out and extra soft gym shirts.

"I love you guys," I said as I took off the pretty, but uncomfortable, nighty.

They passed a look between them, unable to gauge my mood. "We love you, too. So much." Anthony ran his hands along my shoulders as I stepped into the oversized shower stall.

When we'd remodeled our bedroom, we also did the bathroom. It was now twice the size it had been. It had an enormous tub I could actually swim in, and a shower that fit four or five people with room to spare. It had three different showerheads and sprays on the sides. It was a heavenly, tiled masterpiece.

I turned back to them. They looked like lost puppies outside the shower stall, unable to leave me alone. "Come on, then. But I'm in no mood for sex."

They stripped in record time. "Of course not," Elias said as he pulled his shirt over his head.

"We just want to be near you," Anthony added, hopping on one foot to remove his socks.

They stepped into the shower, and I walked into their arms. "I missed you," I whispered, my emotions overwhelming me. "I feel so safe in your arms." The water flow hid the tears rolling down my cheeks.

Hands caressed my hair, my back, my sides. I

didn't realize they were both crying too until Elias let out a sob and clutched me tight against his body, pulling me away from Anthony.

Anthony rolled with the movement and pressed himself behind me, water cascading over us, soothing away the pain and fear.

"At least for a while, I don't want to go anywhere without all three of you," I said, cheek pressed against Elias's chest. The thought of stepping foot out of the manor made my chest tighten and my neck crawl. "I've felt so strong since we left the isle. Not now. Now I feel vulnerable."

Elias's chest rumbled as he spoke. "If you think we're letting you out of our sight, you're crazy."

Anthony laughed behind me. His voice was a little strangled. I looked back and his eyes were red. He was laughing through his tears. "Not even for a minute. One of us has been with you since we got to the hospital."

"Hospital?" I asked. "What hospital?" What the hell happened after I passed out?

"You've been out for nearly a week. A lot has happened." Elias pushed my hair out of my face and, without pulling his body from mine, leaned to the right and back to grab my shampoo. We all shifted to the left to get out of the stream of water while he lathered up my hair. It proved too awkward from the front, so I turned and hugged Anthony while Elias worked his fingers through my hair and massaged my scalp.

"That feels amazing." I'd never doubted that we'd be together again, somehow. They'd move mountains for me if I couldn't do it myself. "I missed you."

I let my head fall back while Elias massaged and Anthony used my upturned lips as an invitation to plant a quick kiss. "I missed those lips," he said.

He grabbed my body wash and pouf and squeezed the gel on it, working it into a good foam before carefully washing every inch of me. I'd told them I wasn't interested in sex, and he was as gentlemanly as it was possible to be when washing my hooha. Even exhausted, mentally worn, and ravenous, I had a hard time ignoring the tingles he created as he washed me.

On his knees in front of me, he grinned, blinking into the water that still splashed over us even though we'd moved out of the direct stream. "You like that?"

"Yes." I laughed. "But not now."

He nodded and smiled while he worked his way down my legs. "It makes me happy to know I cause that reaction in you even when you feel the way you do."

"I think you two would turn me on if I was dead."

Elias's hands paused on my shoulders, where he was massaging. My shampoo dripped down my back. "That's not funny."

Anthony stopped his ablations on my foot as well. "We were really scared, Riley."

Foot in mouth complete. "I'm so sorry. I know you were. But you know, I got a little worried, a bit anxious, but I never truly got scared. I knew, if I couldn't free myself, you'd find me. You'd never stop looking for me."

Elias put his hands on my hips and guided me back to the spray. Anthony stood and grabbed his and Elias's shampoo and made quick work of his own bath. Elias moved away from me to do the same and suddenly the water wasn't as soothing.

I rinsed my body quickly, distracted from my melancholy by the spray they'd installed at exactly the height of my butt. I was able to bend over and rinse all the cracks and crevices and feel my cleanest. *Ahhh. It's the little things in life.*

I jerked my head up when I heard a snort. Elias

and Anthony stood side by side, partial erections on display. *They're not immune to me either.*

"What are you doing?" Elias asked, voice full of laughter.

"Rinsing!" I stood up, wondering why they acted like they'd never seen me rinse my lady biz before.

Anthony's face lit up as he grinned, obviously trying not to. "*That's* how you rinse yourself? You know we have a removable shower head just for stuff like that?"

I tried to remember all the times we'd bathed together. They'd rinsed me many, many times, using the removable spray, but I couldn't remember a time I'd rinsed myself. Our shower time inevitably led to sex, and we sometimes started with that same spray. My cheeks heated as I thought about it.

"Uh, well, yeah. I thought you put this spray in just for me." I shrugged and walked toward the door, a little embarrassed.

They caught me before I got out, Anthony wrapping his arms around me first while Elias turned the water off, then I was in both of their arms.

"Don't ever be embarrassed with us, Coya."

"Yeah, we laughed because it was cute to see you bent over, with that pregnant belly hanging down. Not because you did something stupid or silly."

I rolled my eyes. "Ugh, I know. I know you'd never make fun of me. I'm just such a ninny right now."

They tried to wrap me up, but I shooed them off to put my hair in a towel first, then smiled and opened my arms so they could continue babying me. They needed to shower me with attention, and I needed to receive it.

After several seconds of nuzzling and kissing, they let me go to walk into the bedroom.

"I'll get our clothes," Anthony said.

"I'll get hers," Elias responded.

I sat on the side of the bed and blotted my hair with the towel, listening to them talk about what I might like to wear. "Something comfortable, like yoga pants and a big shirt!" I called.

They came out with comfy clothes for all three of us just as Axoular walked back into the room with a tray piled high with food.

The smell hit me, my new senses overloaded with the aroma of the bacon and coffee. "Ohhh, I didn't realize how hungry I was."

"You haven't eaten for a week," Anthony said, walking toward me bare-chested, wearing striped pajama pants and socks. Elias followed in similar attire. Anthony put on a shirt and handed one to

Elias before taking my clothes from him and crouching to put comfy cotton bikini briefs around my ankles. I dutifully stood, having done this song and dance many times before. They loved to dress me. Sometimes I thought I was their own little dress-up doll.

Anthony pulled my panties up around my hips. I arched an eyebrow at him and ignored how good it made me feel. It wasn't the time. We had to figure out what the hell we were going to do.

"Sorry, Coya. I can't seem to help myself." Anthony chuckled.

Axoular cleared his throat and pulled a small table over from the sitting area, before moving the tray from the other side of the bed where he'd set it. He carefully avoided looking at my naked body.

"It's okay, Axo. You're mine now, even if we haven't really made it official. After what we went through together, I don't want to be apart from you any more than I do them."

"I don't want to be apart from you either, Riley, but we're still new, and I'd like to take it slow. This is new to me, the multiple partner relationship.

"Taking it slow sounds great," I said as my pants were put on me. I took the shirt and put it on myself, ready to eat, not be coddled.

I sat in front of the tray and tried to lean forward and move the cups full of warmed blood in front of the couch for Elias and Anthony. Two identical heaping plates of food were for me and Axoular, so I moved them and the glasses of juice in front of our chairs. By the time I was done I had to sit back and take a breath. Leaning that far forward was murder on my lungs.

The food was amazing. Bacon, eggs, biscuits, gravy, fried potatoes, everything a southern girl could ask for.

Not much talking happened while I ate. Anthony and Elias sipped their blood and couldn't take their eyes off of me.

Axoular ate as much as I did. "My appetite was horrible while you slept," he said.

"How'd you keep me hydrated?" I asked.

"IV," said Anthony. "You pulled it out in your sleep last night. The healer should be here soon, and would've put it back in."

I looked at my arms, and sure enough, a bruise darkened my left arm where the IV must've been.

When I was stuffed and had drunk two full glasses of juice, I sat back and sighed. "Okay. I'm awake, I'm clean, and I'm full and hydrated. I want to see my boys. What time is it?" Our curtains were drawn, and they were blackout curtains, so I never knew what time it was in our room.

"Four in the morning," Axoular replied.

"Too early to see them, then. So, we talk."

Anthony sighed. "We need to plan our next steps. We can't stay hidden in here forever."

Elias stood and walked to the windows, opening the curtains on the dark view of the mountains. "I say we go on the offensive."

"How are we going to do that?" Anthony asked. "We don't know their numbers. We don't know what magic user it is they have on their side, but it's someone extremely powerful."

"So, we hide here forever?" Elias waved his hand around. "That's not an option either."

"No," I said. "It's not." I rubbed my stomach as I contemplated our options. "We'll send the baby away. Surely you know of a safe place we can hide him?"

Elias whirled from the window. "What in the hell are you talking about, Riley?"

"We'll convince them the baby died. When enough time has passed, we'll say he's an adopted Sárkány baby." My heart cracked with every word. Sending my baby away. I'd already missed so much of my boys' lives.

Anthony moved from the couch and crouched at my feet. "That's not happening. We'll contact the Junta. The Shapeshifters are a threat to us all. They're reckless, foolhardy. The Junta will help us."

"The Leyak," I muttered.

"The what?" Elias responded from the window.

"They are the Leyak." I stood and walked around Anthony. "They are the Leyak and before my time in this world is over, I'll make sure my child is safe from them." I filled the cracks in my heart with cement and walked out the door. *I'm Sárkány. I'm woman. I'll make them bleed.*

MY DAYS AND NIGHTS WERE ALL MIXED UP. Another week had passed, one day running into the next. Anthony had called the Junta, who was incredibly unhelpful. They said we were safe in our mountain home, and counseled caution. We were to wait while they put out 'feelers' in Bali.

I shifted in my seat, hidden in the dark in Daniel's room. I'd already sat in David's room for several hours. Elias, Anthony, and Axoular tried, every night, to persuade me to come to bed and leave the boys to sleep. But every time I left one room, I traveled to the other, until I'd spent enough time to be sure they slept soundly and safely.

While I sat by their beds and watched their chests rise and fall, I thought, plotted, and contemplated my options. The healer had been in, and I was measuring at thirty-six weeks, though I was sure I could be no further along than thirty-four. Either way, I could go into labor any day, and we were no closer to a resolution than before. We were in limbo.

I looked toward the doorway to see Axoular there. I could barely tell it was him, thanks to the hall light coming in behind him. After one last glance at Daniel, I joined him in the hall, closing the door behind me. "What's up?" I asked.

"Nothing. Just wanted to see what you've been thinking about."

We walked toward the stairs. "Where are Anthony and Elias?"

"Sleeping. I wish you'd join them."

I shook my head. "I'm hungry."

His face brightened when I said that. "Let me make you some dinner. I have last night's dinner ready to warm up."

"Sure, thanks."

We made our way to the kitchen where he insisted I sit while he heated up the barbeque pork from the night before. I'd smelled it cooking but couldn't muster an appetite at the time.

"Talk to me, Riley. Why have you been hiding in the kids' rooms?"

"I don't know," I said, poking at the pulled pork

with my fork. "I'm so torn with regrets, and then not."

Placing his own plate of food on the table, he sat beside me. "What do you mean?"

"If I'd never met Michael, I might've had a chance at a normal life. I wouldn't have gone through the portal, wouldn't have activated my Sárkány genes, wouldn't have missed out on my children's lives, wouldn't face losing my baby as soon as he's born."

"But?" He put his hand on my knee and squeezed.

"But I might not have had kids. I might *not* have met someone else. I would've missed out on the love I've given and received from Anthony and Elias—and Michael." I smiled at him. "And you." I took a bite and chewed while I contemplated our situation. "Not to mention you and our people would still be stuck in Galdiart, probably dying."

"You have much to be thankful for, and proud of."

"I do." I nodded my agreement. "Absolutely, I do. I also have much to lament, though."

"You haven't had an easy time of it, Riley. No one could argue that."

"But?" He was about to lay some truth down; I could feel it.

"Your children are alive and healthy. You've had not one, not two, but three passionate loves in life. Hopefully soon, four. And the book isn't written yet for that child in your belly. I know you believe you must send him away, but I'm not yet convinced that is the correct course. We still have some weeks, yes?"

Sighing, I nodded. He was perking me up a little despite my determination to be miserable. "You're right. Let's see if the Junta makes any headway."

His words helped, and my appetite roared back with a vengeance. I gobbled down the rest of my dinner.

"Bed?" he asked.

"Yes, please," I said with a smile. "You've been able to pull me out of my funks every time since we met. How do you do it?"

"It's a matter of perspective. Sometimes we get pulled into our own situations and our own problems and... what's the expression? You can't see the garden for the weeds?"

"That works, but I think you're looking for you can't see the forest for the trees."

"Yes, that one."

"It's also called tunnel vision. Becoming so

focused on one thing that you can't think about anything else."

"You never know what the next day will hold. We'll come up with a solution for this mess. In the meantime, we're safe and secure here."

We paused in front of my bedroom door. Axoular pulled me gently into his arms. "It's nice to see you smile. You've been so sad this week." He kissed my hair.

Turning my face up to him, I gave him my brightest smile. "Kiss me, Axo."

He returned my smile, dark brown eyes twinkling. His eyes trailed down my face until he focused on my lips. His mouth descended on mine, and I immediately opened to him.

Axoular was a great kisser. Not too much tongue. Just enough to tease me and make me want more. If I hadn't been hugely pregnant, I would've climbed him. My hormones ignited with the kiss, and I wanted to drag him into my bedroom and rip his clothes off.

Anthony and Elias were in my bedroom, though. And we hadn't discussed sex with Axoular, none of us. "Soon," I whispered when he pulled away.

"Our time needs to be right," he said. "It's our first time, and it should be perfect."

I nodded. He was absolutely right. I had no regrets about my first time with Michael or my guys, but if we could make it great, we should.

"Good night, Axoular."

He couldn't have known how chivalrous and gentlemanly it was, but he pulled my hand to his lips, and let his breath whisper across my skin. "Goodnight, Riley. Sleep well."

I slipped into the bedroom. *Please be awake.* If they were up, I wanted to use their bodies. *They won't mind.*

I stripped down to my birthday suit and climbed into bed. They were asleep together, spooning on one side of the bed. I couldn't help myself, I giggled. I'd never been much of a giggling type of girl, but they were so cute snuggled up together.

Elias's eyes opened when he heard my voice. I sat, totally naked, on my knees at the foot of the bed, watching them sleep.

He grinned. "Well, hello there. Is there a reason you're naked?"

I nodded and smiled. "Axoular made me horny."

His laughter woke Anthony. "What's wrong?" His long hair was a rat's nest.

"It seems our friend Axo has made her horny."

"I can smell that."

I shifted, no longer uncomfortable with the fact that they could smell everything about me. I'd moved from embarrassed to turned on by the fact that they always *knew* when I was turned on and loved discovering different things to make me that way.

"Why isn't he satisfying your itch, Coya?" He furrowed his brow. "We've been over this several times. There is no jealousy. He's become important to you and to us."

"We want the first time to be special. Planned out, maybe have another date night when this mess is settled."

"That sounds like a great idea," Elias said as he moved forward on his knees to reach me. "Would you like some assistance with your current predicament?"

"Yes, please," I said, eyes as big as I could make them as I looked up at him.

He let out a noise that was a cross between a grunt and a groan. "Do you feel like playing, Riley?"

I looked at my knees. "Yes..." I raked my eyes up his bare torso, still trying to keep a picture of innocence on my face. "Sir."

Anthony sat up when he heard that. "This is new, Riley." He had an eyebrow up.

Shrugging, I put my hand on Elias's knee. "It just

popped into my head as Elias came over to me. Is it okay? We don't have to do it."

The bulge in the front of both of their shorts told me they were okay with doing it. Anthony stood on the opposite side of the bed and pulled his boxers off.

Elias sat back on his knees in front of me. "Pick a safe word, Riley. In case we do something you're uncomfortable with. And don't expect us to go very far in your condition."

I nodded. "Barbeque." I could still taste my dinner, so it worked.

They both laughed. "Barbeque it is," Anthony said.

"Put your hands on your knees." Anthony's voice held an edge I'd never heard before. *He likes this.*

I moved my hands. "Like this?"

"Don't speak unless spoken to," Elias answered me. "Look at your hands and don't look away."

Why is this so hot? I feel like I'm going to have an orgasm just sitting here. Blood pounded through me.

Anthony's hand ran across my shoulder blades. I hadn't seen him move from the other side of the room, and I jerked upright with the tickle of his fingers. My eyes moved up and I locked eyes with Elias.

His expression was clear. He liked it too. I

watched his nostrils flare. "Eyes on your knees, Riley." The steel in his voice caused goosebumps to erupt all over my skin.

I moved my gaze back to my knees.

My breathing became more labored. Anthony's fingers didn't go far. He trailed them down my side, which was ticklish. I squirmed and looked up again.

"I won't tell you again, look at your hands."

I looked back down but could see how much Elias enjoyed our play through his plaid boxers. "Please," I whispered. "Stop teasing me."

"We will do as we please," Anthony replied from behind me.

I jerked as a cloth was pressed over my eyes. "Since you're unable to keep control of your gaze, we'll take care of the problem for you."

My labored breathing turned to pants. I trusted them with my life, my body, and my mind. They wouldn't do anything I didn't want them to do, and I wanted them to do. It. All.

"Turn to your right, sit on your butt, and put your legs out in front of you." Elias's voice came from my right, which meant he was standing. I hadn't felt the bed move or heard anything. *He's being all vampy. So hot.*

I twisted around so my feet stuck out in front of me.

"Lie back." The voice was whispered so I couldn't tell who it was, but I was pretty sure it was Elias.

They worked together to help me lie back, because suddenly they were on either side of me, one hand on my shoulder and one hand on my elbow, helping me flatten.

"May I speak?" I asked.

"You may," Anthony said in a husky tone.

"I can't lay on my back for long."

"We know that," Elias answered. "No more talking."

Oh, you wanna be sassy? My brain wanted to smack him, but my lady bits wanted *him* to smack *it*.

Hands clamped around my ankles. They pulled me slowly and carefully until most of my legs hung off the bed and my butt was nearly to the edge. Then, they were back at my side, helping me sit up. I ended up sitting on the very edge.

"Open your mouth."

Here we go! I was nearly giddy with excitement and eagerness. I opened my mouth, but only a little.

A finger tapped my chin, and I opened my

mouth more, but only barely. I had to squash the urge to laugh and tease them.

I was lifted into the air so quickly I couldn't even tell how they'd lifted me. Before I could register it, I was on my hands and knees. The movements had been fast, but gentle.

The slap that was delivered to my backside wasn't gentle. I cried out, surprised more than hurt. It stung, but it was delicious.

"I should've specified. No noises at all," Elias said from behind me.

I started to turn my head to look at him, but then realized I was wearing the blindfold. *Duh.*

He, whichever he was avoided touching me too intimately. It was a tease, a punishment for not opening my mouth.

Pillows were tucked under my chest and sides to help support me.

"Lift your head."

Anthony. He was right in front of me. He must've been on the bed with me, but once again, I didn't feel any movements.

"Open your mouth," he whispered.

More than willing, I opened my mouth as far as I could comfortably.

I imagined, more than felt, his hips flex and realized I was smelling him the way I smelled Axoular, but the scent was totally different. He smelled spicy and slightly metallic.

He pulled his hand away and Anthony stopped moving too. "I know what you're doing, Riley," he said as he rubbed his palm over the burning spot on my butt cheek he'd slapped. "The more you beg for it, the longer it'll take me to give it to you."

I straightened my back. *Stop showing him how he affects you.*

Wiggling my tongue did the trick. "I think she's ready to do as she's told," he said to Elias.

They were changing position, the feeling of a breeze over my skin. They'd moved so fast they made wind. I rolled my eyes behind the blindfold. *I've got you two figured out.*

Carefully, Elias threaded his fingers through my hair. "I know what you're doing, Riley." He spoke in a singsong voice, almost trying to sound threatening. He was having too much fun to be threatening, though.

All control left me, and I moaned—really

freaking loudly. Lying on his back, he pressed his body against my side, moving the pillows so he was the one propping me up.

Anthony increased the friction inside me, putting pressure exactly where I needed it to find a violent release.

This time I was determined not to pull back. I wanted to reach that higher level of pleasure, whatever it was. I didn't even know what I was reaching for, but I knew it was there.

My head thrown back, I moaned low and throaty. "Elias, please bite me."

He obliged, sliding his body under my chest from the side. I moved my hand to let him get into position. He sunk his teeth into the side of my breast.

Anthony must've been watching him, because as soon as Elias bit, Anthony increased the pressure and rhythm inside me.

It was an amazing feeling. His pressure put me over the top again and I screamed their names as I came.

My orgasm didn't seem to end. I rode a wave of pleasure.

"It's too much," I said, panting. Elias nuzzled up to my neck and bit, giving me exactly what I needed. His bite took me over again. It was what he needed.

Elias licked my neck. "Are you up for more?"

I was exhausted and still completely turned on. "Yes. But... don't take your time." I was getting tired.

He laughed and they helped me back onto my knees. Anthony sat back to watch, eyes heavy and sleepy. Elias wasted no time.

He set a furious pace. Every time his hips met mine, I cried out. Without the need for any extra stimulation, every jolt an overwhelming ecstasy.

He finished with a cry. Leaning over it, Anthony lifted me into his arms and carried me to the bathroom. I was deposited onto the toilet, as I always preferred.

I cleaned myself up as best I could while he ran a hot bath with lavender oils. We were already naked, so we sank into the tub as soon as it was full enough. It was perfectly sized for four people. We'd looked for a three-person tub when we built, but this one ended up being perfect, especially now that we would be adding Axoular to the mix.

"I'm sorry I've been distant," I said, floating in the water. "I got caught up in my head. Axoular helped me get some perspective."

"You've been through a lot," Anthony said. "Anyone would get caught up in it sometimes."

"Yeah, but I've been pretty wrapped up in it for a while. Five years, when it gets down to it."

Elias grabbed my foot and began to give me a massage. "I don't think you've been that bad."

"Eli, I've been so angry. Part of that was mourning, I think. And part was the betrayal from Peter. But a big chunk of it was me being stuck in my bad. I couldn't find my good."

Anthony started rubbing the other foot. "What made you realize you were sinking into a depression?"

"I wouldn't call it depression. Situational depression, maybe. My mom dealt with chemical depression, and it had nothing to do with the situation."

He nodded. "What changed your attitude?"

"Axoular. He's really good for me, guys."

"We've noticed. He centers you. Elias seems to be your fun. You laugh with him."

I lifted my head up out of the water and looked at Anthony. "You can't comfort me in the way you'd like to be able to, but you're still my comfort. And you're both my safety. I feel safe and at home with you."

Laying my head back, I continued, "I don't know if I'll ever completely be okay with how it all went down, with the secrets and fabricated stories. But I love you both enough to move past it. I'm so sorry it took me so long to see it."

"Riley, we'll all surely go through moments, days, months like that, where we get caught up in our emotions. You know more than we do, isn't that what marriage is about?"

I smiled at the ceiling while I floated. "Michael was good with that sort of thing, not me. I always got caught up in the emotions and he brought me back to a healing and happy place. He was good at it. I think Axoular is, too." *Basically, I'm on the crazy train and Michael was my conductor.*

Sitting up, I grabbed my shampoo. "I was mourning Michael too, these months. He's definitely dead, and I had to accept that before I could truly move on with you two and Axo."

Elias pulled me close so he could wash my hair. "We've been where you are with mourning him. We just had more time to come to terms with it."

"Going forward, let's focus on us, our kids, and the future," Anthony said.

"That sounds perfect." I smiled at him, and he pushed forward to kiss me while Elias washed my hair. I had one major stress off my chest, and I was ready to tackle the other. Dumadi.

"WHERE CAN WE SEND THEM?" I ROCKED BACK and forth in the chair we'd ordered for the baby. I couldn't wait to rock him in it. *No rocking for you, Riley. You don't get to be happy.*

I squashed back the negative thoughts and focused on the three men sitting in front of me. "Well? Do you know of any safe place we can send them?" We'd been having the same conversation for a week straight. I'd stopped spending my nights in the boys' rooms, and spent my days in my garden, in their classroom helping Tammy. We spent many evenings playing card games. Daniel had become obsessed with them, and I was trying to teach him Rummy. He'd already mastered Uno and had been begging me to teach him poker. When we weren't with the kids, we were rehashing the same subject over and over.

"Who are we sending where?" Axoular had maintained the entire time that we wouldn't have to send the baby anywhere.

"The kids, the baby."

"The kids aren't going anywhere, and neither is the baby," said Anthony.

Elias shook his head. "I don't know, maybe we should. But if we do, Riley is going too."

"Why would I go anywhere?"

"Why wouldn't you?" Elias asked. "Think about it. They want the baby, not you, not me, not any of our kids. Why wouldn't you go with the baby?"

I was floored. It made sense. Why did I have to fight each and every fight? I could leave this one to my husbands and the Junta to sort out. They'd surely be able to bring the Shapeshifters around.

"Okay, so say I go with them. What would you do to change our situation?"

"We'd work with the Junta, give the Shapeshifters an ultimatum," said Anthony. "They'd have to comply, or their leaders would be imprisoned."

Elias, sitting in the overstuffed chair beside me, took my hand. "They can't stand against the combined might of the Unseen. The magic of the Fae, the strength of the Supay. The Mermaids, the Weres."

"And if they really piss us off, we'll call the Reapers," Anthony said. "Or the Vampari."

"We can always gather the Sárkány, too." Axoular shrugged. "For you, they'd come running."

"Wait, what's a vampari?" I asked. "I thought vampires didn't exist as such."

Elias snorted. "It's a coincidence. They're a race of female warriors. They select and train their own members out of the Unseen, hand-picked and all. We don't know how they came about having that name." He shrugged. "They're secretive."

Tammy walked into our bedroom through the open door. "Anthony, you left your cell in the kitchen." She handed him his phone. "Marinus Ash is on there. When I saw his name, I answered."

Anthony jumped up and grabbed his phone. "Yes, this is Anthony."

I listened intently to the one-sided conversation.

"Were you able to make contact? Who did they send? No, I don't know anyone named Ross."

He looked over to me and nodded at Axoular. "Do you two recognize that name?"

I shook my head. "They never mentioned any names."

He listened for a moment. "What about the man that kidnapped Riley and Axoular? What measures are being taken?" He nodded. "Please, keep us updated. We are on tenterhooks here, waiting."

He tapped the screen to shut off the call and turned back to us. "They seem to be trying."

"What are they doing?" I asked.

"They made contact, then the Shapeshifters sent a man named Ross to meet with them. He's like their prince or something."

I rubbed my hand across my face, suddenly exhausted. "Dumadi?"

"They're looking for him. His son, Ross, says he's disappeared."

"Of course, he has," Axoular said. "He's insane, trying to steal a baby."

"So, he could be anywhere, or Ross is hiding him."

Anthony nodded.

"So where are the kids and I going? Do you have any more hidden properties like that one in Texas?"

"Actually, yes," Elias said. "There's a flat in London, and another house close to here, in the mountains. And a beach house in Florida, a cabin in

Aspen, a house in a tiny town in Ohio, and a house in a tiny town in North Carolina."

Anthony continued, "And we have access to houses all over the world. Sort of like an Unseen timeshare program."

"Well, what do you think? Where should we go after I give birth?"

"Probably as nondescript as possible. I'm thinking North Carolina," Anthony said.

Axoular nodded. "I'll go with her. You're not likely to need me unless you want me to gather the Sárkány to fight."

"I won't go before. I won't be without you two when I give birth." They sure couldn't force me to go through that without them, in the name of safety.

"What if we all go until the birth? We can use a burner phone to make any contact we need with the Junta, then travel to New Zealand after to deal with Ross and whatever his solution to this mess is."

"So, he maintains it's just Dumadi being crazy? They don't all want to steal my baby?"

"That's what he said," Anthony walked around the rocking chair and put his hands through the rungs to rub my shoulders. "We will work it out, one way or another, Coya. I promise."

Moaning from the massage, I almost didn't hear

him. "I don't see how. How can we trust this Ross means well? His brother was Peter and his dad kidnapped me. He comes from a family of terrible people. And according to Peter, the Shapeshifters have been trying to kill the Sárkány for centuries." I leaned into Anthony's hands. "We've picked a fine war to plop right in the middle of."

"Hey," Elias said, "You're the one that's a dragon and their mortal enemy."

I swung my head around to Elias, ready to scrap, but he was grinning at me.

"You hush," I said, shaking my head. "I won't be pregnant forever. I'll have this baby and then kick your butt."

"I can't wait," he said, blowing me a sarcastic kiss.

"So, North Carolina, then?" I asked the room at large.

"North Carolina," Anthony and Elias said at the same time.

"I'm going to go sit in on lessons for a while and be near the kids," I said. "You guys decide when we should leave, and I'll start packing. We're taking all the kids. They can have a vacation. Maybe we'll do some activities near the house."

They all stood when I did, like old-fashioned

southern gentlemen. I gave them a bemused look and waddled my way to the classroom.

The kids were sitting back down from lunch when I walked in, and Tammy hadn't returned yet. "Hey guys. What's going on?" I asked.

Stephen, Anthony's oldest, stood and pulled the comfy chair from the back of the room to a round table near the younger kids so I could help them with their math. "We're planning a shopping trip for this weekend," he said. "There are some new CDs out I want to try." I hadn't shown him the marvel that was downloading music yet. I'd have to get to that.

"We?" I asked.

"Me and David."

My Daniel shot out of his chair. "Why can't me and Charlie go?" Charlie nodded his head furiously, looking exactly like Elias. They were very close to the same age and had become fast friends when Daniel and David came to live in the manor. Stephen was thirty-four, a teenager by Supay standards, and David was only twelve, but they got along well and liked a lot of the same music and video games.

I raised my eyebrow. "You mean 'Charlie and I,' and I doubt they're going anyway, Daniel, don't stress it."

"Why can't we go?" Daniel asked, voice cracking.

"We're probably going to go away until the baby is born," I said, apprehensive about their reaction.

Stephen looked suspicious. "To where?"

"Do you know the house in North Carolina?" I asked.

He nodded. "I'm okay with that. It's really close to Charlotte, so we could find a lot to do there. And it's only about a four-hour drive to the beach, and my cousin has a house there."

"See? It won't be so bad," I said. The rest of the kids looked up to Stephen, like they were waiting to see how he'd react before they did. He seemed pleased, so they did as well.

Tammy walked in with Kohbi, wearing a different dress than the one I'd laid out the night before. She had the baby, Rose, fast asleep on her back in a carrier.

"Where's Talem? And what happened to your dress, Kohbi?"

"He's with Danyelus in the barn, and she spilled grape juice all over it. I threw it in the wash so it wouldn't stain."

"Thanks." She was thoughtful like that. I probably should've hated her for raising my sons, but I was grateful to have her. It hadn't been easy to swing back into motherhood, and in some ways, my boys still looked to her. She taught them most days, and they'd thought of her as a mother for a very long time. I spent too much time each day trying to be okay with that. I didn't hold it against her, though. She protected them and loved them when I couldn't.

I spent the afternoon helping Kohbi, Daniel, and Charlie with their math. They were vastly different kids. Kohbi didn't have a head for numbers at all, but she excelled in her writing and English classes. Daniel took a few tries to get it right, but nearly melted down when he got it wrong after that. Charlie was lightning fast at math but wouldn't read a book unless you threatened to take away his video games.

Elias stuck his head in the door about the time we were switching the kids over to do some reading before we let them loose for the day. He nodded me toward the door.

"What's up, Eli?" I asked.

"We've got everything finalized for the trip. When do you want to go?"

"Let's let the kids finish this week's lessons. Friday should put me at thirty-five to thirty-seven weeks, depending on whose calculations you use."

He looked at me like I was crazy. "What are you talking about?"

"The earliest I could've gotten pregnant, the absolute first possible moment was the night the three of us..." I looked back at the kids and found Stephen staring at us, trying to hear what we were saying. I stepped into the hall and shut the door. "When the three of us were together for the first time in your house in town."

It turned out that the house had been rented, even the furnishings. When he got his few personal items out, that was all it took to leave that home behind. I still hadn't contemplated cleaning out the home Michael and I had shared. We'd just paid the rent on it until I could deal. With the baby coming, who knew when it would happen.

"And that was exactly thirty-seven weeks ago?"

"No, that was thirty-five weeks ago. But I'm measuring at thirty-seven. So, I could go any time."

"Okay, let's go this Friday evening like you said. That's just two more days. Can you get everything ready by then?"

"If you'll help me get the kids' stuff together, then absolutely." We walked toward the stairs. The classroom was on the top floor, away from distractions the adults could cause in other parts of the house.

"Of course, we'll help you. You really don't have to lift a finger. We can get Tammy to help, too."

"No, it's okay. I'll do it. I'm not an invalid, just easily tired."

He smiled and threaded his fingers through mine as we walked slowly down the stairs. "Whatever you want, Riles."

I waited for Elias to leave the room before turning to Anthony, who was opening his laptop. I didn't want them to gang up on me if they thought I was being too pushy. "What are you doing about Dumadi?" I asked Anthony. I knew he was trying to protect Riley while she was vulnerable.

"What do you mean?" he asked. "I just told you." He was emailing someone he knew to get us all burner phones and a borrowed car once we took the portal to North Carolina, wherever that was. I couldn't get a handle on the geography of Earth. It was just too big.

"I mean, the man is on the run. He said they knew where this house was, even though they couldn't get through the wards to get to it. For all we know he's hiding in the woods just outside your wards."

"He might be, but like you said, he can't get in."

"Are you content to sit here like prey? I'm not." I tried to keep my voice calm and as neutral as I could, but I wanted to throttle him. Riley was in danger, and her babe as well.

He closed his laptop with a sharp click. "Of course not. I want to go out and find that old man and drain the blood from his body, but I can't. I won't leave my pregnant wife with less than all three of us to protect her until she has the baby and can protect herself. Once the baby is born and she's strong again, I know she can handle herself and we'll go after the lunatic."

"She saved herself from him once. She could do it again." He hadn't seen her. She was glorious, an inferno of rage and retribution. Her hair hadn't burned, as was the norm when a Sárkány let their fire consume their body. It had hung down her back in red waves, made brighter by the flames, stopping just before the slope of her bottom. That's how I remembered that day, watching her walk away from me, shapely thighs and calves flickering.

I could've taken over for her, but since she erupted before I could, her clothes were burned off.

If I'd let my flames out, I would've burned mine off, plus in the amount of time it took to get out of the building, I would've burned all my energy out, giving the Shapeshifters the opportunity to get their hands on both of us again. I'd had to be the voice of reason that day while she saved us.

Anthony was that voice today. "You're right. We must practice patience." I sighed. "I just want her to be safe. She's saving our people, providing a beacon of hope, and through her, we found the Junta, this world, and salvation. Then I got to know her and found her to be simply amazing. How could I not want to save her?"

"Man," he said, chuckling. "You've got it bad, huh?"

"It?" I asked.

"You've been bitten by the love bug."

What did he mean? "Do you have a bug that causes feelings of love? Like a bug as in sickness or an actual flying type bug?"

"It's an old expression. It just means you're experiencing passionate feelings of love for someone."

That made sense. "Oh, well, yes."

"Can I ask a question?" He turned to walk out of the room.

"Of course." I followed him toward the door.

"You're being very calm about the fact that you two haven't been very intimate."

"That's not a question." I knew what he was getting at, but I wanted to make him say it.

"Why haven't you had sex? It's got to be killing you."

I laughed at him and contemplated my answer, pausing before walking out in the hall where we might be overheard. "It needs to be just right. I'm very old, Anthony, by human standards at least. Much older than you and Elias. I've seen marriages prosper and seen them crumble. I'm not saying that moving quickly is a sign of a bad marriage. Just that not treating each other as the most important creatures in the world, that's a mistake."

"She is the most important creature to me. She, Elias, and the kids. You're growing on that list every day, as well." He leaned against the wall, apparently content to allow our conversation to happen in private.

"That is obvious to anyone that knows you. Elias too. She is your center, your focus. The children and her relationship with them bother her, I can see that. She's a stepmom, in a way even to her own children. But that'll ease with time. Elias had the biggest foundation with Riley, and from what she's told me, she fell for you hard and fast. But—our love is different, and it is very new."

"How is it different?" He looked a little offended.

"Nothing bad," I said quickly. I didn't want him to think I was saying our love was better. Just different. "Your relationship, for her, began as attraction and physical lust, yes?"

He nodded his head. "It did, though I was already in love with her before she even knew who I was."

"Okay, but for us, we've been friends for months. We didn't fully know we were interested in pursuing a relationship until very recently. As a matter of fact, I didn't know me entering into this unconventional arrangement was an option. I thought I would admire and care for Riley from afar for the rest of our lives, hopefully finding someone to love along the way."

"You've taken it slow from the beginning, and you want to continue that with your physical relationship?" Anthony asked.

"Yes. And I want to have time to worship her body for as long as I want to."

He burst out laughing. "You're just being selfish. You want her all to yourself the first time."

"Is that so wrong?"

"No... man, I'm just messing with you. You deserve that together. Come on, let's go start some dinner."

I mulled over our conversation as I walked to the kitchen to cook. Having Riley to myself for our first night together would allow us to bond properly, as Sárkány mates should. We deserved a proper bond, even in an unconventional relationship.

Sárkány mates didn't bond for life, but there was a connection that formed with love and sex. The sexual bond, if love was there, triggers the magic in our blood. It was the reason we could transfer knowledge with a touch, and how we bond. When Riley first entered Galdiart I was able to give her the knowledge of the Galdarian language and take a basic understanding of English.

The bond of a serious relationship fades with time if our bodies aren't joined. I'd always dreamed of having such a bond. It was said to increase pleasure and happiness in the bedroom and out. A sort of all-around mood lightener. And bonded Sárkány tended to live longer, fuller lives. If what I felt for Riley was real, and reciprocated, we would have it soon.

The kitchen was spotless, as I'd left it. I'd prepared lunch for the children a few hours before and shined the kitchen before returning to the bedroom to continue our conversation about our options.

I was chopping a potent white vegetable, which I always forgot the name of when Riley and Elias walked into the room. Anthony had gone to fold some laundry and find all the kids for dinner. "Did you hear, Axoular? We're going on Friday." Her smile wavered. She was worried but trying to keep up a brave face.

"I did. We'll hide, for now, get you safe and well and recovered after having the baby."

She grinned. "Then we'll find them and beat them all into submission." Her face brightened, excited by the proposition of being unleashed on Dumadi.

"Yes, indeed," Elias said. "We'll get you back in fighting shape in no time. The house we're staying at has a home gym. I'm actually really excited to stay there."

"Whose house is it?" she asked as she set the table for dinner.

"Michael's mom," he said, looking at her out of the corner of his eye, waiting to see her reaction. I opted to turn away from them and put my chopped eye poison in the skillet, focusing intently on what they were saying while trying to look like I was ignoring them.

"Michael's mother?" Riley said in a weak voice. So much for the bravado I'd tried to help her muster.

"Yep," Elias said.

"Michael's mother's house." She sat heavily at the table. "Has she even met the children? Why hadn't that occurred to me before? The kids have grandparents. All of them."

Elias turned to me and mouthed "Get Anthony."

I pulled out my phone and shot off a text. *Riley knows it's Michael's mom's house.*

The reply came quickly. *Be right there.* He skidded to a stop outside the door. I could see him from my spot at the island, dicing a tomato for the salad. He'd run with preternatural speed and picked right up on the conversation.

Sitting beside Riley, he put his arm around her. "What's wrong, Coya?"

"Their grandparents. How will I face her? I don't even know her name." Riley leaned over and put her head on his shoulder. "I was so busy dealing with everything that's happened, I forgot that Michael had parents. He'd told me they died. Mine really did die." She rambled on like that for several more minutes.

"Why would you be so upset by his mother?" I asked.

She looked up at me with tears swimming in her eyes. "Her son is dead. If he hadn't met me, he might not be dead. He'd be alive and well."

"You can't know that," Elias said. "We don't know if life is fated or if it's total chance."

"I don't believe in fate," she said.

The urge to gasp was strong, even though I wasn't much of a gasping sort of person. "Riley, you must believe in fate. Not everything is fated, but some things are fixed. Inevitable. Like you finding and saving our people. That was fate, prophesied for years and years before."

She looked dazed. "What about your parents? What if it's a Supay baby and then we don't know who the father is? We had that night on the island while Mama Pacha slept in the next room. How will I explain that to your mothers?" Her voice dropped to a whisper. "They'll think I'm a slut."

Anthony burst out laughing. "You're judging yourself by human standards."

"Judgmental human standards," Elias said. "It's common not to know for sure who your father is. Remember, we have many relationships like ours throughout our species, since Supay women are so rare. And we don't allow DNA testing or paternity tests."

She nodded her head, looking a little calmer. "Do you know who your fathers were?"

Anthony nodded. "It was a little different for us. They were trying to preserve the bloodlines. But then so many were killed in the short war with the Aljans that we're the last of the males."

"It's been so long since I had to deal with a parental figure. I just panicked." She put her face in her hands.

I moved on to peeling a cucumber, watching with interest. "I've been meaning to ask about your parents. In Galdiart, our elders moved in with us when they were old enough that they needed caring for. Surely your parents should be living with you?"

Elias grimaced. "You'll say different when you meet them. The marriages between our mothers and fathers were arranged. They're not very old by Supay standards. As a matter of fact, we were their first children. Boys, of course, but that's the norm."

Riley perked up as she listened, interested in the dynamics of their families.

Elias stood and finished setting the table. "They were about our age when they had us, so they're all three around..." He scrunched his face up and pursed his lips. "A hundred and thirty. Maybe a little younger."

Riley raised her eyebrows. "That's pretty old."

"Not when you live for hundreds of years," Anthony argued.

I agreed with him, nodding my head. "I'm closer to their age than yours, Riley."

She looked at me with wide eyes. "I keep forgetting how old you all are. I'm in my mid-thirties. Now that I've changed, I'll stop aging?"

I nodded. "You should. Of course, this is new to us, you being only part Sárkány. But I've never heard of a Sárkány having their full powers as you do and not living for hundreds of years, unless they're killed."

My chicken simmered and the salad was ready. All I had to do was wait on the rolls and we'd be ready to eat. "Call everyone to the table," I said.

It took us several minutes to get everyone seated and served. Daniel had to sit beside Elias's son Charlie, and Kohbi and Jaime had to be side by side. David wanted to be near Stephen, but Stephen was feeling a little smothered by all the younger kids.

Then we got into what to eat. Stephen was the only one on a liquid diet, though the rest of them were picky. Kohbi and Jaime wanted big salads, but I couldn't convince any of the boys to eat one. Riley had to put her foot down and insist everyone have at least a small salad. Finally, they were all settled, and I beamed around the table at them. Little Kohbi smiled back at me, probably feeling some of the same emotions.

We'd come from a desperate situation. Knowing the people back home were safe—I'd just helped with the last supply run. Everyone there was anxious to come here, to be safe and well-fed—and knowing that my people already in this realm were finally living, many of them for the first time ever... That knowledge made me appreciate what I had in that large, clean kitchen full of family. They made mistakes, they had antiquated laws and rules, but all any of them wanted was what was best for each other. And they'd accepted me as one of them without a second thought. I smiled again. I was home.

Axoular didn't see me watching him, but I did. He was intently watching everyone else at the table. I sat to his right, and he would've needed to turn his head to see me staring at him. His chiseled jaw worked, and he swallowed a few times. I was pretty sure I knew what he was emotional about. I understood.

Though I hadn't spent years in squalor, trying to survive like he had, I'd spent years alone, and it did something to me. Being around my new family made me emotional. I couldn't wait to add our little bundle to the mix.

Dinner passed in a blur of conversation. Stephen and the other kids that had been to the North Carolina house before excitedly recounted tales of adventures and fond memories.

"How is this a secret house if everybody knows

about it?" I asked. We needed a place to be safe for a while, not to be able to bowl in the basement.

"It's a Supay stronghold. The secrecy will be in that they don't know where we'll be. We could go to any one of hundreds of homes. This one just happens to be owned by Michael's mother. All of our mothers have homes, as well as aunts and uncles and cousins and a score more we aren't directly related to." Anthony stood and kissed me on the top of my head. "And if they do figure out where we are, the wards there are even stronger than here."

"Why can't we just make these stronger?" I'd rather stay where we were if that was an option.

"Those wards were made by a witch that had leprechaun blood," Elias said. He smirked at me and continued to shovel ice cream into his mouth.

"A leprechaun?" *Is there any mythological creature that doesn't actually exist?*

"Clurichaun," Stephen corrected. "We've been learning about them."

Tammy beamed at her pupil. "Very good!"

Stephen blushed at the compliment. "They're very rare, Clurichauns. To find a witch with Clurichaun blood would be a once-in-a-lifetime opportunity. To get that witch to put wards on a home? I'd say impossible."

"Well, then. We've got two days to pack whatever we want to take with us. Kids," I snapped my finger so the little ones would pay attention to me. "I'm not going to go behind and search for missing chargers, favorite toys, or lucky underwear. You've all done a great job of keeping your rooms clean, you should know exactly where everything is. Does anyone need help packing a fun bag?"

Stephen snickered at the term 'fun bag,' but shut it down at a sharp look from Anthony. His sister gave him a strange look, not understanding what was funny. Little Talem raised his hand. "I need help."

Elias laughed. "I'll help you, little man."

"I'm a big boy," he said with a pouty lip.

"Of course, you are. I'm sorry. I'll help you, big boy."

Our two days of prep passed in a blur, and we were finally lined up in the creepy basement, ready to go through the portal. I'd not been able to resist organizing everything. Lists were a weakness for me. Plus, I relished the opportunity to be involved in the kids' lives.

"Stephen. You were in charge of gaming systems. Do you have a charger for every system?"

He saluted me. "Yes ma'am. I even made a list and checked it off."

Beaming, I moved on, but not before I saw the small blush across his cheeks. I was slowly making headway with him. "David?"

He stepped forward. "Yep?"

"You were in charge of board games, have you got a variety?"

He shook a large suitcase at his feet. "Yep!"

I chuckled. "Daniel?" He'd asked for a job, too. I'd planned on just giving them to the older boys but ended up including all but little Talem.

"Yes, Mommy!" He raised his hand high in the air.

"Did you have everyone pick out one movie to bring?"

"Yes!" He held up a small bag slung around his shoulder that I knew contained a case holding the movie discs.

Anthony leaned forward and whispered in my ear. "You know we have plenty of Wi-Fi and online streaming services for movies at the house?"

I shushed him and moved on to the girls, Kohbi and Jaime, and Charlie. "Did you make sure everyone packed at least two books?"

They all nodded solemnly. "Mommy, me and Jaime couldn't decide, so we brought a bunch."

I laughed. "I did, too."

Consulting my list, I addressed the room. "Did everyone pack underwear?" I paused a few seconds for anyone to shout if they didn't. "Toothbrushes, pajamas. Phones and tablets." Nobody said anything. "Makeup, pads, or tampons."

Stephen and Daniel groaned.

"Hush, it's a normal part of life and you have to get used to it." I finished my list and we waited on Jaime to run all the way back up to her bedroom to get the stuffed bunny she liked to sleep with.

"Okay," I said. "Forward march!"

Tammy led the way, Rose on her back, holding Talem's hand. Anthony followed, carrying all their bags. Then went all the kids, hand in hand with each other and eventually me. "Remember, don't let go and think about your Mamaw's house." Tammy's mind would be what transported them to the right place, but it was good practice for them for future portal use.

Each child was loaded down with suitcases and backpacks. Finally, I went, followed by Axoular and Elias, both also carrying several bags. I was lucky they let me carry my list and hold the kids' hands.

We walked into the large foyer of an open and airy home. As usual, it felt like we'd walked through a waterfall. By then, everyone had used the portal before, so there were no surprises, but it still shocked me every time to feel so wet but be dry. I shook it off.

"Okay, those of you that know where everything is, please show the other kids around. Stephen, can you please make sure all the bags get to the right places?"

He nodded and trooped all the children except Rose off to show them around. Rose stayed nestled on her mom's back.

The men followed the kids and stowed the bags somewhere. I turned in a slow circle while they were gone and looked around. "This house isn't just nice. It's... I don't even know what the word is." It was beyond opulent. I thought I'd gotten a grasp on how much wealth I'd married into, but I was still shocked by the home, even with all the building up they'd done.

Tammy chuckled wryly. "Yeah, it's nice. Listen," she lowered her voice, "what did they tell you about Michael's mom?"

"Delilah? Not much. That she wouldn't think badly of me for having multiple partners. That's about it."

"I—"

She was cut off by a woman's rich voice. A blonde bombshell walked into the room. *Oh, for Pete's sake. She looks younger than me.*

I plastered a smile on my face and held my hand out, intently wishing I'd asked Tammy for information about the grandmother of my children before making this ridiculous journey.

She swept my hand to the side and pulled me into a tight hug. "Nonsense, we're family."

Turning her attention to Tammy, her smile became strained. "Tammy, darling. How is your husband?"

I swear, she sniffed as she said 'husband'. Suddenly, I understood Tammy's apprehension and why Danyelus was all too willing to stay home. "Hello, Aunt Delilah. Danyelus is home, continuing his work." Danyelus was a lawyer of sorts for the Unseen. He represented creatures of all bloodlines in disputes before the Junta courts. He knew the Junta laws in and out. Apparently, something about Danyelus was offensive to Delilah.

She turned back to me and focused on my stomach. "And that's the little problem child. Do we know yet if it's a Supay or a Shapeshifter?"

She just jumped right to the point. "No." I didn't know what else to say.

"No matter. Whatever it is, we'll protect it."

I smiled. Her attitude about the baby was comforting, even if her personality was a little overwhelming.

"Don't you worry. I've had six children. And our healer is the best. I believe you've met her?"

I nodded in the affirmative.

"Good. You'll do great." She put an arm around my shoulders and steered me toward a door behind the winding staircase, all but completely shutting Tammy out. I twisted my head back and gave Tammy a panicked look. She threw her arms up and huffed but followed. "I owe you," I mouthed at her.

"What's that, dear?" Delilah asked.

"Just clearing my throat," I said brightly. "Where are we going?" I really wanted my men back around me to show me around. If we were going to be stuck somewhere, at least it was fun somewhere.

"To the kitchen. You look famished."

I look like a moose. "Thanks?" I wasn't sure what else to say.

We traveled down a short hall and into a kitchen that would have Axoular drooling. "I can't wait for Axo to see this," I said.

"Who?" Delilah asked.

"He's my... Well, I don't really know what to call him." I looked at Tammy for help, but she was rifling through the fridge. Pulling out bottles of blood and fruit juice, she handed the juice to me and popped her blood in the microwave. "When did they start bottling blood like that?" I asked Delilah to turn the attention off of what Axoular was to me.

"It's my new business venture. We haven't even

started distribution yet." She pulled her perfect pouty lips into a wide grin.

"That's great!" I said, not sure where to take the conversation since I didn't know her very well. "When I lived with Michael, I managed a coffee shop and we distributed coffee all over the U.S." *Crap. Don't bring Michael up!*

Her expression dimmed with the mention of her son's name. "Yes, well. This was Michael's idea. He'd talked about doing it when he was a teenager, but once he was of age, he disappeared. Once we found out he'd..." She trailed off, probably unable to say he'd died. I understood. "Anyway, we decided to give it a go."

"I never knew that." She sat at the table, and I joined her, pretending to ignore Tammy sneaking out of the room with her bottle of blood. "He never told me about his Supay life. I thought he was human until last October."

She shook her head. "What he did with you, that was unlike him. It was so out of character."

"So I'm told."

She stared at me, searching my face. *She's looking for what it is about me. She wants to know what I have that's so special that would make her precious son give up his life to be with me.*

"I don't know," I said.

"Excuse me?" she asked, eyebrows arched perfectly.

"I don't know what it was about me that made Michael fall so hard in love. We just met and fell in love. As far as I knew, we had a run-of-the-mill marriage. Money problems, occasional fights, the whole nine yards."

"Money problems!" she exclaimed. "He was wealthy beyond most human dreams. And now so are you. Our legal system honors your marriage to him, you know."

"I know. I haven't been able to look into it much, though. Elias and Anthony have handled the finances. Though it's funny, with Michael, I did and never would've thought I could give it up. With him gone, though, I'm happy to never think about it again." I found myself talking about aspects of myself and my marriage to Michael that I hadn't talked to anyone else about. *Who loves a man as much as his wife besides his mother?*

"Elias and Anthony are good boys. They'll do fine with it. Though now you're married it's theirs as well, besides your dowry."

"My dowry?" What in the hell was she talking about?

"Did they tell you nothing? I would've thought Tammy would keep you informed at the least."

"I've not been myself for a while. Once we came home, I had to overcome a lot. They've been coddling me. All these things about the Unseen and Supay and Sárkány culture that I don't know, they don't have to be learned in one day."

"Of course not. The Unseen world's dowry is different from the humans. It's one-tenth of a bride's total financial value. In Supay circles that's usually still a significant amount of money. That money is set aside, by law, for the bride, should she ever want to divorce her husband and can't be used for anything else. If one of them dies it goes to the heir." She took my hand. "I'm here for you, Riley. If my son was willing to give up everything, including his life, for you, then so will I."

I gaped at her. "Thank you. That means a lot to me. And I'd like to spend time with you, and get to know Michael better through you so that I can tell our children more and more about their father."

"That pleases me more than I can say. Little David won't even remember him," she said with a sad smile. "I have four other sons, but Michael was my oldest. Of course, we don't have favorites with our children. But I was very close to him."

She squeezed my hand and stood. "I see your husbands hovering outside the room."

I twisted to see Elias and Anthony peering into the room.

"Can we come in?" Anthony asked.

"Of course," I said. "We're just getting to know each other."

Delilah met them halfway across the massive kitchen and pulled them both into a hug. The way they responded to her told me they were very fond of her. I'd have to get the details from Tammy about why there was bad blood between Delilah and Danyelus.

After a few minutes of catching up with the men, she excused herself to go find her grandchildren. She said all of the kids were her grandchildren, even the Sárkány. "I claim any children of yours," she said to Elias and Anthony.

Once she was gone, I let out a breath. "Whew," I said. "She's a lot to take. Did the kids get settled? What are they doing?"

They nodded. "Already swimming," Anthony said. He pointed behind me, and I turned to see a few of the kids in the pool with Tammy. I couldn't wait to join them. "Stephen is showing Axoular and David around."

"Isn't she great?" Elias said. "She's the fun aunt. My mom was our teacher, like Tammy now. And Anthony's mom was like a mother hen, always clucking and making sure we drank enough and had warm clothes."

I grinned. I loved hearing about their upbringing. "Were you raised together?"

Anthony nodded. "Yes. Our fathers were always working together. They were generals in the Supay army."

"Whoa. Hold up. There's an army?"

"Of course. Every Unseen species has one. We war with each other too often not to have one," Elias said with a laugh.

"You're so nonchalant about it."

"We grew up with it. Like I said, they were generals. So we moved a lot, just like humans do. Generals must go to their troops, wherever they are." Anthony moved to the fridge and found the bottled blood. "Elias, look. She actually did it."

Elias's mouth dropped. "Bottled blood. It's human?"

"Yeah, we can't make blood yet, not until we get the Council to come into the modern age and let us study the sciences."

Elias nodded. "Well, let's try it."

Anthony warmed some and they sat with me, sipping their bottles. "It's just like bagged," he said. "But much more convenient."

"Not bad," agreed Elias. I watched them discuss blood like wine connoisseurs. Even with months to get used to it, I didn't like to think about the fact that they drank blood. David still hadn't begun to crave it, even though his powers were still progressing. I was hopeful that his Sárkány side would power through, and he wouldn't be dependent on blood to sustain him.

"Show me around this place," I said when they finished their bottles.

The home was beyond my wildest dreams. They'd spent parts of their childhood there, so it was comfortable to them. I think they enjoyed seeing my excitement at every new discovery.

They weren't kidding about a bowling alley. There was also a theater with a television bigger than I'd ever seen outside a real movie theater, and recliners that I knew I wouldn't want to leave.

The hot tub, sadly, wasn't for me until after I had the baby. Too hot. The pool, though, I couldn't wait to get in. It had a grotto and a lazy river. The river snaked around the basketball court and tennis court.

"That's on my list first," I said, causing them to chuckle.

In addition to the entertainment aspect of the home, they had a garage full of cars. "Didn't you make arrangements to make sure we'd have a car?" I asked Anthony. "Are we not allowed to use these?"

"I didn't know they were here. These used to be stored in a garage in Knoxville. They're mostly Michael's."

My jaw dropped. "Oh, wow. Really?" We struggled. Our car broke down frequently. We'd had all those financial problems. He could've pretended to come from money, so we didn't have to spend so much time worrying over bills. "Was Michael's time with me a joke to him? Like a test to see if he could make it as a lowly human?"

"We wondered the same thing a few times," Anthony said sadly, looking out over the vehicles. "Michael, as a kid, and even toward adulthood, he loved his material objects. His cars, the houses. He's got guitars, collectibles, a lot of... stuff."

"We used to give him a hard time about it. Everyone has a thing, you know? Everyone has a vice. He had a bit of a shopping problem." Elias walked toward the closest car, which I was pretty sure cost more than I'd earned my entire life.

"So, we wondered if maybe he was living like he was paycheck to paycheck to prove a point," Anthony said. "Until we got to know you." He smiled at me, love in his eyes.

"Once we knew you, we knew why he did it." Elias turned back to me. "He gave all this up. He gave up his material things, the things he loved. Because keeping them would mean giving you up."

My heart beat faster and my gut ached with missing Michael. "If we'd only known I was Unseen." I didn't know if I would ever stop blaming myself for his death.

Axoular walked out of the back door. "Well, the kids gave me the grand tour. Anyone want to swim?"

I nodded enthusiastically, ready to shove my grief into the back of my mind. "Are Stephen and David coming?"

"I think they're already out there."

I turned to go change to join them and realized I had no idea where our bedroom was. "Uh, I need a guide to get to the bedrooms, please."

Anthony laughed, and all three of them followed me inside, then showed me where we'd be staying.

They weren't kidding when they said the Supay were prepared for poly relationships. Our bedroom had two separate rooms with large beds. "For when we need space?" I asked.

Anthony nodded. "Sometimes people don't like to all sleep together."

I shook my head. "I never want that. But for now, can Axo stay there so he's still close to us?"

He laughed nervously. "My stuff's already in there. We didn't think you'd mind."

"I don't."

Someone had already unpacked my clothes. "Who do I thank for this?"

"Tammy," Elias said. "But don't be too appreciative. She was hiding from Delilah."

I snorted and changed into a maternity bathing suit I'd ordered online, along with a slew of other maternity clothes. They'd come to our PO box the day before we left, and Elias had picked them up for me.

On our way back down to the pool, we were stopped by Delilah. Suddenly, I was thankful I'd put on a cover. I had no desire to be mostly nude in front of a woman that I barely knew that happened to look like a supermodel.

"I'm going to head out tonight since you're mostly settled in. I'll spend some time with the kids then sneak out. This will be our goodbye."

I hugged her, surprised. "You're leaving?"

"Yes, it'd be best if I'm not home. I'm going to let myself be seen out and about shopping in Milan and stay at the Supay flat there. If you were here, they'd expect me to be here with you."

She hugged Elias and Anthony and shook Axoular's hand. "It was a pleasure to meet you."

"Yes, thank you for allowing us to be here."

She waved him off. "Pooh. It's as much their place as anyone, and as far as I'm concerned, you're welcome wherever they are." Apparently, she'd been given the low down on who Axo was.

She left in a flurry of perfume and high heels, off to say goodbye to the kids.

———

We spent a week goofing off around the house. The kids were in heaven. We decided to give them a summer break, and they didn't have to do much work. We figured out Kohbi was a water baby. She'd never been in a pool before. Galdiart was too dry for enough water to swim in. I promised her we'd put a pool in at our house in Tennessee.

The highlight of the week happened while I sat with Tammy after breakfast, sipping on my coffee, and she, her blood. We were in comfy camp-type chairs in the back garden, enjoying the sunrise. Daniel ran out of the house, blood pouring out of his nose. He went straight to Tammy. My heart broke. *He wants comfort from her.*

But he surprised me. He only wanted to tell on Talem. "Talem threw his bowl of oatmeal at me and now my nose is bleeding!" Once he vented his ire at her, he came to me, climbing in my lap as best he could with my monstrous belly.

I'd brought a towel outside to wipe the dew off of the chairs, so it was at hand for his nose. The feeling of my boy tucked around me while I helped him stem the flow from his nose healed a big part of my cracked heart.

———

We were downstairs bowling when it happened. The three-lane bowling alley was crammed full with the entire family playing. I was intently watching my ball as it traveled toward the pins, finally cracking into them. "Strike!" I screamed. As I threw my hands up in the air, my stomach popped, like a rubber band snapping. Clear fluid gushed out of me and splattered all over the floor.

I stared at the wet floor in shock, then looked at my family, who quickly gathered around me. "I guess it's time."

I'd given birth twice before. In hospitals. With doctors, and advanced equipment, and drugs, and Michael by my side.

Before I could take in a single panicked breath, Anthony was by my side, arm around me, whispering in my ear. "Axoular has already got the healer on the phone, see?" I looked around the room until I found him, phone to his ear, grinning encouragingly. Nodding my head, I leaned on Anthony. Elias walked carefully around the mess on the floor and gently turned my face to his. "Let's go to the birthing room and get comfortable. You'll start having contractions soon, right?"

I nodded again, soothed by the actions of my three wonderful men. "I'll clean up the mess if one of the kids will run after some towels."

Axoular, who had moved closer to me while he spoke to the healer, shook his head no. He moved the phone away from his mouth. "I'll get it. Get her comfortable. That sort of thing doesn't bother me at all."

Stephen ran in with a bunch of towels. I hadn't even seen him leave the room. Elias grabbed one before leading me out the door. Once we were away from the prying eyes of the kids, I wedged it up under my dress, between my legs to catch any fluid that would leak while we walked upstairs.

In such a large house it was a long walk.

We'd prepared the birthing suite right after we arrived. It had everything in it I could think of for a safe birth. The healer had stopped by a few days ago and added a few herbs and potions, labeled in a language I didn't know.

"I know everything will be fine," I said. No contractions had set in yet, which was perfectly normal. The water could break hours and hours before the contractions started. I was able to walk normally to the stairs.

"Do you want to take the elevator?" Anthony asked.

"No, but thank you. I'm not in pain." We started up the stairs, moving slow. "Well, no more than I was before my water broke. My hips still hurt, and it still feels like his head is trying to shove my pelvis apart."

Elias chuckled. "It's almost over. And I'd be willing to bet you'll heal quicker this time, with your newfound power."

Axoular joined us on the stairs. "Stephen insisted on doing it. I think he's becoming fond of you, Riley."

I stopped and turned to face him. "Really? He did that?"

Axoular nodded, smiling, and my emotions overtook my rationality. Stephen cleaning up my amniotic fluid was a sweet and mature gesture, but it didn't really warrant the torrent of tears cascading down my cheeks.

Trying to walk forward was difficult, considering I couldn't see where I was for all the tears. Sadness and fear overwhelmed me.

Anthony took pity on me and scooped me into his arms, and we were on our way again. With him carrying me, we got there in no time, and I was deposited gently onto the bed, on top of an absorbent pad. I wiggled out of my panties and Elias brought me a gown. He threw my wet dress and panties into a basket in the corner.

Elias climbed around me and pulled me into his

arms. "This isn't because of Stephen. What's wrong, Riley?"

I sucked in my breath and focused on my emotions. Michael's face and the memories of delivering my boys kept flashing through my mind. "I miss Michael," I said. "I've never done this without him before."

Anthony climbed in on my other side, and Axoular sat at the end of the bed.

"He's here with you, Riley," Anthony said. "He'd never leave you. He loved you with a passion only someone who has also loved that deeply could understand. I think we do, and I think you do."

"Yeah, I think I do," I said. "Even if it's my wishful thinking, I like the idea that he's here with me."

Axoular smiled. "Can I get you anything?"

"No, but thank you." I snuggled into Elias, eyes on Axoular, while Anthony reached over and played with my hair. I absorbed the calm, knowing chaos was on its way.

Axoular's phone dinged, and he checked it. "The healer said to call when your contractions are two to three minutes apart, or if the pain gets too intense."

"Okay. Rakesha said she could help with pain, but I'm a little apprehensive about taking potions."

"I trust her," Elias said. "She knows her business, and she's helped deliver hundreds and hundreds of babies."

"Were you there for Charlie's birth?"

He shifted behind me. "I was, yeah. It was a home birth."

"We've never talked about the kids' moms. I've been scared to ask." It was stupid. Knowing what happened to the mothers of my husbands' children was pretty important, but I'd been in a pretty strong avoidance cycle. Why I chose that moment to finally ask about it, I didn't know.

"She died," he said, voice clipped. "I really don't like talking about it."

"Did she die in childbirth?" I asked. "I can handle it if she did."

"No! Oh, no, sorry." He kissed my head. "We don't really know what happened. She disappeared."

I sat up and faced him. "What? Why didn't you tell me?"

"It happened about two years before Michael died. Charlie was just a baby. Supay women aren't immune to postpartum depression, but it's rare. We assumed Skye went through a postpartum episode and decided to take off. Now, seven years later, though... I told Charlie I think she's dead. I was honest with him."

"Is the Supay life completely full of drama? Do none of you live calm, regular lives?"

Anthony burst out laughing. "We live such long lives, there are times that it's downright boring, and times that the events are exhausting or dangerous, like now."

"Did you love her?" I wasn't sure I wanted to know. *He might've loved people before in life. Don't be jealous, you idiot. You certainly loved before him.*

"Not like I love you. I thought I loved her a great deal, and I don't mean any disrespect to her memory, but my love for you shines like the sun."

"You're not being disrespectful. Were you happy together?"

"Yes, but looking back, it felt more like a great friendship love with her. We, as Supay, are expected to have children as often as we can. It's a societal norm."

"And if someone decides they don't want children?"

"It's uncommon to decide that in a life that lasts hundreds of years, but it does happen," Anthony said. "We don't judge those people. Sometimes, it's not a right fit."

"What about you?" I asked. Before he could answer, my first contraction hit like a strike of lightning. I cried out and sat forward, clutching my stomach. I counted backward from thirty and by the time I got to the number one it was easing.

"What does that feel like?" Axoular asked. "I've lived a long time but never been present at a birth."

"Well," I said, laughing. "You're in for a long day. They start in my back and wrap around to my front. The pain is intense." Breathing deeply, I closed my eyes. "With David, my water didn't break until I was quite a bit dilated. I think I was six or seven centimeters, and the doctor broke it himself. Those contractions were much easier since there was a cushion of water inside."

We sat in silence for a few moments. "Don't think you've gotten out of answering my question, Anthony," I said suspiciously. "Where are Jaime and Stephen's moms?"

"Lily is alive. She's Supay and Stephen sees her on occasion. Molly, Jaime's mom, is human. I told her she died. I'll tell her the truth when she's older."

I looked at him in surprise. "What? Is she alive?"

He nodded; shame splashed across his face.

"How'd that happen? Does she know Jaime is alive?"

He nodded again. "She does." He blew out a puff of air. "You're going to be pissed."

"Probably." If he ripped her baby away from her, I'd kill him, then make it as right as I could with her.

"Our moms were pressuring us to have kids. Stephen was an accident when I was a teenager, though Supay children are never considered accidents. Like I said, it's expected."

"And?"

Elias gave me a squeeze. "He found a human surrogate, Riley."

What the hell? "Is that even an option?"

"No," Anthony said. "It was her egg, my sperm. I paid her handsomely, but I got in a lot of trouble. They were going to imprison me for five years to pay for my crime of involving a human. She had no idea we were anything other than human."

"Why didn't they imprison you?" Axoular asked, enthralled in the story. He had to wait a few minutes for his answer, as a contraction ripped through me again. Axo checked his phone as I groaned my way through it. "Five minutes apart."

"That's surprising," I said. "This early in labor I should be more like ten, based on how I progressed with David and Daniel." Once I caught my breath I turned back to Anthony. "So, why didn't they imprison you?"

"Because she was a girl. Once they determined a human had a girl, they wanted to try it again."

"But sperm decides the sex of the baby," I said. "Surely they know that."

"They do," Elias said. "But we're magical creatures." He rubbed my stomach. "They follow even the most ridiculous leads when it comes to increasing the female Supay population. There are still quite a few pureblood Supay women out there, but they're aging. Many of them are past the childbearing years, and fewer and fewer girls are born every day."

"Did anything come of it?" I asked.

"No. They hired twenty human surrogates across the world. They had three girls and seventeen boys. They did it again early last year with thirty surrogates and had two girls and twenty-eight boys."

"Well, it's a good way to help drive up the numbers of kids if the dads are willing, but it seems a shame to deprive all those kids of mothers," I said. "Those poor babies won't ever know the women that gave them life."

"Our lives aren't always easy. They'll know plenty of love. We cherish our children," Elias said.

"In any case, there weren't that many men willing to do it that way, so the program was scrapped."

"Tell me about Stephen's mom."

Anthony described how she became pregnant. They were childhood sweethearts and dated off and on into adulthood. She had no interest in their plan to find a woman that wanted to marry all three of them, and Elias and Michael weren't that fond of her anyway, so they parted ways.

I sucked in a sharp breath when the next contraction hit. It came on fast and hard. I tried to breathe and count through it, but the pain was too intense.

Axoular checked his phone. "Four minutes."

"What are births like on Galdiart, Axoular?" I asked once the pain was gone.

"Scary." He lay back on the bed and stared at the ceiling. "When I was born, my mother had me in a hospital with modern technology and life-saving techniques. Very few women died in—or as a result of—childbirth."

Axoular paused when he saw me wiggle as a gush of fluid leaked out onto the pad under me. "I'm leaking fluid, and it feels weird." I smiled and shrugged. "Sorry."

"Don't be sorry. I'm thankful to be a part of this," he replied.

Elias nuzzled my neck. "We want to hear everything you feel and go through. We're here with you for this."

"Go on, please," I told Axoular.

"After the war, there were so few doctors and no electricity. In our camp, we had two doctors, and neither were birthing specialists."

"Oh, no," I said. "Is anyone there currently pregnant? I didn't even think to ask that. Just wanted to get out the families with kids first."

"No, the only one that was pregnant already had an older child and came over already with her husband," Elias said. "I helped move them."

Some savior I was. I'd handed the responsibility straight over to Elias and Anthony and focused on my own pregnancy. "I'm sorry. I should've been more involved."

"Riley, this pregnancy has been really hard on you. Was it this difficult with the boys?"

I shook my head as another contraction hit me. "That has to have been faster," I gasped out.

Axoular grimaced as he looked at his watch. "Three minutes."

"Call the healer!" I yelled.

He grabbed his phone and stepped out into the hall.

Anthony tucked himself behind me and wrapped his arms around me. "Do you want to get in the tub?"

"Maybe it'll help," I said as the contraction waned.

Elias climbed out from around me and went into the attached bathroom to run the water in the huge tub.

"Why does she already have a birthing room here?"

"Well, she's got six kids, and three of us are grown and already having kids of our own. Plus, she opens this place up for any Supay that needs it if they ask. We've had a lot of women choose to spend their last few weeks of pregnancy here. Like a little vacation before having the baby and returning to reality."

Elias came back into the room and picked me up as easily as he would the baby when it was born.

Having vampire husbands had its perks, and their strength was one of them. No pickle jar would ever go unopened in our home.

The round tub was positioned in the middle of the room, with a toilet in one corner and a shower in the other. Elias sat me on the toilet, and since I had no undies on, I took the opportunity to pee, flashing Anthony a grin when he chuckled at me. When I was done, I slipped the gown off and stepped into the tub naked. As I sank into the warm water another contraction hit.

It was slightly less painful in the deep tub. I was underwater up to my chest, and the warmth and slight pressure of the water helped with the pain, if only minimally. I managed not to cry out, at least.

Anthony stepped out and was gone for several minutes. He finally returned wearing swim trunks and carrying some for Elias and Axoular.

He climbed in the tub with me, and Elias changed so he could join us. We didn't talk much. I tried to meditate and find a peaceful place to endure the pain.

Axoular returned several contractions later, followed by Healer Rakesha. She knelt by the tub and put her hand on my stomach, eyes closed. "The baby is anxious to be born, yes?"

"Yes," I grunted as another contraction swept through my peaceful place. I was having a hard time finding a place of calm to help bring my baby into the world. "You said something for pain? Will the baby be affected by it at all?"

She patted my stomach. "I've delivered many babies where the mother took the potion and many where she didn't. I've noticed no difference to the babies."

I nodded. "If they trust you, I do, too." I didn't know if I could endure any more of the pain.

She bustled out the door, leaving the smell of cloves behind her.

"She smells good," I whispered.

Anthony, sitting behind me, ran his hands down my arms. "I didn't smell anything," he said.

She returned with a mug of liquid. "It tastes awful, but you'll be glad to have it soon."

I waited for my contraction to pass and took a sip. It burned. *Holy cannoli that tastes like warm pee.* Not that I'd ever tasted pee.

Choking down the potion was difficult, but I finally got it down. Waiting on it to work was even more torturous than before because I knew relief would be coming.

Thirteen contractions later, I still had no relief. "How much longer?" I asked through clenched teeth. I'd long since given up on finding a happy place and I'd left the tub behind, opting to try lying in bed again. Those women I'd watched online having babies in tubs were superheroes. I couldn't do it. "I can't keep this up. It hurts."

She checked my cervix. "You're only dilated to six."

"That's not enough. Not with the contractions this close together."

"I agree," she said. "Time for a more extreme approach."

"What do you mean?" I said, almost yelling at her. My contractions were so close together they were almost continuous, and I'd only been in labor for about four hours.

"Sometimes a human woman will have an epidural at the doctor's request because the pain is to the point of becoming dangerous for the babe. You're not dilating fast enough for your contractions, and I don't have the medicine that'll help you dilate faster. So, we need to take away some of the pain and hope your body will relax and the contractions slow a little."

"Your potion didn't work," said Anthony. He so badly wanted to be able to calm me that he was nearly in tears.

"Try calming me now," I said. "Maybe in this crazy situation you'll be able to. You were able to once when I slept." As soon as I got the words out another contraction hit.

At the same time, I could tell he was trying to calm my mind and body because my head broke out in blinding pain. "Stop!" I yelled. The pain ceased immediately. "It didn't work."

We sat beside the bed for a while, then on the floor and me on a birthing ball, bouncing for all I was worth. After another hour, Healer Rakesha nodded her head and pulled out her phone. "I'm calling Cindy."

I barely heard her over my attempt to not scream out from the pain. Very little time passed before Cindy walked into the room. I was back in my gown, squatting up and down supported by Elias on one side and Axoular on the other.

"Who all is doing this?" she asked.

"I still don't know what you're doing," I said, in between contractions, but I knew another one was coming quickly.

"We're going to split the pain. Witches do it all the time, but for some reason the other Unseen view it as a radical solution."

"Split it among whom?" I asked.

"Whoever is willing to help take the pain. The spell divides it and allows the helper to take half the pain. If more than one person is willing, it'll divide repeatedly and be a lesser pain for everyone."

"If this is possible, why aren't people capitalizing on it?"

"Oh, sorry, forgot that part. The pain can only be given to those with an intimate connection," she explained.

"Like sex?" Axoular asked.

"Not necessarily. It could be a parent, best friend, sister. Anyone that is trusted and loved by the person in pain."

"Then I volunteer," Axoular said.

"Okay. One at a time, please. You two stand back," she said to Anthony and Elias.

"One of us can go first," Elias said. "You don't have to, man."

"I want to," he replied.

Everyone else moved away from me and Axoular hugged me from behind, his hands on my stomach. Cindy closed her eyes and put one of my hands into one of Axoulars. Then she circled our hands with hers and muttered words I didn't understand. Her voice took on a deep, resonating quality, and warmth spread across my body.

When the next contraction came, it was considerably better. I could function through the pain.

"This is amazing!" I exclaimed with a huge grin, then turned to look at Axoular. He'd fallen back onto the bed, clutching his stomach.

I sat beside him on the bed and brushed his hair out of his face. He needed a trim. "Are you okay?" I asked as the contraction waned.

"That was only half your pain?" he asked. "I thought I was going to die!"

"Oh, my. Yes. That was definitely much more bearable," I said, trying not to laugh at his reaction to the pain.

"Can we split it again?" I asked Cindy, turning back to face her.

She was trying to hide laughter. We shared a look, understanding how much more pain we were able to withstand than our husbands, and knowing we couldn't say anything about it to them or they'd be hurt.

"Absolutely," she said. "Who is next?"

Anthony and Elias stepped forward at the same time. She pointed at Elias. "Come on, tough guy. Hold your wife's hand."

She repeated the process with Elias, and I laughed out loud as soon as my next contraction hit— a full minute later. The pain was still distracting, but so much better I began to cry again.

Elias grimaced and rubbed his lower abdomen. "Owwwww."

Axoular sat up. "That's much better than before."

We went through it one more time with Anthony and by the time we all shared the pain, it was no worse than a period cramp, and the contractions spread back out to every three minutes.

After that, it was like a party. Cindy had to hang around and make sure the spell didn't unravel. Healer Rakesha sat her in the corner, keeping an eye on things and checking my dilation every few hours. We had lunch, watched TV, and played a few rounds of Rummy.

After another six hours, it was time to push. My cervix was dilated to ten and I was ready.

Even without the pain, I was nervous. Anthony stood behind me, Elias to my right, and Axoular to my left. I wanted to try pushing from a crouched position. We all crouched down when the next contraction hit us, slightly more painful. All three men gasped when I felt the ring of fire of the baby crowning.

"I warned you," I said. "I pushed David and Daniel out very quickly." I'd had epidurals with both of them. The pain I felt through the spell, while not intense, was distracting and more pain than I ever wanted to feel out of my poor lady bits.

I grunted and watched a wet head appear between my legs. "He's got hair," I said. "Lots of it."

Healer Rakesha helped maneuver him, so his shoulders weren't so hard to push out, and the rest was easy. My baby boy was out, and she immediately put him in my arms. The huge towel under me was moved and a clean one put in its place. I wasn't sure who did it, but I thought it was Cindy.

I sat back on my butt and double-checked. Sure enough, I had another baby boy.

It was hard to tell through the fluid and goo, but I was pretty sure he was blonde. I stared at Elias in shock, tears rolling down my face. "Is he Supay?"

He shrugged. "I have no idea."

Someone handed me a towel, and I pressed him against my chest, rubbing his head gently as he squalled. Rakesha was between my legs, and I felt a tugging as she delivered my placenta.

Once all the mess was cleaned up and the baby as clean as he could be without a bath, we moved to the bed, spell still in place. I had no real pain yet.

Cindy assisted Rakesha and they both promised to stay for a few more hours, downstairs in case we needed them.

The four of us piled into the bed, Elias and Anthony on one side and Axoular pressed against my back.

"What are we going to name him?"

"Michael," said Anthony.

I looked at them, Michael's best friends, and down at the baby that looked just like Elias. "I think that's lovely."

We snuggled together, still bound. The spell helped me ignore the after-birth contractions that were shrinking my uterus. Michael latched onto my breast like a champ, a feat David and Daniel hadn't done with ease.

Sleep finally claimed me while the guys held Michael, cooing over him, and fighting over who got to change him. I was looking forward to being able to share the middle-of-the-night duties with the three of them.

I was jerked from my nap by a particularly painful cramp. I looked at the guys in confusion. They all had looks of surprise and pain on their faces. The cramp lasted a good thirty seconds, like a real contraction.

Axoular checked his phone. "It's been three hours."

"Maybe you should get the healer?" I asked

Elias. Axoular held Michael as Elias jumped up and ran downstairs.

Another contraction followed and Elias zipped back into the room, using his Supay speed. Healer Rakesha and Cindy entered soon after. As they did, I stood, pressure against my hoo-ha forcing me to take action.

"Something's happening!" I yelled.

Axoular handed the baby to Cindy and grabbed himself. "It feels like it did when you pushed Michael out."

I looked at Rakesha in horror. "Twins?"

She snapped on a glove and felt me. "Yes, ma'am. I'm not sure how I missed this. I've never missed a second baby before."

I squatted down again, it having worked so well the first time. Cindy threw a towel under me.

The pain was worse, with the baby coming out of an already sore area. Even with the shared pain, I gasped when I pushed the baby's head out.

"Hurry," I yelled at Rakesha. "It's blue! It's not breathing." I pushed with all my might, and it slid out into Rakesha's arms, skin a light blue color and hair dark brown and wet.

Cindy reached over and sucked the fluids out of the baby's nose and mouth with a bulb. Rakesha held her arms out, and I saw my daughter suck in her first breath, but her blue skin tone didn't fade. She wasn't blue from lack of oxygen. She was just blue.

I fell back on my butt onto the floor. "Twins." I reached for her and Rakesha placed my daughter in my arms. She blinked her violet eyes at me twice before closing them when I wrapped a towel around her. I looked up at my husbands, Axoular, Rakesha, and Cindy. "Twins," I said before I began to laugh.

My laughter turned to tears and I was lifted onto the bed, mess, and all, and hugged in more arms than would fit around me. Cindy placed Michael in my arms and the guys passed the baby girl around, cooing over her beautiful skin tone and amazing eyes.

"I think they have two different dads," Axoular whispered.

I stared at my babies, as different as night and day, and nodded. "I think that's very likely the case."

"WE STILL HAVEN'T NAMED HER." MY LITTLE blue girl nursed, but she wasn't taking to it as easily as Michael did. She'd already made my nipples sore, but I knew they would get better, slowly. "We could be like the celebrities and name her Blue." All three of them gave me a blank stare. "Never mind. Turn on a TV once in a while," I chided.

"Linna," Axoular said, looking at his phone.

I looked down at her fragile, perfect blue skin. "What does it mean?"

"A small blue flower."

"She is definitely a small blue flower." I kissed her head. "Hello, Linna."

She had tiny spots on her palm that I assumed would eventually grow into the spike that would kill people so she could take on their identity. "I'll teach you to be good, and not kill people." She gurgled on my breast. "I'll take that to mean she looks forward to being a good person."

Elias chuckled. "Of course she will be. She's ours."

———

Our days fell into a routine. They helped with the babies. I quickly discovered I couldn't produce enough milk to keep up with both of them, so I pumped every two hours and we supplemented with formula the guys bought in town. The kids got back to their schooling, then in the afternoons spent time playing or swimming. Most of the boys loved the babies, but David, and both girls, were absolutely infatuated with them. We had to force them to leave the babies and go eat dinner most nights.

After a few weeks, I started joining the guys in the gym to get back into my best fighting shape. I knew I'd need my strength.

It was slow going. My body had been through a lot. My hips hurt every day, and I'd been so easily tired when pregnant that I hadn't done anything truly strenuous since we came home from Bolivia the first time.

Several more weeks passed, and my strength returned steadily. Elias had been right. What would've taken months as a human only took about six weeks as a Sárkány. I felt like myself again.

The twins had grown at ridiculous rates. They already filled out their three-month clothes that I'd ordered online and had delivered to a PO Box for the guys to pick up. I hadn't had to leave the house once, with the Healer coming to see me at the house.

The Junta had heard nothing, nor had their Leyak contact, Ross. Dumadi was in the wind.

Tammy wanted to return home, but I was scared to move the kids. If he got ahold of any of them, they could be used as leverage against me. And if he ever found out I'd had a Leyak baby he'd stop at nothing.

Axoular was cooking dinner for our entire brood, and I sat at the table, the eight-week-old twins sleeping in a portable bed beside me. They didn't sleep well if they were separated, and I had to leave them together whenever possible.

"We need to make a move," I said. "I'm strong again. We've been working on increasing my stamina with my fire, and all the time in the gym. It's time."

He shook his head as he chopped peppers to put

in the spaghetti. "Not yet. They're looking for Dumadi and they'll find him eventually."

"You were the one that wanted to go in guns blazing. What happened?" He'd been on my side before, ready to end this.

"The twins were born. I've never seen children be born, much less children I'm growing to think of as my own." He'd really taken to fatherhood and loved to feed them and take care of them. They loved him back and cooed every time they saw him.

Maybe I was jumping the gun, setting him up to be one of the fathers of my children when we hadn't even slept together, but it felt right. He was a part of our family now. He'd even taken to sleeping in bed with us, though Elias and Anthony still hadn't slept beside him. They were like brothers, and he was still just a friend. A good friend, but a friend all the same.

Anthony walked in with Jaime, Charlie, and Kohbi hanging off of his arms like little monkeys. "I've got some hungry munchkins here," he said before giving me a slow kiss. He didn't know it yet, but I was ready to get back in the sack again. They hadn't pressured me and were waiting for me to set the pace. I was ready to set a daunting pace.

Axoular, who had taken over the kitchen, put a plate of spaghetti in front of each child. We liked to eat as a family, but it was difficult with so many of us. We frequently ate in shifts, with the four of us hanging out until all the kids were finished.

I'd also grown much closer to Tammy. She was enthralled with the babies, just like everyone else. We spent a lot of time talking, and she told me many stories about the guys as kids. I enjoyed learning more about them and growing closer to her.

When the dinner was cleared up and the kids were in the theater room watching a superhero movie, I asked Tammy to watch the babies so I could talk to my guys.

We gathered around the pool, the summer heat a comforting friend to Axoular and me. Elias and Anthony didn't ever seem fazed by heat or cold. "It's time to go on the offensive," I said.

"Not yet, Coya. We're having such a nice time here. The kids love it." He took a sip out of his mug. "And I've been in touch with Michael's mother. She's offered the place to us as a home."

Axoular and I had southern-style sweet iced tea. I arched an eyebrow. "She was very sweet, especially to let us come in here and take over while she wouldn't even be here, but living with her? I don't know."

"No, I think she means to give us the house and move."

I'd never lived anywhere but Tennessee. Moving had never even crossed my mind.

"That's something to consider once we're safe. I'm not totally opposed to the idea." Who would be opposed to living in such a grand place? "But what about right now?

Elias shook his head. "I say wait. We've got time. We aren't being hurt by being here. We're safe."

Anthony nodded. "I agree. Dumadi will surface eventually."

Axoular sipped his tea. "I've thought we should hide and wait since the twins were born. I can't fathom risking them."

My shoulders slumped. I couldn't stand the feeling of being trapped, hemmed in. Dumadi had me stuck.

"Riley, what would you be doing right now if Dumadi was dead, and the threat was gone?" Axoular, ever my voice of reason asked.

"We'd be in Tennessee, spending time with the babies, recovering, planning our futures."

"How is that different from what we're doing here?" Anthony asked.

"You're right. We have been taking this time to

enjoy our children and recover. It just rankles that it's forced and not by choice."

"I agree, but we can't let that push our hand too soon." Elias reached over and squeezed my hand.

We finished our drinks and used the rare time with no babies to hop in the pool just us adults. Having a few moments to ourselves to flirt and kiss was amazing.

I swam toward the deep end, intent on doing a few laps while I could. As I crossed over the rope separating the deep end from the shallow, something grabbed my foot and pulled me under. I sucked in a breath just before going under and whirled around underwater to see who was after me. The chlorine stung my eyes, but I didn't care when I saw Elias behind me.

I pushed my foot forward then jerked it back, freeing myself. I knew he could move fast enough to stop me, but he was trying to play fair. I pushed off of his chest toward the other end, coming up for air.

When my nose hit fresh air and I breathed in, I smacked into something hard and smooth. Opening my eyes again, I looked up into Anthony's grinning face. He was lounging against the wall, and I'd gotten turned around under the water. If not for him, I would've smacked into the concrete wall.

Grabbing me under the arms, he braced himself on the side of the pool and threw me halfway across the water. *God, I love being with such strong men. They make me feel like a tiny princess.*

I squealed my way through the air and hit the water with a smack. We played like that for several more minutes, then dried off and changed to go relieve Tammy. The twins were a lot for one person to handle.

That night, after bedtime stories for the little kids and hugs from the big—Stephen gave us a salute from his spot on the couch in the movie room—we got the babies settled in their bed in the room next to ours. I took a long bath, washing the chlorine out of my hair. The guys had already taken showers, but I'd waited until they were gone so I could shave and trim everything properly and pamper myself.

Once I was hair-free in all the right places, I walked out into our bedroom to find them splayed across the bed watching a movie.

They didn't even look away from the TV. Elias's nose twitched. "You used that orange-scented soap I like."

That was all the response I got. I looked down at the teal negligee I'd snuck into the bathroom. It lifted my breasts beautifully. I'd pumped right before my bath, but they were still extra plump compared to before my pregnancy. Under the breasts it fell to my panty line, concealing the pooch I carried. It was worse since the twins, though I'd really not gotten nearly as big as I would've expected, carrying two.

My thong was lace and left nothing to the imagination. I might as well have gone without, but I knew the scrap of material would serve its purpose, turning them on quickly.

I cleared my throat, tossing my damp hair over my shoulder. I wanted to look great for them, but I drew the line at fixing my hair and makeup.

All three of them laughed at a line in the movie just as I faked a cough. I stomped my foot.

"You coming?" Axoular said, glancing my way.

"Depends on you, doesn't it?" I quipped.

He froze, and slowly turned his head back to me in a classic doubletake. "What are you doing?"

"Nothing. Just standing here," I said, giving him my most innocent stare.

Elias and Anthony looked at me when I spoke, jaws dropping simultaneously. "Wow, really?" Elias asked.

"Really." I wouldn't bore them with the details, but I'd finally stopped bleeding a couple of days before. I'd gingerly explored myself, growing more adventurous when I'd not felt any pain. Everything seemed to be in fine working order.

"Well, come here," Anthony said, stripping off his shirt. "Don't waste any time. The twins could wake up at any moment."

I laughed at his eagerness and walked to the bed, rolling my hips, and hoping I didn't look completely ridiculous. I was going for sexy.

Elias's eyes narrowed, and he pulled his shirt off. Anthony's fangs descended. *I still got it.*

Axoular looked at me in terror. "We don't have to actually have sex, Axo."

He ran his eyes up and down my body. "Then what do you call this?" he asked.

"Don't worry," Elias said. "There's lots to do without having sex."

"Yeah," Anthony said. "Worse comes to worst one of us will just bite you."

Axoular looked apprehensive. I looked at Elias, not sure how to proceed. He nodded his head toward Axoular, telling me to go to him first. Anthony nodded his head, so I went to Axo.

He scooted to the end of the bed, and I stepped between his legs. We'd been kissing for a while, but nothing really more than that. I put my hands on his neck and bent over, kissing his lips softly.

He reached up and cupped my cheeks, deepening the kiss. Elias stood from the bed and walked behind me, pressing himself against me and kissing my neck.

Axoular pulled away from me, and I missed the connection to him. There really was something to the bond mess he told me about. I could already feel the tug of it, the need to complete it. I wanted to be his bonded wife. "Scoot back," I whispered.

I climbed up on the bed as he scooted back, sitting on my knees. He spread his legs so I could move in between them. Anthony and Elias moved to either side of me, so they could love me while I loved him. I was pretty sure they knew what I meant to do, though the look in Axoular's eyes told me he didn't.

Reaching for his hem, I tugged up on his shirt until he lifted his arms so I could remove it. His chest was sculpted and strong. "I have a strange request..." I didn't quite know how to word it.

"Anything, Riley," Anthony said.

"It's not for you. It's for Axoular."

"I'm yours, you know that. What do you want?"

"I don't know how to do it, but you did it once..." I looked down at my knees, afraid they'd think I was weird.

He cupped my chin and brought my gaze up to meet his. "Don't be embarrassed. Not with me."

"Can you make your scales come out?"

"You want to have sex with me in my Sárkány form?" He grinned. "That's a turn-on for me, I have to say."

Elias cleared his throat. "If you can figure it out, I wouldn't mind you bringing out your own scales, Riley."

Shivers racked my body. I was also intrigued by the idea.

"I don't know if I can do it," Axoular said. "In this world, it seems to be a defense mechanism. Give me a minute."

He closed his eyes and seemed to be searching himself. I didn't want to distract him, but as soon as his eyes closed, Elias and Anthony began touching me. They moved my hair behind my shoulders and kissed my neck in tandem. I saw them move their heads behind me and knew they were communicating with each other.

I kept my eyes on Axoular, trying to ignore their distractions, but they weren't having it. They moved their faces back to my neck, but instead of nuzzling or kissing, they bit.

My body jerked, pleasure washing over me. I

cried out, my orgasm bursting through me instantly, drenching my thong. They sucked in a breath, smelling my desire as they drank.

What we hadn't anticipated was the milk that would leak from my breasts. My eyes flew open when I felt moisture spread across the silk on my chest. I'd forgotten it would happen. Michael had loved it.

Axoular sat in front of me, covered in scales. He was beautiful. His scales ranged from the lightest gray to the deepest black, and they shined.

"Take your pajama pants off, please," I whispered, milky boobs forgotten. Pleasure still wracked my body as Elias and Anthony still had their fangs in my skin. They weren't pulling on my blood, so I wasn't losing much. They were just letting the pleasure wash over me and lapping up what came out. They pulled back when they heard me speak.

Axoular rose onto his knees in front of me and slid his pants down.

It's gorgeous. Leaning forward, I looked up at Axoular. He'd sucked in a breath the moment I touched him and let it out slowly.

I let go of him and put both hands on his chest. I wanted to explore him, but that would have to wait until we had our night together. Pushing gently, he got the picture and sat back against the pillows at the head of the bed.

I showed Axoular some attention.

I knew it might be a while before he got his coveted night alone with me. I was looking forward to it as much as he was, so I wanted to let him know it.

I tried to make a rhythm to our movements, but Elias must've been too excited.

Elias leaned over me and kissed my neck. "I love you," he whispered.

I twisted around to kiss him. "And I love you."

I looked at Anthony sitting to my right, at the foot of the bed, with a gleam in my eyes. "Do you want to watch?"

He nodded. "I like watching you with them. Is that okay?"

Smiling at him, I went back to Axoular. "Are you enjoying yourself?" I asked.

"Very much," he said. "I'll be paying you back for this," he said. "Just you wait."

"I won't last long if you keep that up," he said.

Wanting to maximize our time together, I loosened my grip so that he could enjoy my efforts longer. He threw his head back, looking more relaxed than I'd ever seen him.

Elias had moved to the other side of the bed, content to watch too. I was pretty sure they were all taking it easy and letting me have my way since it was our first time since the twins.

I turned to Anthony. "Do you have any preferences?"

He had removed his pants

He shook his head no, his face full of anticipation. "Whatever you want, Coya. I've missed your body."

"I've missed yours, too." I straddled his legs, pressing myself against him.

I moved slowly, relishing the feel of him, he lifted me, turning so that he could lay back. We ended up in between Elias and Axoular. Elias had recovered and was growing hard again, something he often did. Anthony never could come more than once, and Axoular was new to us. I didn't know if he'd be content to watch or want round two.

I lost myself in the feel of Anthony. His hands slid up my arm and over my breasts, finding the wet patches there.

The bra of my negligee was fitted, so he slid his fingers into the cups and pushed them down, freeing me. Milk dropped steadily out of my nipples. I heard Axoular suck in a breath.

I turned to find him back in his human skin and aroused again. Apparently, he liked the sight of my leaking nipples. "You can touch them, or lick them," I said as the thought of Axoular spurred me on.

He sat up on his knees and brought his mouth to my chest, trailing his tongue in a circle around first the left, then the right.

"Move up onto your knees, Coya," Anthony commanded. I did as he wanted, and he took over.

Axoular closed his mouth against one breast, and I threw my head back and moaned deep in my throat, amazed at the feeling of his mouth. Breast-feeding and pumping had left me a little sore, but when he swirled his tongue around my nipple and sucked gently, I came unglued.

Elias must've gotten tired of watching because as I closed my eyes and focused on the pleasure, I felt a mouth on my other nipple.

Knowing what it would do to me, Elias let his teeth sink into me just enough to add a stream of pleasure.

I cried out, overwhelmed with emotions, Anthony from below, Axoular's mouth on me, Elias's teeth in me. I exploded into a thousand pieces. I actually had to try to squash down on my orgasm a little, because I literally started smoking. I knew that in the right setting, Axoular and I could make love while on fire, but it would hurt Elias and Anthony.

When he finished, he handed me a towel to clean up. I looked at Axoular. "Are you sure you want to wait?"

"I'm sure. I've enjoyed myself immensely tonight, and one night soon I'll have you to myself so we can bond. I'm afraid that when we join together, we may erupt into flames. That happens a lot with the bond. We may have to be careful when and where we do it."

"I had to fight that off just now. Did you see me smoking?"

"You were smoking, all right," Elias said.

I went to the bathroom and finished cleaning up before changing into pajamas and a nursing tank top. The twins would be awake and hungry any time. "We had quite the adventurous night." I looked at Axoular. "We need to talk later and see if I can't figure out how to bring out my scales."

He grinned. "Okay."

I lifted my leg to climb into bed between them when I heard Linna cry out. "I'll get them, I'm already up."

Picking both of them up had become easier over

time and I soon had them both snuggled into the bed eating, Michael with me and Linna with Anthony.

I sat up with them long after they'd gone to sleep, thinking about their uncertain futures and mine. I watched their dads snore and missed my Michael.

THE MORNING DAWNED ON ME WITH ROCK-HARD boobs. The twins had slept for four hours straight, meaning I didn't wake up and pump, which meant I hurt. I grabbed the hand pumps beside the bed immediately after waking and relieved some of the pressure. Once I was pretty sure I wouldn't leak I made a bathroom run and then hooked up the electric pump to finish the job.

Elias slept beside me, splayed out on his stomach. Axoular and Anthony were gone. I peeked into the twins' room and found it empty, so I snuggled back into the bed, propped up on pillows, to watch the morning news while the pump did all the work.

Eventually, I got tired of the quiet and left Elias snoozing to go find my kids. It was a Saturday morning so they didn't have lessons, and I knew there was no way Kohbi would sleep late. She was a morning person like Axoular.

After spending a few minutes freshening up in the bathroom and putting on real clothes, I wandered around the house until I found the entire family in the kitchen eating. The kids were on their best behavior, as we had a guest at the table. Healer Rakesha sat at the head of the table, eating a stack of pancakes with syrup.

"Hello, Rakesha. What brings you here?" I asked as I walked down the long table, squeezing arms and patting the heads of my various children to say good morning. I leaned over and kissed Daniel on top of the head.

"I just thought I'd pop in and check on you all. I had to make some house calls today, so I added you to my list."

"That's very sweet of you. I wouldn't mind if you gave the twins a once over to be safe, but they seem to be thriving." I paused in front of them, swaddled side by side in their portable bed. Linna had a hint of a smile on her face and Michael looked like he was dreaming of a pacifier as he sucked away with nothing in his mouth.

Axoular winked at me from across the kitchen as he made another stack of pancakes, probably for me and him. All the kids looked like they had plenty, except for Stephen, who was beginning to eat less and less, and drink more and more blood.

"I'm finished," Rakesha said. "I'll just take the twins into their bedroom while you eat?"

"Let me carry one in for you." She plucked Linna from the bed and I grabbed Michael. "Since Elias is still asleep, let's just take them into the living room here."

I placed the sleeping Michael on the couch. Since he couldn't roll yet, he wasn't in any danger of falling off. She put Linna beside him.

"Go eat," she said. "I'm just going to sit with them and get a feel of their auras. It'll tell me if anything is off inside their little bodies."

I nodded and walked across the room to have my breakfast. When I was finished, I peeked into the living room to see if she was done.

She wasn't there. I turned back toward the kitchen. "Has anyone seen Healer Rakesha?" I asked the still-full room. The kids were planning their day and hadn't disbursed yet.

Stephen nodded his head. "I can see the entrance to the living room from here. She never left it."

I stepped inside when I heard a sound, and

walked around the couch, finding Michael laying where I'd left him, one fist worked free from his swaddle. He waved it in the air and watched it move in front of his face. Rakesha and Linna were not in the room.

I grabbed Michael, lava in my gut, and went back to the hallway between the kitchen and living room. "Stephen, are you sure?"

He nodded. "Positive. She never left that room."

That particular space only had one door, so she couldn't have gone out a different way. "Anthony!" I yelled. "She's gone."

He ran in from the kitchen, where he'd been watching me grow panicked. "She's not gone. There's some reasonable explanation."

There was no reasonable explanation. Stephen ran to get Elias out of bed, and we searched the house methodically, top to bottom and back again. She was gone, and she'd taken my vulnerable, Shapeshifter daughter with her.

Anthony got his contact at the Junta on the phone and Elias called Cindy. I walked the house holding Michael, who wouldn't stop crying. He knew she was gone, too.

Eventually, Tammy took him. "He might be picking up your stress, and he might be missing

Linna. Give him here, I'll be calm with him and get him to sleep."

It took me several minutes to actually hand him over. I had to kiss him and squeeze him several times.

I walked back to the kitchen where my men were on the phone mustering our forces. Axoular was even on his phone.

Anthony hung up first. "Well, they were helpful, but then they weren't. They immediately sent hunters to Rakesha's house and found her dead. That wasn't her."

My heart dropped. Until he said she was dead, there was some small chance that there was a reasonable explanation. "I can't do this again. I can't wonder where my family is." My heart screamed at me; a physical pain that made me want to double over.

I ached to hold Linna, and even Michael being several rooms over with Tammy made me ill. "How do I even know that was Tammy who took Michael?" I said, my voice shrill, on the verge of pure panic.

Elias put his arms around me. "The wards should've kept anyone that intended us harm, out. Either nobody wants to hurt us or Linna, or they've got someone that could fool the wards."

"Nobody wants Michael but us. He's not a

unique crossbreed of two species at war. Linna is the only one in any danger," Axoular said, covering his phone. He turned back to his conversation after speaking to me.

Anthony shot him an exasperated look. "I doubt, from what you told us, that they are interested in hurting her. Dumadi just views her as his and claimed her. I doubt he'd mistreat her."

He said the right thing. My panic settled into my stomach as fuel for my rage. My flames grew agitated, itching to destroy. I sucked in a deep breath, smoke flying out of my mouth as I exhaled. "You're right. And he'll die for it."

Elias hung up the phone. "I called our moms and a few friends. Everyone is ready when we get a location. Cindy is on her way with her entire coven. They're meeting us at the house in Tennessee, but Cindy is coming here first to make us a portal."

"What about the kids?" I asked.

"It's safer here, that's why we want to separate them from us. Danyelus is on his way here to stay with Tammy and the rest of the kids. There's no reason any of them would be at risk, but to be safe they're going to get them ready and take them to a location even we don't know." He looked down at himself. "We'll be running out the door in the next ten minutes. Riley, let's go get dressed."

He zipped to the bedroom, and I ran. *This enormous house! Half my ten minutes is jogging to the bedroom!*

He was already lacing up his boots when I entered. "Dress for a fight," he said.

After my naked episode in Bali, Cindy had worked on a spell until she was able to make me a totally fireproof bodysuit. It was such a dark purple it was almost black and made from some sort of spandex and polyester blend, so it clung—but not so tightly it was annoying. I rolled it up my body. It had no seams, buttons, or zippers. It was a feat of magical engineering, and difficult to get on.

Elias helped me tug it up and over my shoulders. I added non-magical boots. We'd ordered dozens of pairs, then tested them out after I gave birth to find the ones that I could move best in. They didn't lace, and if I flamed out, I could slip them off quickly.

I pulled my hair up into a bun, took off my earrings, and grabbed the hand pumps and a handful of bags. I was furious and would probably kill Dumadi, but I wasn't about to be uncomfortable while doing it. Throwing them and a few extra guns and knives into a messenger bag, I slung it over my shoulder.

Elias grabbed my gun and knife belt on our way out and zipped to the kitchen. I caught up with him and put on my weapons as Cindy entered the room. Axoular was right behind her, wearing his own version of the bodysuit. He had a lot more control over his flames, so he only needed a shirt. His was black and clung to every ridge in his chest and stomach. I didn't have the emotional capacity to appreciate it right at that moment, but when he'd modeled it for me, I'd spent several minutes studying it under the guise of making sure it would work. I was really just checking out his bod.

"Ready?" Cindy asked.

I looked around, trying to think if there was anything else we needed.

Stephen came skidding into the room. "I want to go with you," he said, out of breath. He wore an outfit similar to what Elias had changed into.

Anthony wore shorts and flip-flops but would likely change back at the Tennessee house. "Son, you're not ready for open combat."

"I am! I've trained for years, you know that. You trained me!"

"I did, I know. And you're very good. But you're

still growing. You're not at your full strength or power."

"Stephen," I said softly. "I need you to protect my babies. What if they come after Michael or Kohbi to get to me?"

He bristled.

"You'd never let them take my babies, would you?"

"Of course not!" He puffed out his chest. "I'd die first."

"I'm sure it won't come to that, but if it does, I need to know you've got Danyelus and Tammy's backs."

He nodded. "Of course, I will."

"Plus, you know the kids. You can help keep them calm and in line. You'll be on the move. They'll need your help."

He still looked disappointed, but nodded.

I opened my arms and he considered me for a moment before pulling me into a hug. "Be safe," I said.

"You, too." His voice was strangled. He gave his dad and uncle a severe look and ran from the room.

"He's at a difficult age," Anthony said.

"Yeah, he is," Elias agreed. "You were a total douche at that age."

Cindy interrupted them before they could go all bromance on us. "Ready?"

She opened a portal and I ducked through it before it was even really open enough. I stepped out into our living room in Tennessee, and everyone followed behind.

Hearing voices in the kitchen, I moved there and found it full of people I'd never seen before.

Anthony squeezed around me and addressed the room. "Thank you all for coming. I see you've already started scrying."

A short man with a black goatee stepped forward. "They've still got that powerful magic-user. We can't pinpoint an exact location, but we know they're back on Bali."

"How do you know that?" I asked. They'd have to have something of Dumadi's or Linna's to scry for them.

Cindy wedged herself into the room. "I took a minuscule clipping of Linna's hair when she was born. I told Elias."

I glared behind me into the hall where Elias stood.

He shrugged. "I forgot, and now I'm glad she did it."

Rolling my eyes, I turned back to them. "We

need to find Ross. He's Dumadi's son and can help us pinpoint him."

"Yeah, but will he?" a voice said from the back of the crowded kitchen.

I glowered. "He had better."

Anthony pulled his phone out. "I'll call and let the Junta know we're incoming and not to warn Ross."

He squeezed back out of the room. The witches turned back to the kitchen table where they had maps spread out everywhere. I watched them find a different map of the island and return to their spells, continuing to try even though they'd failed before.

Anthony returned quickly. "They're ready for us. He said to have you open the portal into the main conference room. They're ready to back us."

Cindy nodded and walked back to the deserted living room, me hot on her heels.

I watched her circle her arms and speak her ancient language, and again as soon as it was open, I darted through.

The room I entered was an amphitheater, and it was jammed full of creatures of all shapes and sizes. I stopped, shocked by the display of force, and Anthony slammed into my back, propelling me forward.

For an amphitheater, it was small. For a conference room, as Anthony had called it, it was massive. "How many people are here?" I muttered under my breath.

Elias heard me and looked around. "I've never seen it this full. There's gotta be three hundred people here. There's not even room for everyone to sit.

All of the witches streamed in behind us and moved to the sides of the room to stand against the walls and wait for further instruction.

The council, that I'd met at Michael's service, sat at a stone table in front of the stone stadium seats. The whole setup was ridiculous in the modern age, but it reeked of power.

Alexander, the Fae leader of the Junta, rose from his seat in the center of the table and motioned for us to come closer. "Riley, I'm very sorry that we're meeting again under such circumstances."

I smiled, not willing to exchange pleasantries. "Yes, well, thank you. What's the plan at this point?"

"Now that you're here I've sent someone to fetch Ross. He'll be here momentarily, and we'll enlist his help with this mess." He sat back down and scrutinized me, eyes raking over my bodysuit.

I took the opportunity to scrutinize him back. If

I'd been asked to describe what a Fae man looked like before I'd learned that the Unseen existed, I would've probably described Alexander. He was lean, lithe even. Long, shiny black hair framed a pale face with delicate blue eyes.

He wore a suit though. I would've put him in some sort of robes. Looking down at his hands, I noted their softness. He wasn't a man that fought his battles with his fists.

"Have you seen enough?" Axoular growled beside me. I grinned at him, delighted by his show of jealousy.

Sometimes a little jealousy served to make a woman feel wanted.

Alexander inclined his head. "Axoular. I hadn't realized you'd entered a relationship with our Riley."

"Do I need the council's permission to have a relationship?" I asked.

"Of course not. I was simply making an observation."

"She's not your Riley, Alex," Elias said, unable to stay out of it. "Stop being so pompous."

The only indication that Alexander was irritated was a tiny flare of his nostrils. He laughed. "Oh, Elias, always to the point." He opened his mouth to say more, but the massive wooden door to the amphitheater opened and a man walked in flanked by two guards.

I knew they were guards because they wore t-shirts that hugged their massive chests and biceps that said "Guard" in bright yellow print across their pecs.

"Ah, Ross!" exclaimed Alexander. "Thank you for joining us."

Ross stopped near the door and swept his eyes across the room. "What the hell is going on here?"

His hair was red—bright, orange-red. The kind of red that causes fair skin to burn if the sun even peeks out. He had a neatly trimmed red beard to match it.

"Ross, join us." Alexander indicated he should come closer to our group, which consisted of me, Anthony, Elias, Axoular, and Cindy.

He walked forward cautiously, looking out at all the creatures in the stands.

I took a moment to study them while he did. It looked like there were representatives and warriors from every species on Earth. Except for humans, of course. They couldn't be there, even though many of them looked human. I tried not to stare at the beings that were so obviously *other*. I spotted leprechauns, sprites, someone that looked suspiciously like a bigfoot, and more creatures I had no names for with fur or horns or scales.

A large group of who I assumed were Supay took up several rows in the front. They were the most heavily represented species. "How'd all these people get here?" I asked.

"I've had my coven opening portals since I got the first phone call," Cindy whispered. "And every species is required to station twenty warriors here at the keep for policing the Unseen."

My jaw dropped. "I didn't know that. Will the Sárkány have to do the same?"

"Once they're settled on the council, I'm sure they will."

"If you two are finished?"

I turned back to the bench to find the various members of the council glaring at me.

I jolted, shocked I'd let myself be distracted. It was hard to not be fascinated by the crowd, though.

Ross turned to me. "Who are you? What is this?" He was definitely on edge.

"I'm Riley Effler. Where is your father?"

"Why don't we get right to the point then?" Alexander muttered. "Ross, we need your assistance finding Dumadi."

Ross didn't take his eyes off of me. "I've been

trying to help you for months, and all I got for it was imprisoned."

"You've not been imprisoned. You've been free to leave this entire time," said a bearded man I assumed to be a dwarf.

"Yeah, if I agreed to take an entourage with me. Just because I want our people to become a part of the modern Unseen society, and stop hiding, doesn't mean we aren't a secretive and private people. I can't have you all traipsing through our lives."

"Listen to me, you murderous lech," I said, rage trying to ignite my flames. Smoke poured out of my skin. "Your crazy ass father kidnapped my daughter. If you don't help me find her, I'll burn you alive."

Axoular grabbed my arms to keep me from advancing on the redheaded man.

To his credit, Ross looked horrified. "I thought you had her hidden!"

"We did," Anthony said, stepping in front of me. I tried to compose myself. "He killed our healer and took on her personage and probably her memories. Under the guise of inspecting the twins' health, he took Linna."

Ross shook his head. "That crazy old man. He's lost it completely." I stepped around Anthony and Ross addressed me. "This isn't how any of us would've chosen to handle this, but the problem is that Dumadi *is* the leader of the Leyak."

"And?" I asked.

"They'll do as he says. They'll fight for him, and there's no telling what he's told them. I've been stuck *here* so I have no idea if he's returned to our temple or not."

"Well now's your chance to go home," I said. "I'm getting my baby back, one way or another." I turned to the council. "What are we waiting on? Ross is going to help us find his father. Let's go."

"Hold on, we can't just go in guns blazing," Ross said, voice angry.

I stiffened my back, fighting the rage. "And why not? Would your father hurt the baby?"

"I don't believe so. He thinks she'll unite our races."

"As do I. Now let's go." I turned to Cindy. "Take us to the house we stayed at?"

Ross sighed. "This is a mistake."

I whirled on him, unable to contain it anymore. "Listen here. You're going to help me, or I'll kill you. It's that simple." I allowed my fire to lick up my arm, for effect. Half the room gasped. It took a lot of effort to pull it back and not let it consume me. I really needed to work with it more.

Ross's eyes widened. "I didn't say I wouldn't help! I just think you should let me go in and try to get the baby back."

"No." Anthony stepped in front of me again. "We don't know you well enough to trust you. All we want from you is a location."

He nodded. "Okay."

I turned to Cindy, who opened another portal, taking us to Bali. She stayed in New Zealand with the council. "Text me with a specific location and I'll portal everyone in." The portal began to close, but then she stopped and reversed her arms to widen it again. "I almost forgot! Ross!"

"Yeah?"

"What magical creature does your father have that's so strong it can defy my entire coven?"

"He has a Valkyrie, and he has something on her. She doesn't want to, but she has to do anything he says."

"What power could he possibly have over a Valkyrie?" Cindy asked in horror.

"I have no idea. He won't tell me. Peter knew. Peter was the golden child, the warrior, willing to do anything for the cause. I'm not." He sulked, discontent with his lot in life.

She closed the portal, fear on her face.

I turned to Elias and Anthony, who were staring at the spot the portal had been in shock. "What's a Valkyrie? I mean, I know they're from Norse mythology, but what's true about them?" Everyone was freaking out for a reason.

"Not much is known about them," Ross said. "She can do magic, I think. But it's said they can bend fate."

"They're powerful. I actually wasn't sure they really existed," Anthony said. "After learning about the other worlds and portals and stuff, I wondered if maybe they were some of the creatures considered to be old gods. I didn't think there were any on Earth."

"Well, she doesn't work for him willingly?"

Ross nodded.

"Good. We'll use that to our advantage." I walked to the kitchen and peeled the top of my suit down, pulling the hand pumps out of my bag. I grabbed a blanket off the couch on the way. I wasn't shy, but I'd just met Ross, and had no desire to show him my boobs.

Settling down at the table, I pumped while the guys consulted maps. "Where is he most likely to be?" I asked.

"The same temple he kept you in."

"How far is it from here?" Axoular asked. He'd

been quiet, brooding. He didn't know how to react to his daughter being kidnapped. I smiled at him with false bravado. I had no doubt we would get her back; it was just a matter of time.

"Can't you guys make one of those portals?" Ross asked.

"It doesn't work that way. The witch has to have been in the location before," Anthony said wearily.

"So, we'll, what, take a cab?" he asked, smirking.

It did sound ridiculous, pulling up to battle in a bright yellow cab. I snorted. "What's it to you?" I asked him.

"Please listen to me. Let me go to him. I can distract him, grab the baby, and come back here. It will be much safer for everyone." He ran his fingers through his hair, causing it to stick straight up.

"Are you still trying to protect him?" I asked. He had to die. I would not leave him alive to terrorize my family anymore. I didn't give him time to answer. "How many of your people believe the way he does? That the Sárkány are evil and need to die?"

"Is that what Peter told you?" He laughed. "He was so unreasonable."

"Then what's the truth?" I continued pumping milk under the blanket, and Ross's eyes kept straying to the movement of the blanket covering me.

Axoular noticed and slapped him in the back of the head. "Mind your eyes, Leyak."

I winced. "Well?"

"The Leyak want to find a home. We were happy on our planet. We were advanced and prospered. Not here. Here we hide, and sneak."

"You want access to a portal. And he thinks the baby will be able to open or create portals for him," I said.

Ross nodded. "He's said as much. We found a portal here and had it under constant surveillance. When you activated the one in Bolivia, the one here activated too."

"Did you go through it?" I finished with the bottles and covered myself back up under the blanket. Once I was covered, I moved over to the counter to seal the bags and put them in the freezer. We'd grab them on the way home and might need them for Linna. Michael had plenty stored that Tammy had taken with her. I hoped Dumadi had bought formula for Linna and didn't try to give her regular milk.

"We sent a volunteer and waited as the portal went dark and came back to life every time you sent someone through to the dragon world. He never returned."

"You're not from another realm. You're from this

one, albeit another planet, yet still in this realm," Axoular said. "From what we know of the magic of the portals, they transport you to your home realm or here. That's it. Your friend is probably dead."

He shrugged. "We want to try."

"Why didn't he just ask me for some blood while I was there?"

"He took some while you were unconscious. It didn't work. It has to be your finger touching it."

"Well, why didn't he ask me to open it? We could've worked something out." *How ridiculous.*

"That puts all the power in your corner. If he creates a race of mixed Sárkány and Leyak, we can open and close portals as we please."

"Then wouldn't it be smarter to kidnap some female Sárkány and have babies with them?" Elias asked sarcastically.

"That's what I said," Ross bristled, snarling. "I didn't mean it. And I'm not totally sure he didn't already do just that. But he wants your baby because it's Peter's baby. Like I said. Golden child."

Axoular strode forward. "You think he might have Sárkány women hidden somewhere?"

"Maybe. He talked about possibly trying."

It was his turn to fight for control. Smoke wafted over his skin, and he grabbed Ross by his shirt. "You better be wrong." He released him with a shove and Ross stumbled back a few feet, tugging his shirt down.

I heard a noise in the living room. "Did you hear that?"

"I did," Elias said. He crept forward silently to check, disappearing through the door. He returned with one of the witches from Cindy's coven. "This is Leo Price. He's from Cindy's coven. She sent him to open a portal back to the council room if we need one."

"Hello, Leo. Thank you for helping us," I said.

The tall witch nodded his head. "I'm happy to help."

"Shall we?" I said.

"I've already got a cab on the way," Anthony said. "Two, actually."

I couldn't stand any more speculation and maybes and what-should-we-dos. I walked outside to wait on our ride.

The view was breathtaking, I was pretty sure, but I focused on the road, waiting for the taxi to drive up the driveway. The sun normally gave me strength, but I just felt lost.

Anthony walked out and sat on the porch swing. I sat beside him to wait. "This has got to end. When this is over with Dumadi, we're going into hiding. I don't care. I need rest. I need calm. I need to raise my children and love my husbands."

"And you'll have it, Coya. I'll make sure of it." He put his arm around me, and I felt a hand on my back.

I looked up to find Elias and Axoular behind me. "We will find calm, Riles." Elias bent over and kissed my head.

We sat together in silence until the taxi pulled up. Elias opened the door and called into the house. "Let's go."

Leo and Ross came out, looking less than thrilled to be going on our mission. We divided up, Axoular and Elias going with Ross to make sure he didn't try to run. Anthony and Leo joined me.

Ross gave directions to the cab in front of us, and we were off to save my baby. And kill Dumadi.

THE TEMPLE WAS OVER AN HOUR AWAY. WE passed the hospital I'd woken up in. My nervousness was palpable, and I kept shifting in my seat, flexing my legs, and checking my weapon. Leo gave me a strange look the third time I checked the chamber, so I forced myself to put it away.

When we finally pulled up to the front of the temple, I opened the door and slid out, staring at the tourist trap in front of me. Humans milled everywhere, and I suddenly regretted the guns and knives displayed on my hip.

Leo stepped out beside me.

"I wish I'd worn something over this to hide my weapons," I whispered. I was pretty sure no one had noticed us yet, but it was only a matter of time.

Leo pulled out a strange pencil with a very fat

lead. "It's spelled." He drew a rune—basically three squiggly lines on top of each other—on my hand. "It'll draw eyes away from you. You won't be hidden. If you jump up and down and shout, people will still see you. But if you're surreptitious, their eyes will glance over you, noting nothing important to see about you."

"That's handy," I said, peering at the lines on my skin.

He held his hand over it and muttered three words that I, of course, didn't know. The lines glowed for a second and disappeared.

"Aw, I wanted the tattoo."

Elias and Anthony finished paying the cab drivers and joined us.

"Should I bring my coven here?" Leo asked.

"No," I said. "I may be able to handle this myself."

"I doubt that," Ross interjected. "He'll be expecting you."

"He expected me when he kidnapped me and underestimated me."

"He probably won't be as likely to underestimate you this time, Coya."

Anthony was right. "I still don't think we should bring in the cavalry out here."

"I agree," murmured Elias as the cabs pulled away. "Let's get to an interior room. Then our main objective will be to protect Leo as he brings in reinforcements."

Leo nodded. "The entire amphitheater is prepared to come through if they're needed. Nobody takes kidnapping a newborn lightly."

We started toward the temple entrance, walking on a bridge that covered a moat. I hadn't been awake long enough the last time we were there to notice the moat. We walked up to a gate where an attendant collected Rupiah, the local currency, for entrance to the temple. I used my spell to slip through the gate, where I pressed myself against the wall and tried to look unimportant.

Women were required to wear a sarong in the temples, it's a rule. I had no desire to disrespect their religion, but I was on a mission.

The men paid and I peeled myself away from the wall to join them as they marched single file through the crowd toward the main temple.

Ross turned off and went through a door labeled "Private, no entry." It was the door I'd burst out of weeks before.

We retraced the steps I'd taken, through the holy place, and I noticed many of the furnishings had been replaced with similar items. I could tell the difference, though. *Those must've been the ones I torched.*

We went up the stairs, past the spot where I killed the guards, an action I'd not thought twice about. Maybe I should've felt more guilty, but I didn't.

"Why hasn't anyone noticed us yet?" I asked.

Ross chuckled. "Oh, they have. This hallway is normally full of Leyak, going about their daily business. We run this temple, along with many others on the island."

"Why do you look like that, and not like a local?"

"I had a mission a few years ago in the states, and I like this face, so I decided to keep it for a while."

Gross.

We stood at the top of the stairs, and Ross peered into the unusually empty hallway. "Now what?" he asked. "You're the one that wanted to come blazing in."

"Where would they have her?" I asked.

"If you hadn't burned down the room you were kept in, probably there. I'd say we're about to walk into some sort of trap though."

I turned to Leo. "Can you maintain an open

portal?" I asked. I had no clue what a single witch was capable of.

"Of course," he said, inclining his head.

"Okay, can you open it at the top of these stairs once we've gone through to the hall? Then they can come in and follow us as needed."

He nodded.

Ross went first into the hallway. "Maybe if they see me, they'll hesitate."

He was wrong. They didn't hesitate. When he stepped into the hallway, he jerked as he was electrocuted, the floor apparently charged for anyone that set foot on it.

I started to reach for him, to drag him back into the stairwell, but Anthony grabbed me before I could. "If you touch him, you'll be electrocuted, too!"

He was right, of course, and I knew that. I'd panicked. I turned to Axoular, unable to look at Ross's body on the floor. "We *are* fire, can we withstand electricity?"

He shook his head. "No."

"Then we need the witches."

"On it," Leo said. He did the same things I'd grown used to seeing Cindy do, and a wide portal appeared behind us, against the wall of the stairwell.

Cindy came through. "What's the plan?"

I pointed at Ross, lying on the ground. He'd lost his stolen image and lay on the ground with blue skin and dark brown hair. He was far more handsome in his natural skin than he'd been before, and he'd been an attractive man in his stolen face.

"Wow," she said. "Did they electrify the floor?"

"Yeah," Anthony said. "Can you counteract it?"

"I can, but it'll take a minute." She looked back through into the amphitheater. "I need the level two and above."

Three witches joined her, placing their hands on her back while she crouched in the doorway, careful not to touch the floor. "Wait a second," she said, slapping the floor. "He discharged the spell. It's not electrified anymore."

Well, thanks for that.

She stood back up. "Want us to back you up?"

"Probably should," I said as I inched out into the hall. Elias tried to push forward, but I stopped him. "Let me go first, and Axoular. None of us are expendable, but he and I are probably hardier."

He stared at me, deadpan, for a full second before walking around me. "You're not hardier, Riley. Don't be silly."

I shrugged my shoulders and followed him as he approached the first door on the right. The left side of the hall was just stone wall. The right held all the rooms I'd passed by when I escaped.

Kicking in the door, he jumped back in time to avoid the blast of fire that erupted through the door. "Get out!" a woman's voice screamed.

I peeked into the doorway. "Are you Sárk —Minda!"

Axoular pushed me out of the way and ran into the room. "Oh, my god, Minda, are you hurt?"

She jumped out of her defensive crouch and ran into his arms. I tried to pretend it didn't make me feel jealous. *Calm down, Riley, she was kidnapped and sees him as her rescuer.*

"I'm not hurt. I've only been here a couple of days. They keep trying to pay me to have sex with them until I get pregnant, then leave the baby with them!" She burst into tears. "I'm not a prostitute!"

He turned to me with her wrapped totally around him, bawling into his shoulder. His expression was baffled. "Help!" he mouthed at me.

I shook my head. I should've left him to her tears and breakdown, but we didn't have time. "Minda!" I shouted. "Pull yourself together so you can help us."

She dropped her feet to the floor and made a visible attempt to calm herself. "What can I help with?" she asked before hiccoughing.

"They have my baby. Have you seen a small, blue infant?"

"No, I'm sorry," she said. "But I've heard one, so they're probably keeping it close."

"I hope you're right," I responded. "Can you come with us and help search, and possibly defend us if we get into a battle with the Leyak?"

Her expression turned dark. "I hope we do."

Axoular walked out of the room, leaving my husbands and the witches peering in, shocked. I stopped Minda before we joined them in the hall.

"Did they hurt you? Did they rape you?"

"No, thankfully. Every time they came near, I burst into flames, but only enough to make them back off. I really, *really* need sleep, though."

"Okay, I'm sending you back." I pulled her into the hall. "Do you see that portal?"

"Yeah, I'm tired, not blind," she said snottily.

It was difficult not to slap the brat. *She's been through a lot. Go easy.* "Go through it and tell the council lead, Alexander, what's happened. He'll take care of you. He's weird, but he'll make sure you have a safe place to rest and recuperate."

She pulled me into a hug. "Thank you for saving me again, Riley. I have no doubt if I'd slept, they would've raped me. They hinted at it, but I wouldn't let them get close."

"I'm actually surprised they didn't drug you."

"They did when they kidnapped me, but I think I would've known if I'd had sex."

"Of course," I said. "Now go."

She went. I waited until I saw her pass into the amphitheater before nodding at my little posse so we could continue on. A host of faces tried to look through the portal at us, to see what was happening.

Waving at them before turning back to the business at hand, I pulled out my gun, unsure if it would help, but I was trained to fight with it. I felt secure holding it in my hand.

Elias looked to me to lead, waiting until I nodded before he kicked in the door. Somehow, I'd shifted myself into the managerial position of our posse. Me, who had never been in an Unseen war, who had never truly battled anyone except Peter, and he never stood a chance.

You did fight those thugs on the road last year. My inner confidence thought I was a badass, but she was used to being told to shut up. I let her whisper encouraging thoughts in my ear today. I needed her bolstering.

The door flew into the room, ripped off its

hinges. Elias did his job well. That Supay strength, which I rarely had cause to see, impressed me.

Nobody inside. *Dang it.*

Three more doors went down the same way, and at the fourth, we found another Sárkány woman, unconscious. One of the witches carried her out and quickly returned.

Axoular's eyes were red. Not a good sign for whoever stood to fight us. "She appeared to be unhurt," I said. "Hopefully they just recently brought her here and hadn't had time to do anything harmful."

His only response was sparks shooting out of his nose as his chest heaved. *Okay then, let's use that rage.*

I moved forward, not willing to waste any more time. The only door left was at the end of the hall. Based on the structure's layout, I had to assume it was more stairs leading down. We were on the top floor.

We prepared ourselves the best we could. Axoular was a hair's breadth from shooting fire, I had my guns up and my fire wasn't far behind Axoular's. Anthony and Elias's fangs were out, and their hands looked remarkably claw-like. *Something to explore later. I've never seen them like that.*

The witches just sort of stood there behind us. I had no idea what their idea of defensiveness was.

I nodded and Elias kicked the door in. Nothing happened. I inched forward, but Axoular put his hand on my back. "Let me," he growled.

He stepped forward a few feet and his body clenched. I watched his muscles ripple under his tight fireproof shirt. Scales erupted across his body. I could see the ridges of them under the material of the shirt. He leaned forward and fire shot from his mouth.

The structure was made of stone, so no real damage was done, but the door ignited.

"We have to wait for that to go out," Elias said.

Axoular grunted and strode forward, checking first to make sure nobody was hiding on the stairs. He must not have seen anyone, because he grabbed the door and ripped it from its hinges. My mouth dropped.

"I didn't know we could do that," I hissed at him as he walked past us to leave the door out of harm's way. The rest of our party crowded against the opposite wall as he walked by. To them, the flames were intense and burned hotter than any they might've been near like a bonfire or fireplace.

Once the door was gone the rest of the flames

rapidly burned themselves out while we waited on Leo to close the portal at the other end of the hall.

When the coast was clear and the portal down, I advanced us down the stairs. We were in a strange position at the bottom, exposed once the door was opened. Axoular and I hadn't been on that side of the temple before, not that we could remember. We had no idea what we were in store for.

"Quietly or quickly?" I asked.

Elias shrugged. "They know we're here."

"Quickly then," I said. I tested the door handle but found it locked. I stepped back and he kicked it off its hinges.

We spilled out into the same holy room we'd entered before. The stairs had taken us in a big circle. "There's got to be another way out of this room. The upstairs won't be all of it."

"Spread out, but buddy up. Don't be more than a foot from your buddy at any time," Anthony said.

"Elias, stay with Anthony. You two are already used to fighting together and are more effective. Plus, if Axo or I burst into flames you can't get close."

Neither one of them looked happy about it, but they did as I asked, crossing the room with two witches to search the walls.

I turned to the walls on the right side of the room

where we'd exited and pointed to an enormous tapestry on the wall. "It makes sense that the most likely place in the entire room is behind there."

Nobody responded, so I strode forward and jerked the tapestry away from the wall, Axoular on my heels. Nothing was behind it but stones.

I turned in a circle, studying the walls. Several spots held shelves and cases full of religious artifacts. I moved to study one, maybe there was some sort of lever that could be pulled to make the wall move.

One of the witches near me, I was pretty sure her name was Circe, huffed in consternation. "You know, this temple isn't anything like the other temples here. I've stayed in Bali many times. It's a favorite vacation spot for my family."

"Okay," I said. "What's different about this one?"

"Most of them are open air. Some have springs that you can get into to be blessed. A couple are underground. But I don't know of any other structured like this. This is too... too..." She looked around, trying to think of the right word. "It's western. Like something that would be built for a Christian church or something."

I turned in a circle, trying to figure out what we were missing. The outer structure was large. There was definitely a way out of this room besides the way we came in.

"Underground?" I asked Circe.

"Yeah, if this was more like one of the cave temples, there would be a cave entrance up there at the end of the room, and this structure could've been built around it to protect the entrance, but it wouldn't have been considered the temple, it's too modern, even though it's made out of stone."

I walked toward the area she indicated. The wall looked normal. Like a stone wall with no breaks. There were tables running along the wall and gold plating in the middle, almost like a picture frame. It was beautiful, especially with the artifacts on the tables. I didn't spare them much energy though, as they were too far away from the wall to help or be a hidden lever.

You're thinking like a human. Think like a magical being.

"Is there a spell of revealing that you could do?"

"I'm not strong enough." She turned around, looking for Cindy, who had made her way over to search the opposite walls with my guys. "Cindy!" she called in a whisper-yell.

Cindy didn't hear her, but Anthony did with his supernatural hearing. He turned and spoke a few words and Cindy and her buddy came jogging over to us.

"Let's try a revealing spell, we think there might be a door to a cave temple on this wall."

"Sure," Cindy said brightly. "Those are fun."

Leo walked over to see what we were up to, and Cindy explained.

He pulled out his weird fat pencil. "I brought this."

Cindy's eyes lit up. "Good thinking!"

He walked over to the middle of the wall, in the center of the gold plating, and drew a rune that was like a complicated V. Cindy, Circe, and Leo placed their hands on the wall around the symbol and closed their eyes. Leo muttered and Circe mouthed what seemed to be the same words, but Cindy said nothing.

Interesting. I wonder if they don't have to say the spells out loud as they get more powerful.

Stepping back, they focused intently on their symbol. It didn't disappear like the one on my hand did. It did, however, begin to glow.

"Ha!" Circe said. "I knew it!"

The glow intensified, and everyone but Axoular and I looked away. We weren't bothered by bright lights. The light blinked out with a pop, and the wall changed.

They didn't see it because they'd covered their eyes, but Axoular and I saw the moment it shimmered away. Behind the illusion of the wall stood a woman in a stone doorway.

Axoular roared and I unholstered my gun as quickly as I could. "Who are you?" I asked.

She stepped forward, rolling her curvaceous hips.

I had to be honest with myself. The woman was the sexiest creature I'd ever seen, but also one of the most dangerous.

Elias's eyes recovered the fastest. "Valkyrie," he inclined his head. "We have no desire to fight you."

"I bet you don't," she said, voice deeper than mine, and I had a husky voice. It wasn't masculine, just rich. "I would kill you."

"What is your name, Valkyrie?" I asked.

"You may call me Kára."

Anthony's mouth dropped. "*The* Kára?"

She inclined her head. "You must leave here now. I don't want to kill you, who would not be welcomed in Valhalla." She studied me. "You might be welcome by Frejya in Fólkvangr."

I couldn't help feeling a little proud hearing her

words. Her demeanor of power and elegance made me want to impress her. I looked around at my group and realized they were all in a state of awe.

"No disrespect, Kára, but I need to get past you."

"I can't allow that, Dragon. I must protect this space."

"I'm Riley, Kára, and I can help you. If I kill Dumadi, will his hold over you break?"

Her face blanched. "He has no hold over me."

My lies are necessary, Dragon. He holds my children.

I blinked. She'd spoken but her lips hadn't moved.

I'm in your head, Dragon.

"We will fight you, if necessary," I said, but at the same time tried to think at her. *How can we help you?*

Her mouth moved, but I couldn't hear the words she said to cover our conversation. *We must find my children before he dies. If he dies before he reveals their location, they'll starve to death wherever they're hidden.*

Anthony snapped out of his reverie. "Valkyrie, you don't use magic, not as these witches do. Your power is different. How are you able to block the spells of these witches?"

I looked around and saw my wonderful backup entourage of witches staring at Kára with narrowed eyes. They'd joined hands behind me and muttered under their breath. I hadn't even noticed.

"That is for me to know, Supay."

Anthony raised an eyebrow, then looked at me, at a loss how to proceed. The Valkyrie, from what I knew of them, were the fiercest warriors known. We didn't want to fight one and be slaughtered, nor did we want to fight one and kill her, risking a war with the others.

Dragon, I don't wield the magic protecting me from your spells. They're using me as a power siphon. If you can get around me and find the warlock that is nearby and kill her, my powers will only be in battle. And I highly doubt you can kill me. Feel free to try. If you succeed, I only ask that you find my children. I'll go home to Freyja and await the coming Ragnarök.

"Right then, only one thing to do," I said, raising my gun and firing in rapid succession. *Please don't die.*

She moved before I had time to pull the trigger the first time, rolling to the right. I stopped wasting bullets and holstered my gun, grabbing Cindy and running through the door, away from the fight. *Don't kill my people!* I wasn't sure if she'd hear the shout from my mind, but I tried.

Cindy jerked away from me. "What are you doing?" she hissed, looking around in the dark cave. We had no light and no idea where we were going.

I pressed my lips against her ear. "We gotta find the magic-user that is siphoning energy from the Valkyrie," I spoke as softly as I could, and luckily, she heard.

I looked back toward the entrance to the dark tunnel and watched as someone flew past the door, having been thrown if my guess was correct. *Be safe.*

Leaving them to their fight, I inched forward. The tunnel grew darker and darker as the light of the worship room dwindled.

Cindy squeezed my hand and put her lips to my ear. I grimaced as she spoke. Her hot breath tickled. "Can I risk a light?"

I put her hand on my face, so she'd feel my motions and nodded, leaning close to whisper, "Dim."

She rustled around and a tiny fireball appeared in her hand. *Well, I could've done that.*

The tunnel widened into a dead end. *This isn't right. They're messing with us again.* I turned to Cindy. "Reveal," I breathed.

She nodded and took out a knife, pricking her finger. I tapped her shoulder and held my arms out in a "What the heck?" gesture when she turned to me.

She pulled the fireball close to illuminate her face and mouthed, "No pencil."

Dang. I nodded my understanding. *I should've brought Leo, too.*

I grabbed her arm before she touched the wall and leaned in to ask one more question. "Can you siphon energy from me?" I asked. I was afraid this battle would primarily be magical, with not too much muscle needed once Kára stopped fighting my guys out there.

I heard a roar from Axoular and snapped my head toward the barely visible tunnel entrance, worried. Cindy squeezed my arm, bringing my focus back to the task at hand.

She nodded her head. She'd be able to channel my strength. I hoped it was enough to kill that warlock. I also hoped Cindy was up to the challenge. What I knew about warlocks was how to spell warlock and not one more thing.

She took her bloody finger and smeared it over my forehead. I furrowed my brow. *Why is everything magical gross?*

Grinning like she knew what I was thinking, she put her hands on my head and touched her forehead to the bloody spot on mine. I felt a tug in my chest, and she pulled away, nodding, and smiling. She'd done it.

I didn't feel any different until she squeezed more blood out of her finger and rubbed it into the fancy V shape on the wall. She focused on the rune, and when she did, I felt a tug in my chest again, but this time it was accompanied by a tingle. She was using my inherent magic to reveal the hidden passage or room.

Apparently, my inherent magic was a teensy bit powerful because there was no shimmer this time. There was a deafening pop and the walls rumbled.

Being in a cave tunnel during a rumble wasn't and would never be on my bucket list. I shrank back, ready to bolt.

Oh, god, Linna is in here. I can't leave without her.

Cindy looked at me in shock. She hadn't expected it either. The rumbles stopped and we grinned at each other, turning to face the opening in the rock that had appeared.

"They know we're in the tunnel now, with that noise. No sense in hiding," I said.

She shrugged. "You're one seriously powerful creature. Did you know you could do that?"

"Nope. Axoular knows what all I can do, but he's been waiting to show me slowly. Most Sárkány learn this stuff throughout a long life. I haven't had that opportunity."

As we spoke, we eyeballed the doorway, apprehensive about entering another dark cave. "Let's go," I said.

She brightened the ball, using her own power. I didn't feel any tingles. We walked in side by side, her arm out ahead of us so the ball would illuminate the room.

A curvaceous woman stood at the other end, wearing a cloak. *Finally, one of these magicals wears something I'd expect.*

"Hello Cindy," she said, smiling. Her face was long, angular, almost serpentine. I expected a tongue to dart out at any moment.

Cindy froze beside me. "Remember the rumble," I whispered, reminding her that she had my power at her disposal.

Apparently, she heard me because she smiled. "Hello, Meg. How've you been? Still doing magic for the highest bidder, I see."

"Like you don't?" Her voice had a hissing quality to it.

"I only take jobs for people that aren't evil, you know that."

"You don't have the power to hurt me," Meg said.

"Maybe. Care to find out?"

She smiled. "I hoped you'd want to play."

Cindy threw the fireball in her hand at the warlock. It was completely ineffective, but it distracted her so I could draw my gun and shoot. The sound of the gunshots was overwhelming in the cave, and I cried out, not that anyone would hear it.

I felt a little tingle in my chest, and Cindy touched her hands to my ears, clearing up the ringing and pain.

Meg was pressed against the back wall of the cave, holding her hand to a gunshot in her shoulder, probably healing it. Cindy wasted no time, using her moment of vulnerability to throw lightning at her. I felt the tug and tingle in my chest. She put a lot of power behind it, but Meg sidestepped it.

I had moved a little slower and was able to change the trajectory of the fireball I sent her way, and it winged her on the shoulder, catching her robe on fire. She waved her arm over it as she watched us, not even flinching at her flesh sizzling from my extra-hot flames.

"Enough," she roared, and went on the offensive, throwing fireballs and energy balls at us in rapid succession.

I hit the floor, but Cindy threw her arm up and pulled on my magic. The balls hit her defensive energy wall and fizzled out. While she protected us and she threw useless balls, I pulled on my fire, trying to get a narrow stream of it and conserve energy.

I almost came out of my skin when someone touched my back. My stream of fire erupted into a fireball that hit the wall behind the warlock, doing absolutely no damage.

I turned to find Axoular there, bleeding and hurt. He didn't miss a beat though. By the time I'd fully turned my head his way he was throwing spurts of fire at the warlock from behind Cindy's defensive wall like a champ. He was definitely better at it than I was.

"What about the others and the Valkyrie?" I asked as I focused on my stream of fire again. My idea was that I could move the stream like a water hose and Meg wouldn't be able to stop it, but the evil warlock put up a shield of her own with her left hand while throwing balls of increasing power with her other hand.

"She noticeably weakened, probably when you engaged this one here." He stopped throwing fire that was doing no good, and I pulled in my stream.

I yanked him close to Cindy and grabbed the arm she wasn't using. "Channel him too," I said. She grinned and closed her eyes, splitting her focus between the shield and Axoular.

The shield, which I couldn't actually see, must've flickered while she was distracted, because the next thing I knew, I was slammed against the wall, the breath knocked out of me. Axoular ran to me, running his hands over my body. I pushed him away, put my hands on my knees, and tried to breathe.

"Are you okay?" Cindy yelled, both hands pushing toward the warlock.

Once I could suck in a breath, I yelled back. "Yeah! Get her!"

She laughed. "This feels amazing!"

I looked at Axoular with a little bit of fear. I hoped she didn't take in too much power.

He shrugged and turned back to the warlock, who was backing up step by step. "How do you have this much power?" she asked, panic in her voice.

It was my turn to laugh as we unleashed more

fireballs on her while Cindy battered her shield with energy. At least, I assumed that was what she was doing because our fireballs began to slip through it.

Suddenly the room was filled with people, Elias and Anthony flanking me, and the witches running up behind Cindy and putting their hands on her back.

Leo sucked in a breath. "This power!" He looked back at Axoular and me. "It's too much."

I gave him a helpless look but had to stop sending fireballs. There were too many people in the way, and I didn't know where Cindy's shield ended.

Once Cindy had her coven around her, it was over quickly. The warlock couldn't withstand the combined power of our Sárkány magic and the witches.

"Kára?" I asked Elias, watching Meg weaken.

"Unconscious. I got the feeling you didn't want her dead."

"I didn't, thank you."

He kissed my hair.

"Was anyone hurt in there?"

"Hurt, yes. Dead, no."

"Oh, good," I said, casually, as if I wasn't watching a coven of witches suffocate a warlock with energy.

She writhed on the floor, gasping for air. "Stop!" she screamed.

"You've needed to die for a very long time, Megan Lee." With a final tingle of energy from my chest, the warlock was crushed and breathed no more.

Cindy dropped to her knees, sobbing. Leo put his arms around her, and I ran forward.

"Are you okay?" I whispered, crouching beside her. "That was some intense magic."

"It's not that," she said through her sobs. "Megs was my sister."

I rocked back on my heels. What had I made her do? "I'm so sorry."

Leo stood, pulling Cindy with him. "I'll leave Circe with you to make portals, but this is where our coven leaves you. I can't make her continue, and we're much less effective without her."

"I understand," I said. "Thank you for your help. We'll be in touch." They slipped out through a portal that didn't take them to the Junta. Leo had to pick Cindy up and one of the other coven members picked up the dead warlock and followed, into what I was pretty sure was the mountains of Tennessee.

RILEY

We watched the portal close. I was thankful for the witches' help—we'd certainly already be dead without them—but I was scared about what was coming.

"Now what?" Anthony asked.

"Now we go through that door." I pointed at a wooden door that I hadn't noticed in the corner. I turned to Elias. "If you could?"

He rubbed his leg. "She got me pretty good, and I'm not totally healed yet."

Anthony laughed. "Got it." He kicked the door in with as much force as Elias had.

We've got to explore this strength thing a bit more. It's hot. I felt like we hadn't been using their strength to its fullest potential.

I created a fireball for light, and Axoular did the

same. We walked through first, having no idea what else Dumadi could've set up to kill us.

The next room was circular and had six doors leading off of it, each in a different color. "Seriously?" I asked. "This is some Alice in Wonderland stuff." I sighed. "We gotta go through them one by one. And are we still in Bali? I feel like we might be somewhere else. This does *not* seem like an underground temple to me," I said.

Circe breathed deep. "It smells like the ocean, so that doesn't help."

"Wherever we are, we still have to get through those doors," Axoular said.

"Okay. One at a time." I walked to the first door on the right. It was blue. I turned the handle, unlocked. Nerves assaulted me. There was no telling what I'd find behind that door. *I hate that Leyak psychopath!*

The door opened but nothing was behind it. "We'd have to spell that one, to reveal the hidden opening," I said. *What if Linna is behind it, or Kára's kids?*

"Where did they even get this stuff?" Anthony asked, inspecting the stones in the door. "They're supposed to be non-magical."

"Let's try door number two," Elias said. He

opened the next one, green, and stepped back so we could see what was behind it. Another dark tunnel.

"No," I said. "Should we check the others or explore this one?"

"Check the others," Axoular said. He walked up to the purple third door.

"I really like the color purple. Maybe this one will be good luck." He opened it and jumped back. The room behind it was painted stark white and filled with harsh fluorescent lights.

"These are definitely portals then," I said. How else would you get a fluorescent light in a cave?

"Of course, they are. Which means we have to pick the right one to go through because they'll probably close it behind us."

"I can get us back here, now that I've been here," Circe said.

"And if it's spelled so you can't?"

"Maybe we should call in some backup," Circe said. "Don't we have all those people in the amphitheater waiting to help?"

I'm an idiot. "Of course. Can you open us a portal? But wait just a minute. Let's look behind all the doors first," I said.

I moved to stand in front of the fourth door, painted black.

Axoular opened it, and I gasped. The room behind it was a nursery, and it was full of babies in beds, ranging in age from infant to probably nearly three years old. I lurched forward. "Linna?" I called.

Anthony grabbed me from behind. "You can't go in there yet. The room smells of a trap."

"Whatever you do, do *not* close that door. Will you hold it open?" I asked Circe.

She nodded and took the handle from Axoular. "Do you see your baby in there?"

I searched, but there were several cribs that I couldn't see inside unless I entered the room. "Not from here. Those babies shouldn't be in there alone!"

"It strikes me odd that none of them are crying," Circe said.

I stopped, about to walk to the fifth door, and looked back into the fourth. "You're right. They're all asleep or cooing gently. That's not normal behavior for babies, not for all of them to be content at the same time."

"All the more reason not to enter that room," Elias said.

I sighed and nodded to Circe so she could close that door. "Open it back up," I said once it clicked closed. She shook her head, probably thinking I was crazy, but I couldn't stop myself. That room had babies in it.

"We're wasting time," Axoular said. "That room is just a trap for you."

"No!" I said, striding forward and jerking the door open. I had to make sure she wasn't in there. It was the first door I'd actually touched myself, and as soon as my skin touched the handle I was sucked through a portal, the feeling of water washing over me.

I felt a hand grab my shirt, but instead of being jerked back into the cave, I was pretty sure whoever grabbed me was pulled forward with me.

We stepped into another cave, hopefully in the same area as the one we'd left, so we weren't too separated from the rest of the group.

I found Anthony beside me. "I couldn't let you go alone," he said.

"You were halfway across the cave from me, ready to open the next door."

"I moved quickly."

The cave was well lit, with torches hung along the wall. It was massive, so deep I couldn't see the other side.

I turned in a circle, the part behind me just as

massive. "I guess it's up to us now since I fell for their trap."

"Indeed, you did, Ms. Effler," Dumadi's voice came from the shadows. "I suspected you would make it past my Valkyrie and warlock. Though I'm sad to know they're both dead."

He thinks I killed them both. Good. No need for anyone to know Kára is alive. Maybe he'll release the children.

I gave Anthony a look and hoped he knew not to correct Dumadi's mistake about the Valkyrie." What do you want, Dumadi?"

"My son surely told you. He was always vision-less and spineless. I was saddened but not surprised when he ran to your ridiculous council."

His voice seemed to come from a different direction every time he spoke.

"Where is my daughter?"

"My granddaughter is being spoiled rotten as we speak. I would not harm her for the world. This attack is unwarranted."

"Unwarranted? You can't kidnap babies! Or women. We rescued the two Sárkány women you had in the rooms near where you kept me. *And* you murdered my healer!"

"They would've been paid handsomely for their

efforts. You, however, have no claim to this child. She is the heir to the Leyak throne now that Ross is gone."

"Throne? Since when do you have a monarchy?" He was off his rocker. Ross had told us they had a democracy, with his family being voted in as leaders since they left their planet.

"I've been putting plans in place to change that. Beginning with my granddaughter, I'll unite our races under one rule, and we'll find a new home to begin again."

Anthony stifled a laugh. I gave him a look, none of this was funny.

He made no efforts to lower his voice. "I'm sorry, Riley, but this guy is ridiculous, like he's trying to be some dramatic bad guy from a play or old movie." He turned away from me and spoke to the room. "Get real, man. You can't win this! The standing Unseen army is descending on these caves as we speak. If that doesn't work, the council will send out a conscription and the full might of the Unseen will annihilate you. This is just ridiculous."

"Do you think one Valkyrie and one warlock is the best I can do?" Dumadi's voice dropped. He was pissed. "You're not even supposed to be here, Supay."

Anthony shrugged. "Sorry, dude. She's my lady and I'd follow her into Hell."

"How do you know you didn't?" Dumadi laughed softly, but whatever magic he was using to project his voice made the chuckles bounce off of my eardrums like a throbbing headache.

"I'm done with this," I said. "Let's find our baby."

I strode forward, intent on checking out the entirety of the cave to see what all was in there. I found the far wall and just had to hope he'd used up his magical assistance in the other part of the cave and didn't have any more hidden walls.

Anthony zipped over to the wall nearest us and got a torch, then zipped back to me. I tried to watch him do it, but he moved too fast for my eyes to follow.

"Thanks," I said when he joined me a few seconds later.

"I'll always be here for you, Coya. I know Elias and Axoular would be here too, they just couldn't grab you with me in the way."

"I bet they're pissed," I said with a grimace. *They're probably raging right now.*

"You know they are."

We made it to the back wall and found signs of someone camping out. It looked like Dumadi had been staying there. There was a pallet full of blankets and pillows, and clothes piled neatly up. Canned goods were stacked beside the bedroll, with a can opener and a box full of trash from the food he'd already eaten.

Judging from the smell coming from the closed pot beside that, he'd been down there a few days. "Eww, gross," I said.

"Dumadi? Why are you hiding in here?"

"I'm not hiding. I've been waiting."

"Waiting on what?" I asked.

"You."

The torches all flickered out at the same time, and Anthony grabbed me and jerked me against the wall. A whizzing sound, followed by a thud on the stone by my right ear caused me to jerk my head. "I think we're being shot at." I dropped to the ground and felt around. Anthony kept one hand on me, so he dropped with me. "Yep," I said, finding his hand and putting the arrow I'd found into it.

Another whiz and thud right above my head. "Fudge."

"Give us some light," Anthony said.

"If I do, it'll give him light, too."

"He can already see us somehow. We're just lucky he doesn't have the best aim."

"Follow me," I said, shuffling to the side and

grabbing a big handful of the blankets from Dumadi's bed before crawling forward as quickly as I could. Anthony rustled behind me.

When I got to what I hoped was the center of the room, I created a fireball and lit the blankets on fire. They wouldn't burn long, but maybe they'd give us enough light to find him. When Anthony realized what I was doing he zipped back and grabbed the rest of the bedding and clothes, piling them on top of the flames.

I stepped around the fire, painting myself as a giant bullseye, backlit by the flames, but I had a clear sight of the rest of the cave. Dumadi stood against the back wall, skin a vibrant blue, darker than Linna.

Something in me unhinged because I saw a bundle of pink blankets at his feet. He had her with him.

I screamed, and my flames burst out. I had no desire to faint this time, so I stamped them back while I snatched my gun from its holster.

Stopping myself just in time, I didn't fire. If I did, the noise would burst the baby's eardrums, and I didn't have a witch to quickly heal them, meaning she would suffer.

Also, I couldn't risk any possible ricochet hurting the baby. Without my gun or my fire, I was helpless unless I could get close. "Anthony," I whispered. "I don't know what to do."

"Make him think you're going to shoot him. Take your time aiming," he said.

I didn't know what his plan was, but I did as he said.

"Freeze!" I commanded. "I've got a hell of an aim, but I'd rather not shoot this gun in here. Walk forward slowly and you'll get out of this with your life."

Dumadi looked down at the baby at his feet. "I think not," he said.

As soon as he looked down, Anthony zipped forward.

He grabbed Dumadi so fast, the man didn't have time to process what was happening. One second, he was standing beside my baby, the next he was held up by his throat in front of me.

He gargled, trying to talk. "Let him speak, please," I said. "There is more information I want from him."

Anthony sat him on his feet and loosened his grip on his neck marginally, but before he could speak, I cut him off. "Anthony," I said. "Will you keep him here for just a moment?"

"Of course, Coya."

"Mind his hands. They have spikes."

Anthony twisted Dumadi around, so his hands were behind his back. It looked painful.

I rushed over to the pink bundle on the floor and snatched it up. It was a pillow swaddled into several blankets. "You sneaky bastard!" I screamed. "Where is she?"

I ran back to him, throwing the pillow at him. "Where is she?"

He coughed around Anthony's grip. When he'd turned him, he'd put his arm around his neck. Anthony loosened it so he could speak. "She's safe, I told you. But no matter what you do to me, you won't get her back."

"Why not?" I snarled.

"Because I convinced my people that she was our salvation, our way to a new home." His eyes glinted. He was completely mad. "She'll save us and take us to a place where we can thrive."

"Not by force."

"If we raise her properly, she'll never know she wasn't born to loving and doting parents that raised her to be the next Queen."

"That's enough. Can you knock him out for now?" Anthony nodded and squeezed Dumadi's neck until he slumped forward in a faint.

"Do you think he's lying?" I asked.

"Yes. If he had the support of the entire race of Leyak, he wouldn't be hiding in this cave. I think he blackmailed Kára and paid the warlock. Where's the rest of his devoted people?"

I contemplated his words and our options. "We gotta get out of here. Can you carry him?"

"Of course."

I jogged to the other end of the cave, where Dumadi had been hidden. Quickly scouring the perimeter, I stopped when I felt a breeze.

Running my hands along the wall, I found a seam. This wasn't magic, it was just a carefully concealed door. There had to be a latch or something somewhere. I ran my fingers all over the seam, looking for any indentation. The light from the fire had faded, and it was getting really dark. I focused on my internal flames and allowed one hand to ignite so I could see.

Feeding the flame to make it brighter, I moved my arm up and down until I saw a tiny crack perpendicular to the door. Applying pressure to it made it sink inward with a scrape, and the door moved, at a snail's pace, of its own volition. As soon as the opening was wide enough for me to squeeze through,

I went, praying to come across something, anything that would help me find my daughter.

Bolting down the passageway, I tried to hold my hand up and wave it back and forth as I looked at the walls to see if there were any other branches I could follow.

The passage veered off to the right, and upward. Soon I came into another big open area, but it wasn't as large as the one Dumadi had been in. Anthony zipped around it looking for another exit. The darkness made everything more complicated, and I wouldn't let myself think about what sort of creepy crawlies were probably being attracted to my light.

We were in another room with no exit. Either one was hidden, or we'd passed a different way out in the dark.

I screamed with frustration, throwing my glowing hands up in the air, and happened to look up as I did. There was a ledge, just above eye level, not five feet from me. "Anthony, look."

He saw it and grinned. Dumping Dumadi on the ground with a thump, he crouched down then launched himself into the air, landing nimbly on his toes on the ledge. "I can't see very well," he said. "But, this goes somewhere." He hopped back down and picked Dumadi up, throwing him up onto the ledge.

"Can you jump?" he asked. "We've never tried that with you."

"I have no idea," I said. Crouching, I was about to give it my all when I heard the faintest whimper come from whatever was beyond the ledge. "Oh my God, did you hear that?"

"I'll bet I heard it better than you did," he said with a relieved laugh. "That was my daughter."

The sound of her voice gave me the strength I needed. I doused my flames and pushed off the ground as hard as I could, flying into the air without an ounce of grace.

I landed on Anthony, moving too fast to know how to catch myself.

He used some of that Supay strength and caught me, barely, so we didn't hit the ground.

I lit my hands again, feeling the drain from the flames. *Not much longer now. You're almost there.* Running forward, we weaved through a maze of passages, stopping whenever we heard Linna's sweet voice to reorient ourselves.

The problem was that caves echo, so more than once we were fooled and went in the wrong direction. Anthony's excellent hearing was helpful though, and we only lost our way a couple of times.

Finally, we entered a small room that was lit with more torches. Two little girls sat on cots, the older holding my baby.

I cried out, relieved and overwhelmed, and dropped to my knees in front of the girls. "Are you okay?" I asked, smiling at Linna. She fussed back at me.

"We're okay," the younger girl said. "But I really gotta pee."

"Okay, give me just a second, sweetheart," I said, taking Linna from the other girl and clutching her to my chest, suddenly full of milk and aching.

In all my haste and the rushes of adrenaline I hadn't even considered my breasts since we arrived at the temple, but that had to be hours before. They were like rocks.

I handed Linna to Anthony, who had dumped Dumadi onto the empty cot. He kissed her and unswaddled her to make sure she was unhurt. She wore one heck of a soggy diaper. "What are your names?" he asked.

"I'm Hildr, and this is Herja. Do you know where our mommy is?" the older child said.

"We do, and we'll take you to her. I'm Anthony,

and this is Riley. Are there any more diapers here?" Anthony asked.

Hildr helped Anthony find the diapers and change Linna, and I took Herja to the corner and squatted in front of her to give her some privacy so she could pee. I showed her how to squat and hold her panties out of the way.

"But Ms. Riley, how will I wipe?"

"Sweetie, you're gonna have to learn about drip-dry."

I helped her bounce when she was done to knock off all the urine she could, then she waved her little butt in the air a little before pulling her panties and shorts back up.

"I can feed her as we find our way out," I said. "Let's go."

"Girls, did he leave any food in here? Are you hungry?"

"Yes, but we ate it all this morning. I tried to be brave, but I can't reach the torches and I couldn't leave them to go out into the dark. Herja wouldn't go out there," Hildr said

"You did the right thing, Hildr. You would've gotten lost in this maze, and we wouldn't have found you. We're taking you to your mommy now, but it might be a long walk. Can you keep up with us?"

"We are Valkyrie. We will keep up."

I hoped she was right. I didn't know if I had the stamina to hold one of them and the baby. Anthony couldn't hold both them and Dumadi.

He'd grabbed two torches and handed one to each girl. We continued the way we'd come, and since we now had access to torches, we were able to use them to find the likeliest exits.

We continued on until we came to a split. *Go straight or turn?* Anthony dumped Dumadi and held the torches very still in the crossway of the passage. The flames settled, then a tiny, imperceptible breeze tugged them straight, so we kept going.

After several more times testing the passages with the torches, we finally began to feel a breeze. I hadn't realized how much I missed the feel of air moving over my cheeks until it tickled my face. The caves had been fairly cool, but stifling.

Our steps hastened with the promise of escape. After another ten minutes or so of walking up the same incline, we reached a door, painted green. "Could it be?" I asked.

I took one of the torches, shifting the baby as far away from it as I could. She'd eaten her fill along the way, relieving my aches and knocking herself into a milk coma.

Rattling the door handle and pushing slowly, he peeked out, then laughed out loud.

His laugh was followed by a loud, "Yes!" from the room beyond.

"I know that voice," I said, grinning.

Anthony pushed through the green door, into the room with six colored doors. Elias sat on the floor in front of them, looking at us like he couldn't believe what he was seeing. His eyes darkened as he saw who Anthony held.

The purple door was open in front of him, and he held a rope in each hand. One rope was attached to the door handle and the other trailed through the doorway.

Jumping up, he tugged on the rope and yelled, "Come out, they're here!"

Axoular came out, followed by at least a dozen people I didn't recognize.

"What are y'all doing?" I asked, amazed.

"Looking for you and Linna," Axoular said as he looked me over. Once he determined I wasn't in immediate danger of dying he took the torch, handing it off to a man that looked human, so he could be any number of creatures. When it was gone, he pulled me into a tight hug, curling around Linna.

I felt Elias behind me, pressed against me like I was his lifeline. "Are you okay?" he asked.

"I will be as soon as all of my children and you three are with me at home." I laughed, overjoyed to be reunited with my loves with Linna in my arms.

The witches immediately opened a portal to the Junta, and we wasted no time going through.

We were met with applause and shocked cries. "Did you not think we'd make it back?" I asked.

I looked down at myself. The parts of me that were exposed were covered in dirt, as was my suit. It had done its job though and had even protected me from any scrapes or cuts along the way. I'd bumped into too many cave walls.

Dumadi was handed over to the Junta's prisons, with the promise he'd be extensively questioned, and they would be in touch once they figured out how to communicate with the general Leyak populace.

We gave the Junta a rundown of everything we could remember of the caves. The second-best part of the day, though, was watching Kára's face when she was brought into the room.

"They wanted to arrest her, but she laughed at them and told them they were welcome to try," Elias whispered in my ear as her girls ran to her and she enveloped them in a hug. "But she was actually pretty hurt after our fight. We tried not to, but she wouldn't stop. We had to hurt her to subdue her so we could continue the search."

"She seems fine now," I replied.

"Yeah, she said she just needed time to commune with Frejya," he said in my ear.

"That's really cool," I said. "I wonder if they are a result of the portals too, like Supay and Mama Pacha."

"Probably," Axoular muttered, having listened in on our conversation.

Once Kára had a few minutes with her girls, she walked up to me and put her hand on Linna's head. "The Valkyrja owe you three life debts, Riley, leader of the Sárkány."

"No, please. I just did what any mother would've done."

"You are brave, and if you tire of this life, we'll find a place for you in the halls of Fólkvangr."

I blinked at her several times before I could find the words to reply. "You honor me, Valkyrie. I'll keep that in mind."

She inclined her head at us and walked out the huge doors of the amphitheater, her girls following.

Once she was gone, we said our goodbyes, offered help if anyone needed it, and thanked everyone profusely. We promised to throw a huge party in the mountains as soon as we got settled back in at home, and all who had volunteered or participated in our daughter's rescue would be invited.

We got a lot of cheers from that, especially from the werewolves. "They've wanted to hunt deer in our mountains for a long time," Elias said with a chuckle.

"I thought the location was hidden?" I asked as we walked toward a portal back to the house in North Carolina.

"It is, but most people know the general mountain range we live in."

I sucked in a huge sigh of relief when we stepped through and into the living room. "This place is already starting to feel like home."

Elias grinned. "I hoped you'd feel that way."

"When are they supposed to call?" I sat on our bed pumping while my guys passed Linna around.

"Every day at six eastern time. They'll call and if we answer, great. If we don't, they move on to the next safe place."

"We owe Danyelus and especially Tammy a huge favor. They dropped everything to help us," I said as I finished.

"I was thinking about that. What if we took this house and gave that one entirely over to them? Technically that house belonged to Michael, too, so now it would be yours." Anthony rocked Linna back and forth as he spoke.

"Seriously? How many homes do I own now?"

Anthony and Elias exchanged a glance and Axoular laughed. "That look they just gave each other," he said, "makes me think there's lots to tell you."

"Well, first you were pregnant and easily overwhelmed. Then you were kidnapped. Then you had the babies and were recovering, and Dumadi hung over our heads." Anthony handed Linna over to Axoular, who had been patiently waiting his turn.

"Now, we're home, it's only a matter of time before our entire family is here, and things can calm down. We can go over the estates, businesses, finances, and all the other important things," said Elias, itching to hold the baby, based on the way he kept touching her.

"How much longer until they call?" I asked.

"Another four or five minutes," Elias said, checking his phone.

I groaned. "I'm going to run this milk to the freezer real quick."

We'd gotten home and all showered, eaten, and had a nap. Linna hadn't been put down once since I took her from Hildr's arms. She'd eaten again, and I had just finished pumping the rest of what she didn't eat.

In the kitchen, I marked the bags with the date

and laid them flat in the deep freeze alongside the rest of the liquid gold.

I stopped in the kitchen and sank into a chair, overwhelmed. I didn't let myself dissolve into tears, but I sat there for a few moments and tried to come to terms with what had happened over the past few weeks, the past few months, the past five years.

It had been a lot.

When I had come to some shaky terms with the insanity of my life, I returned to the bedroom, all smiles. *Sometimes a girl just needs a moment.*

Linna was out like a light, and Elias had just hung up the phone. "They're on their way," he said. "I just got off the phone with Leo, he's on his way to get them."

I jumped up and down with a squeak. "Excellent!"

We moved into the living room onto the couches, knowing the portal would open there. "What happens if someone tries to open a portal where someone is standing, or where a piece of furniture is?"

"That's why we keep certain spots open and free of furniture. It'll cut it in half. But if a person is standing in the way it won't open."

I harassed them with random questions as they

popped into my head, trying to pass the time until Leo opened the portal and brought my family to me.

Finally, after ages and ages, a portal opened in front of us and Tammy walked through carrying Michael, followed by Danyelus with a screaming Rose.

Tammy looked like she was ready to break down in tears, but grinned when she saw us. "I'm so happy to see you guys," she said, laughing while tears slipped down her cheeks.

"Rose has a bellyache, and Michael must be having a growth spurt because he's eaten every hour today," she said, depositing Michael in my arms.

Linna woke with a screech as if she could feel her brother close to her. I walked over to Axoular, who held her, and put them side by side so their faces touched while I listened to Tammy talk about the kids.

"Charlie skinned his knee, that's why he's crying," she said.

A sniffling Charlie walked through, held by Stephen. Stephen deposited him into his dad's arms, and Elias grinned, squeezing him tight. His tears stopped once he was in the comfort of his dad's arms.

David walked through holding Daniel's hand,

which he snatched away as soon as they entered the room. "Hey mom," David said, walking over and kissing the twins. "Hey Linna. I'm happy you're safe."

"I gotta get away from Daniel," he whispered to me. "He's driving me crazy."

I winked at him. "Go, escape."

"Daniel!" I exclaimed. "Can I have a hug?"

He grinned at me toothlessly. "Look," he said, pointing at his mouth. "I lost a tooth."

I raved over his missing tooth and hugged him tight, eventually letting him go so Axoular could take them to the kitchen and make dinner. They claimed they were starving.

I followed, holding Michael. "Are you sure I can't make it tonight?" I offered.

"I'm sure. I love doing this for the family, and I'm good at it."

I smiled at him, love and thankfulness squeezing my heart. "We have a lot to catch up on, now that we're safe."

He paused in his prep, putting the knife down. "You're mine, as soon as possible. I can't wait another day to be bonded with you," he said, quietly so the little ones sitting at the table couldn't hear.

His promise made shivers dance down my spine.

Dinner was chaotic, with everyone excited to be together again. Once they'd eaten, we sent all the kids older than little three-year-old Talem off to play or watch tv, whatever their choice. They were exhausted, as were we all.

The twins slept peacefully in their portable bed in the corner, and we made quick work of the dishes, sending Tammy and Danyelus off with their two to relax alone for the evening.

When the dishes were done, the kids occupied, the babies asleep, we sat down at the kitchen table to talk. "I want to bond with Axoular," I said. "In the eyes of the Sárkány, it'll marry us, but not in the eyes of the Unseen, so we need to plan a marriage ceremony for all of us now that we're four, not three." I chose my words carefully, stating, rather than asking, what I wanted.

Having three husbands would be a lesson in not allowing myself to be bowled over. I wanted to start as I meant to live, as a team. Everyone on the team would have valid opinions.

"That sounds great. We can have that big party for the Unseen and have the wedding at the same time," Anthony said while Elias nodded along.

The conversation went faster and easier than I expected it to be. Axoular didn't say much, mostly he just stared at me, probably looking forward to our night.

We finished our drinks, and I hooked up the pump while we talked about the events of the past few days. Axoular's eyes kept straying to my nipples being manipulated by the suction of the pump.

That man only had one thing on his mind, now that we were about to do it. I grinned, putting the milk into bags, and labeling them. Once everything was cleaned up, I looked at Elias and Anthony, who were smiling from ear to ear. "Can you two handle putting all the kids to bed alone tonight?" I asked.

They nodded their heads simultaneously, ribbing each other and chuckling.

"Oh, stop it, you act like teenage boys, losing their virginity behind the bleachers," I scolded as they chuckled harder.

Axoular stood, "I don't know what that means, about teenage boys, but they can laugh all they want to—I get to bond with you tonight."

He held out his hand and I took it, nervous, feeling a bit like a teenager myself.

"Let me take a minute to freshen up," I told him.

I headed to our bedroom and went into the attached bathroom. I'd had a shower but hadn't bothered shaving my legs at the time. I hopped in the tub and made quick work of my legs and some of the stubble on the hoo-ha.

It was hard to focus on shaving, I was so turned on. I wanted to run out and attack Axoular, but I managed to keep myself in check and make everything pretty for our first time.

I walked out into the bedroom naked. I didn't have the patience for a negligee.

Axoular sat on the bed in his boxer briefs. When I walked out his nostrils flared and his eyes glowed red for a brief second. "You are the most beautiful creature," he said.

I approached him slowly. We hadn't intended on spending our time in our bedroom, in case it took us a while and the guys wanted to go to bed, but there was no reason we couldn't make out like the teenagers we'd talked about.

He looked up at me as I moved between his legs, lowering my lips slowly down on his.

We spent a few moments like that, exploring each other's mouths, then I pulled back. I grabbed my robe from the back of the closet door. "Which guest room should we use?" I asked.

He walked over to the balcony and looked down at the pool. "There's nobody in the pool, and it's getting too late to expect any of the kids to go out there. I think we should go to the pool house."

"Oh, okay." Did he expect us to get that loud?

He probably heard the apprehension in my voice. "Just for the privacy," he said.

"Whatever you want," I said. Bonding with him was important to me, but to him it was everything. He was as excited as I probably would be on the day I wore a fancy dress and walked down an aisle toward him. Whatever he wanted was what he'd get.

He led me, hand in hand, down the stairs. We snuck past the kids watching a cartoon in the movie room and out the back doors that opened on the pool. The pool house wasn't huge, but it was a fully furnished apartment, with tile floors and lots of absorbent rugs so parties could happen in and out of the pool.

The bedroom and bathroom were one large, airy room, with floor-to-ceiling windows that had built-in shades on the inside. He lowered all the shades while I moved toward the bed, pulling back the blankets.

"Are there any words we should speak?" I asked.

"No," he said. "If our love is real and pure, the bond will happen."

I grinned. "Awesome."

He joined me on the bed, laying down beside me. I quirked an eyebrow at his boxers, and he shed them. "You manscaped!" I said with delight.

Elias and Anthony always did, but I'd noticed before he'd gone all scaly the other night that his hair had been a little long.

"I don't know what that means," he said, looking worried.

I giggled. "It means you trimmed the hair down there."

"Oh, yeah of course. Isn't that what you were doing in the bathroom?" he asked as he untied my robe and looked at my neatly trimmed hair.

I nodded. "Do you like a woman to be completely shaved?"

"Honestly, Riley, I'm almost two hundred years old, and I've never met a woman that I was attracted to that I became turned off because she had hair or not."

I burst out laughing. "So, basically, you don't care what I do with my hair?"

"That's right," he said, running his hand over it.

He bent his head down and kissed me, pushing my robe over my shoulders. I arched forward and let it fall behind me while he sent tingles straight down.

I was in no mood for extensive foreplay. "I don't want to wait," I said as he ran his tongue across my bottom lip.

He sat up, crossing his legs in front of him. "Okay, but first, I want you to find your Sárkány side."

Oh, yeah. "Okay!" I sat up with him crossed my legs, too. "What do I do?"

"Close your eyes and find your fire."

I'd gotten good at doing that, so I focused myself and found the flames licking around inside me. "Okay."

"My true nature is a force, pushing to get out. It feels like my skin is crawling, and I need to let it out. Similar to the fire."

I searched inside myself, breathing deep and searching. My flames tickled at me, delighted to have me meditating on them again. They liked the attention.

"Feel your skin," he whispered, running his hands up and down my arms.

I moved my attention to my skin, trying to feel it from the inside out. After a few minutes, I felt the tingling. It began at my chest, between my breasts, and extended outward until even my scalp prickled.

I shivered to the point of almost giving me an

orgasm. I groaned out loud and opened my eyes. When I looked down, I found Axoular covered in his gray and black scales, and my own body was covered in shades of green.

"I did it!" I said in delight.

He growled, eyes red. "Yes, you did." Apparently seeing me naked in my Sárkány glory really did it for him.

I had to spend a few moments studying myself. Everything was basically the same as when I was in human skin, but dark, forest green. Axoular wasted no time. The feel of my milk releasing felt amazing in my new skin. It was more sensitive. I felt the breeze from the air conditioner blow across my skin and I hadn't been able to feel it before.

He pulled back to reposition and I leaned forward to check out my lady bits. The hair was gone, but my hard scales came around my hips and down my stomach like arrows, pointing at my sex. The skin there was a little darker than grass and shimmered slightly.

"I can't wait much longer, Riley," Axoular said. "I need you."

I smiled, enjoying the need in his voice. "You can have me."

He growled and pushed me to lay flat on the bed.

Laying my head back against the pillow, I put my hands on his chest.

He gave me pleasure that was almost *too* intense right before I shattered.

Once he knew I had recovered, he kissed me, saying, "You are mine now, Riley Effler. Mine," he said.

I tried to catch my breath, but he gave me no opportunity. "This is how I claim you, Riley," he said.

He was close. "We must go at the same time for the bond to complete," he said. "I'm very close. Are you?"

I shook my head. He felt amazing, but I wasn't quite there.

When he saw my head move, he sunk his fingers into my hair, close to my scalp, and grabbed a handful of my hair, pulling me up closer to his body. "You will come when I tell you to, Riley."

Oh my, yes, Sir. I nodded my head frantically/ My moans turned throaty as I grew close to an orgasm.

He asked me again. "Yes," I cried out. "Please!"

My orgasm took over my senses and when I

opened my eyes again, we were both on fire, joined together in a flaming bed. I screamed out, but not from fear. The waves of pleasure continued to shoot over my body, and from his moans, he felt the same. It was the most intense, longest orgasm I'd ever experienced.

When the pleasure finally released me, I pulled away from him and ran to the side of the room, not sure what to do about the flaming bed.

Axoular was prepared though. He grabbed a fire extinguisher from the kitchen and doused the bed quickly, leaving a smoking, stinky mess.

I looked at him as he looked at me, shocked. "Was that it?" I asked.

"Can you feel me?" He grinned. "I was afraid the fire would happen. That's why we're out here."

I felt him, tucked away in the back of my mind. I couldn't tell what he was thinking or feeling, but he was warm, like I could feel his flames. "You're there."

"Happy wedding night, wife," he said. "Let's go find a quiet place to continue our evening." I smiled at him, and we grabbed towels to walk back to the main house, after making sure the fire was out.

I wasn't sure what was next with the Leyak or if we were completely safe, but after what we'd been through, I knew we could handle it. I had my family back—finally—safe and whole.

Need more from the Unseen world? Check out book 3, War of Wings. Or, read on for chapter one!

BASK IN MAGIC CHAPTER ONE

THE CRACK OF MY HEEL SNAPPING ON THE concrete stair sent a jolt of dread down my spine. My body turned into one clenched muscle as time slowed, and I fell to the pavement. I saw the pain coming and tried to twist myself, so I'd fall on my side, not straight on my hands.

The sound of a bone snapping in my shoulder registered before the pain. I continued to tumble down the never-ending row of stairs, growing angrier with every bounce and jolt of pain. My life had been a joke from the moment I'd left home eighteen years before, and the thought of dying by falling down was infuriating.

My hip bounced off the edge of a stair, launching me further into the air. *No! This is not how I go out. I don't accept it.* With that thought, I watched the unyielding ground coming toward my face, and I'd had enough.

Throwing my hands in front of me, I screamed. All of the anger and frustration of my life poured out of me in a screech that I was sure had everyone within a mile radius looking my way.

I froze in midair, shaking. My yell dwindled to a gasp as I pulled my head up to look around me. The courthouse stairway had been bustling when I began my tumble, and all the people that had previously scurried about, worrying about their everyday problems froze, turned toward me, staring. I assumed they were looking at me, I couldn't see much without my contacts.

A jerk on my spine explained why they stared. I tried to turn my head and found myself face to face with an enormous purple wing, slowly beating up and down. Whipping my head around showed me the twin on the other side. *Who is standing behind me, holding wings up?*

My mind might've been a teeny bit fuzzy. I moved my legs to turn myself completely around but jerked my gaze downward when I felt nothing under my feet. I was floating a good two feet off the ground.

Breathing hard, I did a double-take when I saw

my hands. My mind couldn't compute what it was looking at.

My skin was purple. Purple and black. *It's a bruise from falling. A crazy, huge, scaly bruise.*

"It's a bruise," I whispered. It was easy to believe since I couldn't see clearly anyway.

The crowd in front of me laughed and pointed. Some of the people clapped. I smiled in relief. It was a stunt. Some crowd magician or performer had caught me mid-fall and managed to make it look like a big stunt. "Tada," I said, voice shaky. *I must be in shock. I don't feel any pain from my fall.*

I peered over my shoulder, but couldn't see past the big, fake wings. Squinting, I looked closely. They were incredibly realistic. Veins pulsed in the membrane between the bones, and the scales covering them shimmered in the sunlight. I squinted harder to try to see the details without my contacts in.

"That's enough," a voice behind me hissed in an accent I couldn't quite place. Maybe British. "They think it's a show. Come down from there and get lost."

"Whoever you are, I can't see you. Thanks for stopping my fall, but can you get me down now?" I craned my neck to see who was talking to me and why they weren't putting me down. The wings kept flapping, and I realized I'd risen another foot. "This is starting to freak me out, and I think I'm probably injured and in shock."

"It's not funny. If you don't stop this now, I'm going to notify the Junta!" The voice still whispered, but he'd begun to sound irritated. "What are you, anyway?"

"What are you talking about?" My own voice rose in pitch as his words registered. He thought I'd done the stunt myself. Where was the person responsible? "If you didn't do this to me, someone else did. Can you please help me down?"

The owner of the voice walked around me, glaring. "Are you kidding me?" he asked. "You're going to expose us if you don't stop." His accent wasn't British. Maybe Irish. I'd never been able to travel as I'd once hoped to, and his accent was so refined I couldn't put a finger on it.

More people gathered around. He looked at the crowd and smiled. His features were indistinct, but I saw a flash of teeth, and I could tell his hair was dark blond. Or maybe light brown. "Thank you for coming, everyone." He produced a velvet bag from inside his coat pocket, stuck his hand inside, and transferred whatever object he'd kept in the bag to his pocket. It looked like a magic wand, but I couldn't tell with my contacts out. Probably a prop for the show.

"Please, if you enjoy the illusion, leave the beautiful lady a tip." He flourished the bag and a good dozen people strode forward, dropping bills and change.

Mutters from the crowd astounded me. "So realistic," one lady said.

A man took my bruise-covered hand and gave it a soft kiss. "Perfection," he murmured against my knuckles.

My jaw dropped.

The man who'd collected the tips stuffed the bag back in his coat pocket and grabbed my hand once the last person moved on and people stopped being impressed. He tugged, and my body responded. I lowered to the ground with a jolt. With one hand on my shoulder, he turned toward the big wings behind me. Placing one hand on my arm, he grabbed the edge of the wing and pulled it toward my body. It crumpled, but that wasn't the part that made me moan.

I *felt* his touch on the wing. His hand on the wing was as real and warm as his other hand on my arm. I shook my head, my long black hair coming loose from the clip. I had a fleeting thought of surprise that it had stayed put during the fall.

Watching the wing fold toward me was almost like an out-of-body experience. How was I feeling the muscles bend and the sides of the wing touch each other as they crumpled?

My stomach filled with acid. I looked in the other direction and watched—and felt—as the same happened on that side. "How?" I asked the strange— and I was pretty sure he was hot—man helping me.

Once they were contained behind my back, he circled to my front. I looked up and back to see the massive wings rising over my head. When I rolled my shoulders, the wings moved accordingly. It felt like someone had their fists pressed into my shoulder blades.

A finger on my chin forced my gaze downward, and I squinted to get a real look at the person helping me. He was the definition of lithe, and his body seeped sex appeal. His suit had to have been tailored for him, the fit was too perfect. His light brown— dark blond?— hair was shaggy enough to be sexy, but not so long he needed a haircut.

My jaw dropped, and I temporarily forgot the insane predicament I was in. The man was drop-dead gorgeous. "Who are you?" I asked.

His green eyes flashed. "*What* are you?"

What the hell does he mean? I raised my hands to pull my hair out of my face and put it back in the clip and was distracted by the bruises. Both arms were entirely purple. I needed to find my purse and get my glasses out so I could get a better look at everything around me.

I rubbed my eyes and was shocked to feel the contacts moving around on my eyeballs. They'd survived the fall after all. I looked around and saw my purse lying at the top of the stairs, where I'd begun my descent. I couldn't believe it was still there with all the people around.

When I lifted my foot to walk up the stairs, I discovered my balance had changed. The wings attached to my back threw my equilibrium off. I teetered backward; arms windmilling as I tried to catch my balance on those steep stairs. I heard a shuffle behind me, and then I was pushed forward.

I turned back to find the handsome stranger with one eyebrow cocked. "Do you normally have so much trouble staying upright?"

"No. I'm not a clumsy person at all. I'm just having an extremely strange day." The broken heel didn't help.

He nodded; expression masked. I figured out my

new balance—barely—and tottered up the stairs to grab my purse. As I bent, I realized the back of my blouse was in shreds and hung on my body from the shoulders. *Lovely*. It had been my favorite.

Swapping out my contacts for my glasses, I tossed the disposables down in my purse. I blinked my eyes behind my glasses and rubbed at them as I slowly walked down the stairs, mindful of my balance. The fuzziness wasn't going away.

As I reached the bottom where Sir Studly waited, I pulled off my glasses to clean them. Maybe they were smudged and that was keeping me from focusing properly.

"So, what are you?" he asked as I used the bottom of my shirt to clean the lenses.

I looked up at him to respond that I didn't have the first clue what was going on, but the words didn't come. I could see him. I could see him *clearly*.

Oh, yeah, he's hot all right.

A group of teenagers across the street walked past with cell phones pointed at me, probably taking pictures. I could see the details of their cases as clear as I could see the faint beginnings of laugh lines in the corners of Studly's eyes.

He snapped his fingers in front of my face, bringing my attention back to him. "What are you?

Don't you dare change back until you're out of sight. People think you're dressed up for some stunt now, but if you change back to human in front of them, they'll get freaked out." He looked around at the people milling about. "You're lucky humans do their best to believe the world is utterly non-magical."

I finally found my voice as I dropped my apparently unnecessary glasses into my purse. "What in absolute hell are you talking about? I'm a person. Magic? Why can I see clearly without my glasses? How did someone attach wings to me? What's going on?"

My frantic voice drew a few stares. He put his arm around me, wings and all, and laughed nervously. "Okay, calm down, the show's over." He lowered his voice. "Did you drive here?"

"No, I took the bus." I marveled at the feeling of his warm arm around my wings. How could I feel something someone had stuck on me? It made no sense!

"Fine. Come with me. I'll get you out of here." He tugged me toward the side of the building, where I knew a parking garage to be.

I jerked out of his arms. "Why would I leave with a total stranger?"

"What species are you?"

Oh, for Pete's sake. "I'm a human, what else?"

"Look closely at your arms."

I rolled my eyes, but I also couldn't stop myself from looking down. With a gasp, I brought my arm closer to my face. "Are they scales? How did you get them on me?" What I hadn't been able to see with my glasses and contacts was that the colors on my skin I'd thought were bruises were something else entirely. They looked like scales.

"I didn't put anything on you, lady. I was walking out of the courthouse, minding my own business when you exploded into this purple and black *thing*."

"Why'd you help me?" I couldn't take my eyes off of my lizard-like skin. I twirled my wrist around and watched them overlap each other. "How is this happening?"

"I have no idea. Are you going to let me help you further?"

My brain finally caught up with the events of the day. I'd almost died falling down the steps, but in a moment of extreme panic, I seemed to have sprouted wings and flown instead of breaking my neck in the middle of downtown Knoxville. A strange man apparently thought I was some other species and wanted to help me. *Yeah, right. More like he wants to stick me in a cage and run tests on me.* I rolled my shoulders again, shocked that there was no pain from what I had been sure was a break.

"Okay, I guess the joke's done. It was all a stunt!" I said brightly as I pulled away from him. "Gotcha!" I pointed around randomly with a huge smile plastered on my face. "There are hidden cameras everywhere. If you wait here my assistant will be right along to have you sign a waiver to be on camera." I grabbed his hand and pumped it up and down, then turned and scurried down the sidewalk, limping with only one heel still intact. I turned once, before I rounded the corner, to see him staring after me, a confused look on his face.

I had driven to the courthouse, but he didn't need to know that. Once I turned the corner and was out of sight, I doubled back around the rear of the courthouse to go to the parking garage without him seeing me.

It was a long walk around the enormous courthouse. I contemplated my fiasco of an afternoon while I trudged along. I wouldn't even have been at the courthouse for whatever-the-hell-that-was to happen to me if I hadn't been told to appear so papers could be served. The postcard notice I got in the mail said if I didn't go to pick the papers up, I'd be served at work, and to save embarrassment, I should go in.

Of course, I'd received the notice in the mail on Saturday, so I had to wait until I got out of work on Monday to find out who in the world would want to serve me with papers.

It had been an old credit card that I hadn't been able to pay. I'd lost my job the year before and had to take a lower-paying position. I'd gotten behind on bills. *Perfect. Since I can't afford to pay you, sue me so I have to pay you* and *the court costs.*

My thoughts grew more morose with every step. I owed everybody and their mama money. My boyfriend disappeared into the night right after I lost my job, leading me to believe he was only with me because I made good money as a pianist for the local symphony.

I'd found work with the local school system, teaching piano, and accompanying their choirs and orchestra—for half the pay. All in all, my year had gone to hell. The last thing I needed was to be taken to court, so I'd have to find a way to pay them.

The shiny blue paint job on my sedan was a welcome sight. A large glass of wine called to me, all the way across town from my tiny, one-bedroom apartment. Pressing the button on the key fob, I unlocked the car, opened the door, and stooped to sit, but the stupid wings banged against the top of the car. They were too tall.

I looked up at them behind my head, craning my neck to see. "Argh!" I yelled. "Now what?"

Reaching behind my back, I tried to grab the large bone along the top of one of them so I could tug them off of my back, but I jerked my hand back when touching the wing caused it to flex outward. *Crap!* They were fully extended again.

Slowly rolling my head from one side to the other, I tried to gauge their span. Longer than my arms, they had to be four feet wide each. There was no way they were going in my car.

"I think it's time to admit you've grown wings." I jumped when I heard his voice. His approach had slipped past me in my attempt to figure out the wings. The wings started flapping again when I jerked, pulling me off the ground by about three feet.

"What have you done to me?" I looked down at the ground, marveling at the feeling of weightlessness. I'd never felt so light in my life. Not with my thighs.

"I'm trying to help you." He crossed his arms and stared pointedly at my wings.

All the wind left my sails. I didn't have the first

clue what was going on, but I had to accept the wings were attached. I couldn't continue to deny that I had feeling in them. I could feel the whisper of the gusts of air flowing through the garage on the soft skin covering them.

I focused on them and imagined them pulling inwards again and they complied. I dropped to the ground with a thump. I would've been flat on my face if he hadn't been there to catch me.

Slumping against him, I sighed and ignored how strong his body was under the suit. "Okay. I don't know what to do. Help me, please."

He put his hand on my shoulders and squeezed, pulling me upright. "I'm happy to." With quick movements, he opened the front and back doors to the sedan before looking around. "Crouch down here, if we're lucky we can get you to change back to human, and if anyone sees they'll think you've just taken the costume off.

I dropped to my knees. "How am I supposed to change this? I don't know how it happened."

"I've spoken at length to some wolf shifters about how they change."

Wolf shifters. "You know? I reckon I must be dead. Is this some sort of crazy version of Heaven?" I sighed as he stared me down. I wasn't dead. "Okay. Lay it on me."

"They say they center themselves. They're cognizant when they're shifted, every shifter I've ever known is. They describe the change much like meditation. Apparently, if you can shift, you can unshift."

Right, okay. Find my center. I couldn't sit on my butt, the wings hung down too far, but I could settle back on my knees. I couldn't twist to see how far back they went on the pavement, but I could feel the rough concrete against them. The feeling wasn't pleasant, and I didn't like the idea of the beautiful wings encountering dirt and oil on the pavement.

I closed my eyes, but meditation was the last thing on my mind. My studly stranger's face, with his aristocratic nose and dimpled chin, was. I cracked an eye to find him standing with his back to me. His suit pants hugged his rump like a dream. "What are you?" I asked. "If I'm some special species and humans are ignorant, then you're not human either."

He didn't even turn around. "I'm Dannan."

"That tells me so much."

"Shouldn't you be focusing?"

I snorted. "Listen, my heart is going a mile a minute. I need a few moments to calm myself down before I'll be able to consider meditating. "So, what is a Dannan? It sounds like a yogurt."

It was his turn to snort. "Humans would call me an elf or a fairy. Actually, not only humans. Most of the Unseen call us the Fae."

Fairy. I was standing in the presence of a real-life, sexy Legolas. It was about time my dreams came true. "And what is the Unseen?"

"It is a name we use to encompass any being that is *other*."

It was all true. "Thank God, or whoever or whatever deity there is out there."

He turned. "Oh?"

"I've prayed for the impossible to be possible since I read Anne Rice when I was a teenager."

"I'm not familiar with Ms. Rice's works."

"She writes about vampires and other creatures." I'd fallen in love with Lestat and continued to fall for every leading male vampire I'd read about ever since, from Edward to Eric and all in between. "Do vampires exist?"

He chuckled. "In some form or another. Most every creature you've ever heard of exists, though the legends may be skewed."

Sir Studly's head whipped around, and he crowded in, blocking me from view. I saw a pair of legs walk by. Studly nodded his head. "Just trying to get the costume off."

A voice reached me from behind the car. "I saw that! It was some trick."

"Thank you," Studly replied. "We're thinking of taking the show on the road, maybe trying out for that talent show on TV." I couldn't see anything, so I contemplated his accent. It wasn't Scottish. I kept leaning toward Irish.

The stranger's voice laughed and faded away. Studly turned back to me. "Are you calmer?"

"I think so." My heart had stopped racing. People thought it was a costume, so I was in no real danger of anyone freaking out—besides me. I closed my eyes again and sucked in a deep breath, counting out slowly as I exhaled.

It occurred to me I had no idea what his name was. I couldn't exactly call him Sir Studly. "I'm Jen, by the way," I said without opening my eyes.

"Roan. Nice to meet you. Focus." Smiling, I did as he said.

I'd never been one to meditate. If I needed to relax, I grabbed a bottle and a friend. Not to say I was a lush, I drank maybe twice a year, but when I did, I drank myself into oblivion and relaxation.

Focus. My breaths rattled in and out as I ignored

the itch on my left butt cheek. I was failing miserably.

"When are you at your happiest?" Roan could probably tell it wasn't going well.

"When I'm playing."

"What do you play?" His voice was skeptical.

"Piano, guitar, violin. A few other things." I determinately didn't open my eyes; I had no desire to see the skepticism in his face.

"Play."

"Play? What do you mean?"

"In your mind, play. Picture yourself wherever you're happiest playing, and play."

I doubted his advice would work, but I gave it a try. The last time I'd been truly happy playing was with the symphony. I didn't mind accompanying the kids, but I absolutely loathed teaching them.

The stage was dark, and the auditorium was full. A spotlight hit me, decked to the nines in a black evening gown. The white keys of the piano glowed with promise.

Chopin flowed from my fingers; Nocturne in E-flat major committed to my memory. My fingers flew across the keys as the light, haunting melody filled the air. My back swayed, and my hands moved up and down the piano keys.

I sucked in my breath as the orchestra joined in, moving me to play better, to make them proud, and to reach the audience's discerning ears.

At the end of the piece, I sat my hands in my lap and opened my eyes. My hands were pale again, the sort of pale that required SPF 50+ and a sun hat. I blamed my Irish mother.

"Well done," Roan said. "You did it." His grin was infectious. He was truly proud of me for accomplishing the transition.

I smiled up at him and climbed to my feet. He offered me a hand since I rose so slowly. I'd sat there so long my feet had gone to sleep and didn't want to move. "I didn't even feel the change."

"It's described as a tingle across the skin, or a tickle, usually."

Shrugging, I closed the back door and grabbed my purse from where I'd dropped it beside the car. "Well, thanks. We should exchange numbers. I'm sure I'll have questions about what happened today." Boy would I.

He pulled a cell phone out of his pocket and tapped it a few times before handing it over to me. I typed my first name, Jen, and then hesitated. *He doesn't need to know my full name.* Jen was enough information.

After taking his phone back, the one in my purse dinged. I pulled it out to find a text that said, "Roan Harrington."

"Thank you, Roan Harrington," I said as I slid into the driver's seat.

"I'll be seeing you again, Jen." He nodded his head and turned, walking across the garage while I sat behind the wheel of my car, dumbfounded.

Now what?

OTHER SERIES BY L.A. BORUFF

Prime Time of Life (Paranormal Women's Fiction)

COMPLETE SERIES

Series Boxed Set

Complete Series Volume 1

Complete Series Volume 2

Borrowed Time

Stolen Time

Just in Time

Hidden Time

Nick of Time

Witching After Forty (Paranormal Women's Fiction)

A Ghoulish Midlife

Cookies For Satan (A Christmas Novella)

I'm With Cupid (A Valentine's Day Novella)

A Cursed Midlife

Birthday Blunder

A Girlfriend For Mr. Snoozerton

Fae

The Meowing Medium (Paranormal Cozy)

COMPLETE SERIES

Series Boxed Set Coming Soon

Secrets of the Specter

Gifts of the Ghost

Pleas of the Poltergeist

Demons and Demigods (Paranormal Romance)

COMPLETE SERIES

Series Boxed Set Coming Soon

The Devil's Delight

Chaotic Creations

Divine Deviations

An Unseen Midlife (Paranormal Women's Fiction
Reverse Harem)

Bloom In Blood

Dance In Night

Bask In Magic

Surrender In Dreams

Tales of Clan Robbins (Paranormal Western Romance)

Outlaw of Ladies

Lady of Outlaws

Princess of Thieves

Alpha of Exiles

Coven's End (Paranormal Reverse Harem)

COMPLETE SERIES

Series Boxed Set

Kane

Voss

Quin

Jillian

Academy's Rise (Paranormal Reverse Harem)

COMPLETE SERIES

Series Boxed Set

Hell Fire

Dark Water

Dead Air

Lucifer's War (Paranormal Romance)

COMPLETE SERIES

Devil's Consort

Devil's Assassin

Valentine Pride (Paranormal Reverse Harem)

COMPLETE SERIES

Series Boxed Set

Unicorn Mates

Unicorn Luck

http://www.books2read.com/Leola3

A Platypus and Her Mates

The Firehouse Feline (Paranormal Reverse Harem)

COMPLETE SERIES

Series Boxed Set

Feline the Heat

Feline the Flames

Feline the Burn

Feline the Pressure

Magic & Metaphysics Academy (Paranormal
Academy Reverse Harem)

COMPLETE SERIES

ABOUT L.A. BORUFF

USA Today Bestselling Author L.A. (Lainie) Boruff lives in East Tennessee with her husband, three children, and an ever-growing number of cats. She loves reading, watching TV, and procrastinating by browsing Facebook. L.A.'s passions include vampires, food, and listening to heavy metal music. She once won a Harry Potter trivia contest based on the books and lost one based on the movies. She has two bands on her bucket list that she still hasn't seen: AC/DC and Alice Cooper. Feel free to send tickets.

Printed in May 2023
by Rotomail Italia S.p.A., Vignate (MI) - Italy